Praise for Mary Herbert . . .

"*The Clandestine Circle* . . . has an excellent, imaginative plot. It is suspenseful, exciting and often impossible to put down. It . . . has a little bit of every-thing: action, adventure, fantasy, romance and comic relief. An exciting page-turner."

—*Florida Today*

Flight of the Fallen . . .

Reluctantly, she opened her eyes . . . and choked on a cry. Her eyes blinked with sudden tears. She crawled to her knees and knelt on the blanket, her heart pounding.

The light she'd thought was the sun actually emanated from a huge metallic dragon. Her large expressive eyes gleamed down on Linsha with pleasure. Her sleek head and polished horns glowed with a pale translucent gold light of their own.

"Iyesta!" Linsha whispered in delight.

The dragon inclined her head to Linsha until her gleaming nose almost brushed Linsha's head. Giving a slight nod, she lifted her neck and plunged her nose into the leaves of the Tree's canopy. Gently the apparition snipped two leaves from the vallenwood and let them fall to Linsha's side.

The bond formed between a dragon and a human is worth the effort to forge it, the dragon's voice said inside her mind.

"How?" Linsha begged. "How do I help him?"

The Tree of Life will guide your hand.

"Will you stay and help me?" Linsha cried.

There was no answer.

THE LINSHA TRILOGY

City of the Lost

Flight of the Fallen

Return of the Exile
(2005)

THE LINSHA TRILOGY

FLIGHT OF THE FALLEN

Mary H. Herbert

FLIGHT OF THE FALLEN

©2004 Wizards of the Coast, Inc.

Distributed in the United States by Holtzbrinck Publishing. Distributed in Canada by Fenn Ltd.

Distributed to the hobby, toy, and comic trade in the United States and Canada by regional distributors.

Distributed worldwide by Wizards of the Coast, Inc. and regional distributors.

Cover art by Matt Stawicki
Map by Dennis Kauth
First Printing: September 2004
Library of Congress Catalog Card Number: 2004106798

9 8 7 6 5 4 3 2 1

US ISBN: 0-7869-3245-7
UK ISBN: 0-7869-3246-5
620-96556-001-EN

U.S., CANADA,   EUROPEAN HEADQUARTERS
ASIA, PACIFIC, & LATIN AMERICA   Wizards of the Coast, Belgium
Wizards of the Coast, Inc.   T Hofveld 6d
P.O. Box 707   1702 Groot-Bijgaarden
Renton, WA 98057-0707   Belgium
+1-800-324-6496   +322 467 3360

Visit our web site at **www.wizards.com**

An author deals with numerous people in the process of producing a book, and one of the most important of those is the editor. The editor is the author's guiding hand through the morass of writer's block, a shepherd over the rugged miles of revision, and a cheerleader in times of success. I have had the pleasure of working with a succession of talented editors at TSR and Wizards of the Coast, and to them I respectfully offer my gratitude.

Jim Lowder — you never forget your first

Bill Larson — always the gentleman

Rob King — with the great sense of humor

Pat McGilligan — a talented author in his own right and especially to Mark Sehestedt for his terrific support, his endless patience, and his imaginative ideas that have added life to these books. (You can blame him for the ending of this one!) All my thanks.

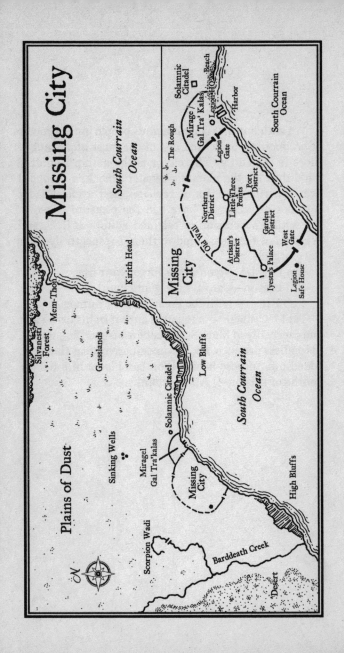

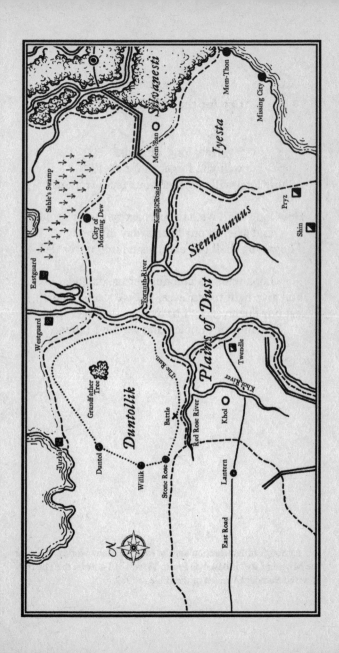

"Cry for the Missing City" [1]

How long, oh gods?
will you forget us for ever?
how long will you hide your faces from us?

How long shall we have perplexity in our minds,
and grief in our hearts, day after day?
how long shall our enemies triumph over us?

Look upon us and answer us, oh gods;
and give light to our eyes, lest we sleep in death,
lest our enemy say, "I have prevailed over them,"
and our foes rejoice that we have fallen.

1.) Songs of lamentation are the same in many worlds. "Cry for the Missing City" is based on Psalm 13, verses 1-4 from the The New Revised Standard Version of the Bible c. 1989.

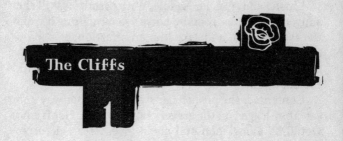

The Cliffs

Linsha stiffened her legs in the stirrups and lifted herself upright in the saddle. Over her horse's ears she looked straight across and down into the deep, rolling waters of the southern Courrain Ocean. Guilded with the light of the sun setting behind her, the sea lay spread out before her in a vast expanse of water and sky.

Out of habit she scanned the land to her left and right. To her left far in the distance she could just make out the smudge of smoke rising from the cooking fires in the port city of Mirage, the Missing City. She spared only a glance for that troubled city, for she did not want to dwell now on failure and disaster. To her right were only the cliffs that rose sharp and sheer from the water to the reddish-tan lands of the Plains of Dust. There was nothing that way that held her attention either. There was only the sea and the friend she sought.

She stood as tall as she dared on the fractious buckskin horse and studied the water carefully. Ah, there! She saw it. A brilliant metallic flash of dark gold beneath the surface just beyond the breakers. Close behind it, she could just make out a pod of dolphins frolicking in the waves.

Linsha slid from her saddle. With practiced skill she slipped the bridle from the horse's mouth, hung it from the saddle horn, and gave him an affectionate slap on the rump. Tossing his head, the horse wheeled and cantered away. He would be back in his pen by nightfall, Linsha knew.

Contented, she pushed her sword out of her way and sat cross-legged on the gravely earth to wait. Her friend would be along soon and could give her a ride back. Meanwhile she could enjoy a few minutes alone, away from the crowded caves, the grim faces, the constant noise, the endless planning, the ever-present danger. She pulled in a deep lung-full of cool, salty air, closed her eyes, and leaned back on the palms of her hands. A brisk wind pulled at her auburn hair. She drew in a second, longer breath and let it out in a slow sigh.

She felt a few ants investigate her fingers, but they weren't the vicious, red, biting variety, so she let them alone. A small bee buzzed by her ear as if investigating a flower, then it drifted away on the currents of the wind. The sound of the surf at the foot of the cliffs filled the quiet with a rhythmic wash of sound.

For a while, Linsha simply sat and let the tranquility sink in. She was so tired, so worn from weeks of battle and fear, that she made no effort to maintain her usual heightened awareness. She just let herself drift on a slow tide of drowsiness.

Something brittle crackled behind her.

Linsha snapped alert. Apprehension and surprise splashed over her like ice water, swiftly followed by anger. Couldn't she be left alone for even a minute?

She straightened and was starting to turn her head when she heard—

"Well, well. Look what we have here. Move a muscle, and a dozen spears will find your body."

Linsha's surprise and indignation chilled to fear and cold fury. In both edges of her vision she could make out several heavy, male-looking forms positioning themselves behind her. She had little doubt the speaker was not exaggerating about the number of weapons at her back.

"Stand up, you Solamnic whore," demanded a different, coarser voice.

"But Gortham just told her not to move," piped up a younger, definitely dimmer individual.

Linsha heard a collection of sighs, curses, and grumbling behind her and felt her fear lessen just a little. These were not the brutally efficient Tarmaks but mercenaries—mercenaries without effective leadership it seemed.

Without waiting for another contradictory command, Linsha held her empty hands out in plain view and pushed herself to her feet. She turned and faced her captors.

Twelve heavily-armed men of questionable parentage glowered at her from about twenty feet away, their spears lowered toward her. How had she let them get so close?

One man with a heavy leather jerkin and a bearded face leered at her. "See? I was right. It's that Rose Knight with the ruddy hair. We could have a little fun with this one."

"No," growled a taller man, the voice of the first speaker, Gortham. "There's a bounty for this one. We turn her over to the Tarmaks. They'll pay."

"And by the time we divide it twelve ways there won't be enough to buy a decent ale," the bearded man said.

A third man joined in. "There's no decent ale left anyway. The brutes took it all."

"Let's get our fun out of her now," the bearded man insisted. His thick hands tightened around his spear, and he took a step closer.

"The cap'n said to bring prisoners," Gortham said. "Especially Solamnic Knights."

Linsha studied the soldiers while they argued. Although the Tarmaks controlled most of the Missing City and its close environs, the mercenaries, who had been hired by the dragon Thunder, participated in the invasion shortly after midsummer of that year and still held the palace and grounds of the dragonlord Iyesta's lair. They rarely bothered to patrol or involve themselves in the subjugation of the city, and Linsha had the impression the Tarmaks merely tolerated the unruly mercenaries until they saw fit to rid the city of their presence. Still, that didn't make the hired soldiers any less dangerous.

She took a calculated step back.

Behind her the rocky ground sheered off in a cliff edge that plunged down into the roiling water of the sea. She guessed at this point along the coast she had about ten running steps to the edge before the cliff dropped thirty-five to forty feet to the water—water that she knew was very cold.

She slid another step back.

"Stand still, woman!" bellowed Gortham.

"Drop your weapons!" shouted the bearded man.

"How can she do both?" the literal-minded youngster asked.

Several voices chorused, "Shut up!"

The mercenaries tightened their half circle and moved closer to trap her against the cliff edge. Several drew their swords, others their knives.

Linsha's hands turned damp and cold. Her stomach twisted into a knot. Slowly, she unbuckled her belt and let her sword and dagger fall to the ground. Her feet eased backward another step.

At least these men were not carrying bows, she noted. One had a crossbow slung across his back, but he hadn't made a move to remove it.

The mercenaries, seeing Linsha unarmed, advanced.

"Watch her hands, buckos," Gortham said. "She may have blades in her boots."

Or up her sleeves, Linsha silently added. But she didn't show her enemy anything but her heels. Quick as a pickpocket, she spun and sprinted forward.

She took the seventh step over the edge of the cliff.

Crucible's farewell

2

insha had a scant moment to point her feet, straighten her body, and clamp her arms to her chest before she plunged into the sea. The cold water hit her like a physical blow. It closed over her head and pressed in on her body in a fierce assault on her senses. Pain raced through her head and limbs. She struggled upward through the surging water and broke the surface, coughing and gasping for air. Her heart raced in her chest; her lungs ached.

A wave lifted her up and carried her close to the towering stone wall of the cliff. She forced her sluggish arms and legs to move, to pull her out of the waves' undertow and away from the stone barriers. There was no safety against those wet, slick walls, only bone-breaking death.

The cold bore into her skin with frozen needles that numbed her muscles. Her limbs became heavy and weak. Her saturated clothes and boots weighed her down until she could barely keep her face above the rolling, tossing water. With a desperate heave of her arms and shoulders, she threw herself upward above the surface just enough to scream, "Crucible!" before she fell back.

Salt water washed into her eyes and nose. A cold fog closed around her awareness until she saw nothing more than the gray water that surrounded her. Her eyes stung from the bitter cold and salt.

Now would be a very good time for him to appear. The thought ran through her mind in a desperate wish. She had trusted her life to him too many times, and he had never failed her. This would not be a good time for him to start.

A wave slapped her in the face, filling her nose and mouth with briny water. A huge, swallow washed down her throat. She gagged and choked and fought to free her face from the frigid wet. Her eyes cracked open and gave a blurred glimpse of the cliff overhead. She was too close. The tide was coming in. She should have remembered that. A few more waves and she would be battered to a pulp.

Something gray and sleek broke through a wave nearby. Its dorsal fin slid tauntingly close to her hand then slipped out of sight. Something else bumped by her leg. Linsha tried to cry out but she was too full of seawater, too numb with cold.

Then she realized another form moved under the water close by. It was visible only as a pale shape in a tossing swirl of grays and blacks and whites, but it was huge, and as it drew closer, Linsha saw glints of gold where slanting rays of the setting sun pierced the waves and caught the polished scales of the big creature.

Water surged up around her, and a draconic head, large and lethal-looking, broke to the surface and stared at her curiously with eyes like ancient pools of fire.

Just what in the name of any god do you think you're

doing? A powerful masculine voice spoke in her mind. *It's too cold for you to swim.*

Sputtering, Linsha could only manage to point a weak finger toward the clifftop.

The dragon rose a little higher in the water and lifted his head to study the cliff just as another wave washed over them. The combination of wave and dragon surge was more than Linsha could manage. She felt herself pushed relentlessly toward the solid stone and knew this time there was nothing she could do to stop it. She closed her eyes and braced for the impact.

Instead of stone, something else scraped over her skin. She felt teeth close gently over her torso and lift her out of the sea. Her eyes flew open in surprise. Water cascaded from his jaws, leaving her flopping like a fish across his tongue. Her eyes grew enormous, but she was too busy coughing on sea water to argue this treatment. Several of his teeth closed too close to her chest and legs for comfort.

"Crucible, what—!" she gasped before his head swung up and jolted her against his back teeth. Her words were lost in the noise of claws scraping against granite. The dragon erupted from the sea, sending water in all directions. Linsha saw the cliff wall swing past.

The forty-foot cliff offered no difficulty to a dragon who tipped well over a hundred feet from nose to tail. He swarmed up the wall, water streaming from his bronze scales. At the top, he paused and peered over the edge.

From her vantage point in Crucible's mouth, Linsha felt a bit silly. She supposed she looked like a bedraggled dragon snack dangling out both sides of the bronze's mouth. But she had to admit, she had a wonderful view of the mercenaries.

A weak smile stole across her mouth.

The men hadn't departed. They were clustered about, frozen in a tableau of group surprise. Every one stared at the dragon, each set of eyes aghast, every jaw opened in shock. Linsha felt Crucible's hot breath blow across her back and heard a rumble begin in the depths of his throat like the movement of lava across cold stone.

Linsha's sword fell from the nerveless fingers of the bearded man. The sudden loud clatter made them all jump and broke the stunned silence. Shouts of anger and fear filled the evening. A few brave men hurled their spears toward Crucible, but most took to their heels and fled toward the dubious shelter of the distant city.

Grumbling, Crucible ignored the spears that bounced off his scales, and in one flowing movement, he slithered over the edge of the cliff and placed Linsha carefully on the ground. She landed on her hip and shoulder, rolled once, and sprang into a defensive crouch. All the movement proved too much for her abused stomach, and she found herself on her knees retching seawater onto the dry ground.

The remaining mercenaries lost all traces of bravery. Flinging down their weapons, they bolted after their racing companions.

Linsha wiped her mouth and sighed as she watched them go. Bad decision, she thought. Bronze dragons were fairly good-natured, and with some flattery and groveling, the soldiers who had stood their ground might have talked their way into a prisoner pen at the Wadi. Now they were dead men. Few dragons could resist fleeing prey.

Crucible roared and spread his wings.

Linsha, still kneeling, covered her head against the storm of dust and gravel as the big bronze leaped

9

skyward. In moments the wind of his passage moved away, the screams of the hunted soldiers faded, and the normal sounds of wind and surf mercifully returned.

Linsha sank back on her heels. Once again she found herself sitting on the clifftop, watching for Crucible, only now she was soaked, streaked with mud and dragon saliva, and cold to the bone. She shivered, as much from the chill of the wind on her wet clothes as her body's reaction to the past few minutes. What had she been thinking? To jump over a forty-foot cliff into deep, icy water in the hope a dragon would notice her and bring her out safely! The fact that her plan worked quite well did not excuse the lunacy. She shivered again and did not stop.

Feeling weak and shaky, she shoved herself to her feet and began to trudge toward the range of low hills to the north. Better to warm herself with exercise than wait and die of a chill. She picked up her sword as she passed it and when her numb fingers could not manage the buckle, she slung the scabbarded blade across her back and continued walking, dripping as she went.

He would be leaving.

She saw it as clearly as she had seen the magnificent spread of his wing sails glowing like oiled vellum in the light of the westering sun. His wing had healed. He could fly again. There was no more reason for him to stay. Just when she was getting quite comfortable with his presence, he was going to leave her. Of course she could not lay any blame at his taloned feet. She and her difficulties could hardly compete with an entire city. But she would miss him.

She did not look up when the flap and rush of dragon wings announced his return. Carefully he touched down to the ground in front of her and tucked his wings against his body with an obvious air of satisfaction.

Linsha stopped by his stocky foreleg, looked up, and let her gaze travel up his entire height. Even years after her first glimpse of him, she never ceased to marvel at his power and handsome proportions. His body was long and well-muscled, tapering to a broad tail. A ridge of spines joined by webbing, characteristic of all bronzes, topped his neck and tail and helped drive him through the water he loved. His horned head was wedge-shaped and covered with a tough hide of dark bronze-colored scales. These scales began as a deep burnished gold on his head and back and lightened down his sides and belly to a pale bronze that gleamed like newly wrought metal.

Crucible tipped his head. "What are you doing out here?" he rumbled. "I thought you were out on patrol."

"We returned early. Sir Fellion broke his arm in a fall. I thought I'd come out and meet you."

"So you rode out alone?" He sounded angry.

She gave a light shrug. "You were out here."

Even she heard how frivolous she sounded. Frivolous, overconfident, and senseless. She should know better than to rush out alone from the Wadi and sit like a practice target on the edge of the cliffs. She was lucky the mercenaries had been looking for prisoners and not bodies to loot.

"What if I hadn't been here?" the dragon demanded.

"I wouldn't have come," Linsha said. But to her surprise, she felt a tightening in her throat and the prickle of sudden tears, tears that had sprung out of nowhere. She bit her lip and used the pain to damp down her feelings. She knew this day had been coming for some time. "So when were you going to tell me?"

He stared down at her with luminous eyes, standing

so still she could see her reflection in the amber depths. "Today. Tomorrow. My wing is finally strong enough to bear a long flight. Now that you know, I will leave tonight."

"So soon?"

"I have been gone too long. Sanction was still under siege when I left. We have had no word of its fate since. I must go back. There is no telling what those fool Solamnics have done."

Linsha nodded, ignoring the comment about the Knights of Solamnia. She knew he was needed in Sanction. She knew, too, her friend, Lord Bight, was in constant danger and that Crucible was his guardian. The bronze had to go back. Yet all the forewarning, logic, and common sense in the world did not make this parting any easier.

"Will you be able to get past Sable?" she asked.

The black dragon Onysablet, commonly known as Sable, had drowned the land between the Plains of Dust and the southern Khalkist Mountains and built her swampy realm on the rotting corpse of the earth. For years Crucible in Sanction to the north and the brass dragon Iyesta in the south had maintained a tenuous truce with the unpredictable black by playing on her fears and greed to keep her off-balance. But Iyesta's death that summer changed the balance of power. Without an ally in the Plains of Dust, the safety of Sanction and its secretive guardian was thrown into serious question. If Sable caught Crucible alone, trying to fly over her realm, she would not hesitate to tear him to pieces.

Crucible knew full well his danger. "I will travel at night and stay to the east of Shrentak. I will be gone from her realm before she knows I am there."

Crouching down, he thrust out a foreleg. Still cold

and wet, Linsha gratefully climbed up his leg and shoulder and seated herself on the dragon's warm back in a spot in front of his wing joints and just where his neck ridge ended. He didn't like to carry riders usually—complained it interfered with his wings—and refused any who dared ask. But he had made an exception for her once years ago in Sanction and since then he had grown quite comfortable with her on his back. A favor Linsha thoroughly enjoyed.

She vividly remembered riding the brass Iyesta once into the desert to pay a call on another dragonlord, Thunder. Iyesta, however, had been over three hundred feet long and wider than a masted ship. When Linsha tried to sit astride the great brass, her legs stuck out in both directions. All she could do was hang on to Iyesta's back like a cowbird perched on an oxen. One shrug of Iyesta's shoulders had been enough to send her into a free fall over the Plains of Dust. It was not an experience Linsha cared to repeat.

Crucible was different. Not only was he shorter and more streamlined, his shoulders were narrower and offered a place at the base of his neck where his backridge ended that suited Linsha well. They had fought together, bled together, and worked together for almost three months now and formed a bond as affectionate as many dragonriders and their life-long mounts.

Yet Linsha shut her mind to all of that. As close as Crucible was to her, his first loyalty was to Sanction and Lord Bight. She had to respect that or she would not be worthy of his friendship—or of her status as a Rose Knight in the Solamnic Orders. She knew all too well the necessities of responsibility and loyalty to one's chosen cause.

"Ready?" he called.

Linsha held on with hands and knees as Crucible

13

sprang into the wind and with a powerful thrust of his wings, he rose above the bleak land and angled north toward the eroded banks and sandbars of Barddeath Creek. To the west, the sun touched the purple horizon and began its descent into darkness.

They flew without speaking in the gathering dusk until Crucible tilted his long wings to brake his descent and touched neatly down. Linsha swung a leg around, grabbed his wing, and lowered herself to the ground.

They had landed at the mouth of the deep, winding canyon called Scorpion Wadi where the remnants of Iyesta's proud militia and survivors of the Missing City had taken refuge after the Tarmaks invaded the city. Linsha knew there were sentries hidden in the rocks and along the high walls, and eyes watched her carefully. But the militia knew her and Crucible and would leave her alone.

The bronze dragon lowered his head and curved his neck around to enclose Linsha in the circle of his neck and body. Unable to trust her voice, she gazed up at him and gently touched her fingers to his long nose.

"Do you still wear the scales?" he asked.

She tugged a gold chain out from under her soggy tunic and showed him the two disks that hung around her neck. One was brass-colored and gleamed in the fading light—a gift from the dragonlord Iyesta. The second was slightly larger, edged with gold, and darker in color. It had been given to her by Crucible and had saved her life at least once.

"Keep them near," he told her. "Magic is dying around us, but there is a little of our power inherent in our scales. It may protect you."

Linsha knew it was why he had given her his scale three years ago in Sanction. She always wore them.

She tucked the scales back under her clothes. They

were a pact of friendship and reassurance to them both, and a way to say good-bye.

"Give my regards to Lord Bight," she said.

He straightened and lifted his head to scent the wind.

Linsha moved away. Sadly she watched him crouch and spring upward. His great wings caught the air and lifted him above the bonds of the earth.

The downdraft of his first beat nearly knocked her off her feet. Ducking down, she shielded her eyes against the dust and the grit until the draft passed, then she lifted her eyes to the north. Rising high on a wind from the sea, the bronze dragon caught the last rays of the setting sun. His scales flared with golden light, and he glowed like a comet against the darkening sky. Moments later he passed out of sight, and the fire winked out. The sun vanished. Night settled over the plains.

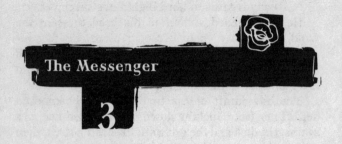

The Messenger

3

Lady Linsha!" Her name rang down the canyon and echoed off the high rock walls.

Linsha looked up from the stone and the sword in her lap, cocked her head for a moment, and went back to work. The Scorpion Wadi was a deep, curving canyon with a complicated maze of caves, tunnels, washed-out gullies, and eroded stone walls. Voices carried in odd ways through the Wadi, so it was often difficult to tell where the caller was located.

Not that Linsha bothered to find out. She had finally managed to steal another few minutes away from the crowded, noisy camp, and she was in no mood to help someone find her and ruin a rare moment of sulking.

"Lady Linsha!"

She continued to ignore the call while she ran the honing stone along the edge of the sword blade. Her name bounced off the rock walls and went unheeded.

"It might be important, you know," a raspy voice said from the shaded ledge of a nearby outcropping.

"They'll find me," Linsha replied in a tone as hard and uninterested as the whetstone in her hand. She flipped the weapon over and began to sharpen the opposite edge.

"It sounds like young Leonidas," prompted the voice.

Linsha's clear green eyes narrowed and her lips tightened to a thin line. Couldn't she enjoy a bad mood alone for just a little while?

"All right, all right," she grumbled. "Go get him."

An owl, brown and creamy in color, hopped off the ledge and glided silently out of the side gully and into the main canyon.

Linsha paid scant attention. The whetstone in her hand continued its raspy journey along the length of the sword blade. From guard to tip. Again and again. Slow. Steady. With even pressure and fierce concentration. The stone evened out the inevitable nicks and honed its edge to a killing line.

If only, Linsha thought wearily, there was a whetstone somewhere to take the nicks and bluntness off her soul. She felt as battered and worn as the sword in her calloused hands, and there wasn't anything she could do about it in this place.

Hooves thudded in the canyon close by then clattered into the dry gully where she had chosen to retreat. She didn't bother to look up. Varia had been right. The one who called her name was the centaur, Leonidas. She could recognize those hoofbeats anywhere. Feeling perverse, she ignored the new arrival and bent over her sword.

"Lady," a male voice said, then she heard an audible intake of breath.

Leonidas may have been a gangly buckskin stallion barely out of colthood, but he had been a friend to Linsha through the long, bloody summer, and he had learned early to recognize many of her moods, including

17

her occasional bouts of temper. Although she normally kept them in check, once in a while something would slip loose and she would erupt like Mount Thunderhorn. Since Crucible left two days ago, even the lowliest camp potscrubber stayed out of her way.

"Before you throw that sword at me, I have a message. Lanther sent me to tell you we have captured a prisoner who has news of the eggs."

Something twisted in the pit of Linsha's stomach. Her hand fell still.

The eggs. In the name of Kiri-Jolith, why had Iyesta left those eggs in her care? They had been the bane of her summer. The great brass dragonlord had meant well, Linsha supposed, when she'd made a human promise to look after the clutch of brass dragon eggs that she'd left to incubate in the hot sands in a labyrinth under the city. Linsha assumed at the time that vow was simply a gesture of respect. None of them, including the sleeping mother dragon, had ever suspected Iyesta would be dead only a few days later. Then the mother brass was murdered, the eggs disappeared, and the promise made by a Rose Knight of Solamnia became a matter of honor.

Linsha suspected the Tarmaks had the eggs, for reasons known only to them, and she had tried everything she could think of to learn their whereabouts, only to be thwarted at every step. As far as she knew, the eggs had vanished. But what if they hadn't? What if the Tarmaks had hidden them somewhere and someone else knew about it? It was a chance she could not ignore.

"Lady, did you hear me?"

The sudden, insistent voice jolted Linsha's attention back to her surroundings. She hadn't realized she was staring blankly at the ground. For an answer, she slid the sword into its battered scabbard and rose to her feet.

"I heard you." She sighed and raised her arm, wrist straight out, in an invitation. There was a flutter of wings and the owl, Varia, came to land on her forearm. Sidestepping delicately, the bird made her way up to Linsha's shoulder and settled comfortably close to the woman's head of auburn curls.

Linsha turned her face to let the owl's soft feathers brush her skin. The scent of owl, mingled with cedar, desert wind, and dust filled her nostrils. A bit of down tickled her nose, causing her to sneeze a gust of air that fluffed out the owl's feathers across her chest.

Varia gave a throaty chuckle. She was a rare bird—one of a kind as far as Linsha knew—who had appeared in the forested mountains outside Sanction and adopted Linsha as her own. They had been inseparable for years and were very familiar with each other's personalities.

"Are you through sulking?" Varia asked.

Linsha smiled. "Not yet, but I'll work on it."

She could never remain sullen for long. It was too much work. Her temperament was naturally optimistic. Like her parents and her grandparents, she was a fighter who sought to find the positive in any situation—even one as dire as the circumstances she found herself in now. As long as there was a scrap of hope, the Majeres managed to find it.

Her bad mood ebbed a little, and instead of nurturing it as she had since Crucible left, she let it go. She really needed about two months of sleep, steady meals, and easy duty to feel normal again, but she could at least do herself a favor and let her better nature take over.

She saw Leonidas watching her dubiously, like a man watches a cobra from a distance, and she offered him a faint smile as an apology. "Thank you for bringing Lanther's message. Where are they?"

The young centaur swished his black tail and stamped a hind foot as if to say, "about time!" What he said aloud was, "They're on the way to the Post."

She looked at him closely and saw for the first time the dark patches of sweat on his sandy-colored hide and the dust on his legs. He had traveled hard and fast to reach her.

Without wasting more time, they hurried down the trail through the Wadi, wending a way between high stone walls tinted with late afternoon shadow. Smoke and smells from the cooking fires wafted down the canyon on a capricious wind. Voices bounced off the rock walls. A mile from Linsha's chosen retreat they came to the edges of the camp that had sprung up in the canyon that summer after the death of Iyesta and the fall of the Missing City to the Tarmaks.

In the open plains that surrounded the port city, the Wadi was the only defensible position large enough to provide sanctuary for more than a few people, and in desperation, they had come in the hundreds. Someone had made a complete head-count shortly after the fall of the city and numbered 892 men, women, children, centaurs, elves, kender, and miscellaneous sorts living in the canyon. That number had changed often as more refugees and escaped slaves arrived, as a few displaced families left to seek shelter on the Plains of Dust with relatives and clans, and as people succumbed to wounds, disease, and conflict. It was a population mostly of fighting men and centaurs made up of remnants of the dragonlord's once-proud militia, the City Watch, the Legion of Steel, and a few tenacious survivors of the Knights of Solamnia. No one knew exactly how many people remained in the Wadi, and most people were too tired to care.

As Linsha and Leonidas walked the narrow paths

of the camp, they passed corrals and pens that were nearly empty, tents and huts and caves where people slept, clearings where a few children played, and groups of people bending to a myriad of tasks. Everyone was busy, for there was always work to be done. No one sat and did nothing, except the wounded. A few people nodded or waved to the Lady Knight and her escort, but most paid little heed. They concentrated on their work with the joyless weariness of people who knew they had nowhere else to go.

They were a disreputable looking bunch, Linsha observed. The mercenaries she had met two days before looked better equipped and certainly better fed. The people she saw now were dirty, lean from thin rations, and hollow-eyed from exhaustion that went bone-deep. Living in a strong, defensible sanctuary was well and good if there was enough food and water to go around, but here there usually wasn't. The refugees didn't have the means to grow crops, and any hunting party or scavenging patrol ran the risk of being caught by the Tarmaks or mercenaries. Several patrols had disappeared without a trace while too many others were found slaughtered.

Food was not the only thing that had become hard to replace. Weapons, clothing, saddles, horseshoes, tools, medicine, armor, rope, and blankets were all in short shrift. Everyone made do the best they could with makeshift repairs and crude replacements. The dead of the enemy were stripped whenever possible, and a few supplies had come in from the barbarian tribes to the east and the centaur clans to the north. But it was not enough. It was never enough. And no one knew what would happen when winter set in. Winters on the southern edge of the Plains of Dust received the brunt of the fierce winds and cold from the southern glaciers. They were long and hard and difficult enough to deal with when there were snug walls, warm fires, and plenty of food.

Linsha wished for the thousandth time that Crucible had not left. Crucible had provided a valuable service by tracking down and killing cattle from Iyesta's scattered herds to feed the hungry in the camp. He also served as a powerful guardian to the encampment.

"I miss him, too, you know."

Linsha started at the voice beside her ear. She had been so deep in thought she'd forgotten the owl on her shoulder. Sometimes, she swore, Varia could read her mind.

"Who? Crucible?" Leonidas snorted. "We will all miss him. Especially at meal time." He shook his shaggy head and looked around the camp. "I wonder how long it will be before the Tarmaks know he is gone."

Linsha had wondered the same thing. And what would the Tarmaks do about it?

Shortly the activity of the camp fell behind them and they passed through a fortified earthen wall recently completed. Sentries stepped out, saluted the Lady Knight and the centaur, then faded back out of sight. The camp was nearly two miles from the mouth of the Wadi and could be reached only along a narrow path that hugged the canyon floor between towering walls pockmarked with caves and scarred with gullies, washouts, and dead ends. It was a perfect place for an ambush.

At the mouth of the Wadi, Crucible had triggered a landslide that blocked all but a pathway barely wide enough for two horsemen to ride through abreast. There, cleverly disguised at the juncture of the massive slide and the canyon wall was a small complex of stone shelters and holding cells that represented the headquarters of the beleaguered force. The refugees simply called it the Post.

When Linsha and Leonidas approached, they saw three men and a centaur standing around a rough table laden with maps. The men, bent over the table, were talking and gesturing all at once. The centaur stood slightly apart, his arms crossed over his chest and his face impassive as he listened. He was a stranger to Linsha—a tall, rangy horse-man with a reddish-blond beard and mane and a coat the color of polished cedar.

"Who is that?" Linsha asked her companion.

"I don't know," Leonidas replied, curious himself. "From the look of the harness he wears and the white color of his arrows, I'd guess he's from Willik."

Willik. Linsha tracked through her memories for that name and found it. Willik was a centaur settlement in Duntollik, the free human-centaur realm pressed precariously between four dragon realms. Until recently the harried people of Duntollik had maintained a mutual protection pact to help defend their lands from the green dragon, Beryl, to the west, the blue Thunder to the south, and black Sable to the north. Only Iyesta to the east had given them any aid and support. Now that two of the four dragons were dead, Linsha considered what was happening in that land that would bring a messenger so far from home.

The group around the table glanced up when they heard Linsha and the centaur. Pausing in their discussion, the three men waited for the two newcomers to arrive.

These three men, Linsha knew, were the reason the small fighting force in the Wadi had held together as long as it had. They were the backbone, the spirit, and the strength of everyone who sought refuge in the canyon.

By sheer weight of seniority and forceful presence, Falaius Taneek, the commander of the Legion of Steel, had assumed overall command. Bluff, blunt General Dockett of Iyesta's once-proud militia became his second-in-command. Knight Commander Jamis uth Remmik of the Solamnic Order grudgingly filled in as third ranking officer.

Although the Solamnic commander would have preferred to keep his Knights separate, he was realistic enough to know they had nowhere else to go. He could not pull them out, for their small numbers could not easily strike off across the vast Plains of Dust on their own without supplies, horses, or support, nor could he withdraw in good conscience. He had not received orders to retire the Solamnic Circle from of the Missing City, and Lord Knight Remmik based his life on the strict adherence to the Law. Instead he curbed his feelings and stayed with the eighteen Knights who were left from his garrison of seventy-five and lent his considerable talents to scrounging supplies and building defensive fortifications.

As she drew near to the men, Linsha felt her teeth grind. Only Falaius and Dockett looked pleased to see her. Sir Remmik deliberately angled his body to keep his back turned to her so he would not have to look at or speak to her. The Knight Commander had never forgiven her for several alleged crimes and for surviving the Tarmak attack on the city when most of his favored Knights had been slaughtered. He had declared her blacklisted to all Solamnic Knights, although he'd never had time to send a full report to the Grand Master in Sancrist, and ordered the Knights of the Circle to behave as if she did not exist.

Linsha found his attitude ludicrous. She knew she was innocent of the crime he despised her for, and in the close proximity of the Wadi, it was difficult to avoid someone who struggled beside you to survive and whom you had worked with for more than a year and a half. Linsha took perverse delight in being unfailingly polite and friendly to Sir Remmik and forcing him to acknowledge her in the presence of others, even when she preferred to punch him in the sneer on his aristocratic face.

This day, however, enough traces of her bad temper remained to kill any thoughts of playing nice to Sir Remmik. Striding up to the table, she spoke warmly to Falaius and General Dockett, nodded to the centaur, and passed her gaze over the Solamnic Knight as if he did not exist.

The Legion commander and the militia general were used to such hostilities between the Lord Knight and the exiled Lady Knight, but the centaur looked surprised by their rudeness.

"Lanther just arrived," Falaius told Linsha. "He's in the pens." He held out a hand to stop her before she turned. "Lady Linsha, this is Horemheb of the Willik clan of Duntollik. He has brought us news you might find interesting."

The centaur's eyebrows rose at the plainsman's use of the Solamnic title, and his eyes slid from Sir Remmik to Linsha and back in surprise.

Linsha didn't blame him. While Sir Remmik still wore the formal blue and silver tunic of the Solamnic Circle and made an effort to keep it clean and repaired, she had lost her armor and her uniform months ago to battle, blood, and exile. Now she wore a stained and battered tunic that looked a little worse for her dunking in the sea, a leather corselet that was two sizes too big, and pants she had washed and repaired so many times there wasn't much left of the original color. Her boots had holes in the soles and were held together by bits of rope and leather strips. Her auburn hair was shaggy and unkempt, her nails were dirty, and she was thinner than she had been in years. An owl perched on her shoulder. She hardly looked the part of a high-ranking Solamnic Knight.

Leonidas beside her chuckled and, giving a salute to his kinsman, said, "Do not be fooled by appearances. It takes more than a fancy coat to make a warrior."

A rude snort brought Linsha's attention to Sir Remmik's face. Anger suffused his lean features and creased heavy frown lines around his nose and across his high forehead. "That's true, horse-man," he said fiercely. "It takes morals and obedience to a higher law."

Linsha's temper, already straining at its bit, lashed out. Ignoring Varia's warning hoot, she leaned forward, her hands on the table, and held him with her eyes. "It also requires an open mind and the ability to see beyond the end of your nose. The Tarmaks killed Sir Morrec. I told you that, but you refuse to accept anything that does not conform to your own fantasies."

Sir Remmik leaned forward as well, the other men forgotten. "You have no proof."

"I cannot drag the Tarmak leader before you to admit to his complicity," she retorted. "I have given you my word as a Rose Knight, something which even to you should be inviolate."

"You were tried and condemned before a council of your peers. You are an abomination to us. Your word means nothing!"

"A pretty use of logic!" she spat. "That council was of your making. You—"

Falaius held up a hand between them and said calmly, "We've heard this before."

Embarrassed, Linsha stepped back. Why had she

let Remmik goad her again? She knew better than to engage in an argument with him, especially in front of a stranger—or Falaius and Dockett. Sir Remmik had convinced himself and much of the Circle that she had killed their commander, Sir Morrec, during an ambush on the night of the great storm. His evidence of her alleged guilt was the presence of her dagger in Sir Morrec's back and the fact that she had been the only one of the honor guard to survive. She had failed to defend her superior officer, and she had failed to die. In Sir Remmik's eyes, that alone was enough to condemn her to exile and, if possible, death.

Thankfully neither the militia nor the Legion fed on Sir Remmik's idea of the truth. They accepted Linsha into their ranks, gave her sanctuary, and protected her from Sir Remmik's wrath. Falaius had even offered her a place in the Legion, an honor for which she was truly grateful. But in spite of the fact this was the second time members of the Order had tried to convict her and blacklist her, the Solamnic Knighthood was too deeply ingrained in her bones. She wasn't ready to give up on it yet.

She bowed apologetically to the centaur. "Forgive us. It is an old feud."

Sir Remmik backed away, too, and had the grace to looked slightly ashamed.

On the woman's shoulder, Varia huffed out her feathers and made a low-throated grumbling sound of indignation. Although she had a vast range of sounds and voices, she preferred to remain quiet in the presence of strangers.

"As I was saying," Falaius said, "Horemheb has come from Duntollik with news."

The rangy centaur shook his head as if he couldn't quite believe what he had just heard, then returned to his business. "In truth, I bring news. But I came to seek news as well. For years we have kept a close watch on the blue dragon, Thunder, since his realm borders on our own. Many times he has flown over Duntollik to spread terror and raid our villages. I think he would have driven us out long ago if Beryl and Sable had not forbidden him to seek more territory. Lately, though, our chieftains have grown concerned. We have not seen either Iyesta or Thunder these past three months, and news from the Missing City has completely stopped. I was sent south to find out what is happening."

Falaius pointed to the maps and said to Linsha, "We have told him of the storm, the invasion, and the fall of the city. Since you are here, you can fill in the rest."

Sir Remmik had not left the table, and Linsha could feel his pent-up anger radiating off him like heat waves on the sand. He had never fully believed her story of the death of the dragons—he didn't want to believe her part in it—and he probably feared she would lie again. Linsha pushed him from her mind and let her thoughts slip back to midsummer and the dark-drowned caverns below the city. In her mind's eye she saw them again, the huge corpses, two withered and reduced to heaps of bones and scales; one rotting in the sands of the empty dragon nest.

"They're dead," she said at last.

Horemheb started as if stung. "Both of them? By the gods! What happened?"

"The Tarmaks brought an Abyssal Lance. Thunder used it to kill Iyesta during the storm. Crucible and I and a centaur named Azurale turned it against him and killed him just after the city fell. Their bodies are beneath the Missing City, so the news has not spread quickly."

The Willik centaur rubbed his bearded chin. He

looked stunned. "Falaius has told me of the Tarmaks, but who is Crucible, and what is an Abyssal Lance?"

"Crucible is a bronze dragon who helped us for a while. He has since returned to his lair near Sanction." Linsha paused, took a deep breath, and went on. "The Abyssal Lance is a vile weapon. I was told a few were made during the Chaos War. A Dark Knight presented one to the Tarmaks—the Brutes as you might know them—who used it as a lure to overcome Thunder's fear of Iyesta. They convinced him to help them invade the city in return for a large share of her treasure." She grimaced. "As soon as Iyesta was dead and the Missing City had fallen, the Tarmaks left the lance for us to steal, knowing we would try to kill Thunder."

"Why would they do that if he was their ally?" Horemheb asked, still trying to absorb the monumental news.

Linsha lifted her free shoulder in a shrug. "You know Thunder. He was vicious, greedy, and unpredictable. I think they hoped we would rid them of him before he became a problem for them."

"They wanted Iyesta's city for themselves," General Dockett said.

"They won't stop there. I believe they want her entire realm."

Linsha turned at the sound of the new voice and grinned at the tall man coming to join them. Lanther's eye caught hers, and his weathered face broke into a matching smile of pleasure. Dark-haired and lanky, he had been a formidable warrior once until a serious injury two years ago had left him with a limp and a livid scar down his right cheek. The injury had sent him into semi-retirement in the Missing City while still in his forties.

He stopped beside her, gave Varia a wink with a

29

bright blue eye, and bowed gravely to the messenger. "Your pardon for the interruption," he said.

Introductions were made again to acquaint Horemheb with Lanther. The centaur studied the Legionnaire carefully and nodded once. "You have seen your share of fighting these past years," he observed.

Lanther laughed, a sharp sound of grim humor. "What gave it away? The scars or the limp?"

"Those, and the tales that are told about you in the City of Morning Dew. I went there before I made my way down here, and they are still telling stories of your rescues in the tavern."

"Ah yes, the *Sunken Ship.*" Lanther turned to Linsha, who had never been to the City of Morning Dew and said, "It's an old boat they grounded at the edge of the swamp and converted into the city's only tavern, inn, watering hole, gathering spot, and gaming house. All the Legionnaires go there to sit around and tell wild stories of their exploits."

She crossed her arms. She knew the tales, too—of his dangerous trips into Sable's black swamp to rescue slaves and escaped prisoners—but she couldn't helping asking, "So who did you have to rescue from the tavern?"

"Two barmaids and a confused crocodile."

His comment brought several smiles, a chuckle from Dockett, and gave them all a moment of lighthearted humor—something rare in that canyon. As soon as it faded, Horemheb returned to his questions.

"What did you mean they want Iyesta's realm?" The centaur asked, unable to disguise his alarm.

Lanther tapped a forefinger on a map. "The Tarmaks do not seem content to stay where they are. From the news I have picked up from prisoners and our few spies in the city, the Tarmaks are building a new army—one equipped for a land campaign rather than a seaborne invasion."

Sir Remmik agreed. He despised the Legionnaire, but he knew the business of supplies, shipping, and organizing an army, and he, too, had been keeping a watch on the port. "They are receiving several ships a week—filled with reinforcements and supplies. They have already outstripped us in numbers, and they are far better equipped."

"Where are they coming from? I thought these Brutes were only a slave race controlled by the Knights of Neraka?"

Linsha shook her head. "We don't know. Even their mercenaries have no knowledge of their origins."

"At least we've seen no indication of Dark Knight involvement," Falaius added. "The Tarmaks seem to be attacking us on their own initiative."

Horemheb rubbed a large hand across his face and looked pensive. "I will have to get this news back to Duntollik. If this realm falls to these Tarmaks . . ."

He didn't need to finish. They all understood the pressures of Duntollik's geography.

Linsha, the men, the centaurs, and Varia stared down at the maps scattered across the table. No one had to explain the grim truth staring them in the face. The forces of Iyesta had refused to admit defeat even after the city fell. Led by the three commanders, they had formed a thin line of defensive positions, fortified outposts, and roving patrols anchored on the Scorpion Wadi that surrounded the Missing City in a rough half-circle. At first they had waged a successful campaign to keep the mercenaries and the Tarmaks confined within the boundaries of the city. But as the weeks passed and the numbers of besiegers dwindled, the effort to contain the Tarmaks had become little more than a waiting game. Before too long, Iyesta's forces would either have to find another way to keep fighting or retreat back into the empty Plains of Dust.

"How long do you think it will be?" Horemheb asked quietly.

"If they are planning a campaign for this year," General Dockett replied, "they will have to move before winter."

Linsha stirred, remembering what Falaius had told her. The centaur had come with news of his own. "What about your people? What is the news from Duntollik?"

A look of frustration marred the centaur's face. "We are watching and preparing what we can. Something is happening in Qualinesti. There have been large troop movements over the border and a great deal of activity among the dwarves in Thorbardin. Sable has been quiet, but we heard disturbing news from Schallsea."

The men bent over their maps again, intent on gleaning every bit of information from Horemheb's news. Soon they were asking questions of their own, jabbing at the maps, and talking to the centaur.

Linsha listened for a moment, hoping to hear the news about Schallsea, then felt herself pulled back by a hand on her arm. "Come see this prisoner who spoke of the eggs," Lanther whispered. "He won't last much longer."

She turned to go, but Horemheb stopped her with one last question. "Lady, where is this Abyssal Lance you spoke of? Do you still have it?"

Linsha could not speak for a moment through the welter of emotions that suddenly assailed her. Anger, shame, dismay, and regret whipped on by a deep-seated fear—all charged through her thoughts.

"I don't know where it is," she said at last. "We were

forced to leave it in Thunder's body, and when we returned to retrieve it, it was gone."

She said nothing more, nor did she wait to hear any possible disappointed comments or critical remarks from anyone. She'd already heard them all or said them to herself. She turned and walked away with Lanther, leaving Leonidas, Horemheb, and the men to finish their discussion.

Into the Labyrinth

4

The prisoner huddled against the wall of the stone cell. There were only three holding cells in the Post, all carved into the rock wall of the canyon and all large enough to hold at least five large men. The prisoner, the sole occupant of his cell, looked small and pathetic on the floor, like a pale pile of bloody rags.

Linsha eyed him critically. "Another one?" she said with some disapproval.

Lanther was not known for his ability to treat enemy prisoners with kid gloves. He was usually a patient and deliberate man, but almost two years ago he had spent too many days in the hands of Sable's guards after they caught him in the swamp. He still bore the limp and the scars to prove it. Since that time he had little patience or mercy left to offer uncooperative enemy prisoners.

He shrugged at her question. "In truth, we found him like this. I think the mercenaries left him out in the Rough to die."

The Rough, the rock-strewn, scrubby grasslands on the outskirts of the Missing City certainly would have finished off a wounded man—if the wild dogs, the lions, or the ants did not find him first.

Linsha looked closer at the prisoner and realized the tatters and rags she had taken for his clothes were just an undertunic and some leggings. There was no sign of boots, cloak, outer tunic, vest, jerkin, or even armor. The man had been stripped of everything but his undergarments.

"Did your men take—?"

"We would have if he'd had any, but he was left the way you see him. I think he irritated someone." He pulled the rough wooden door open further, lifted a torch from its bracket, and thrust it into the gloom.

The two stepped inside. Varia dropped from Linsha's shoulder and glided into the darkness of the cell. Extending her taloned feet, she landed gently on the wounded man's back. The prisoner did not move. The owl craned her neck to study the man's face half-hidden by his out-flung arm.

"This one is dead," Varia hooted softly. She hopped to the ground close to his head.

Lanther swore and hurried over. Rolling the man over, he held the torch over the slack, battered face.

A stink of urine, sweat, and old blood rose from the body. The corpse's face stared glassily through half-closed lids. He was a young man, Linsha noticed, too short to be a Tarmak and too well fed and heavily muscled to be one of the townsfolk still living in the city. A mercenary, probably. He had been viciously beaten on his head and torso and whipped across his back. She also noticed some odd burn marks on his temples. What had he done to deserve such treatment?

She knelt beside the body and closed the bruised eyelids. "Leonidas mentioned the eggs?"

Lanther irritably pushed a hank of dark hair out of his eyes and glared down at the corpse. "Gods blast it. I wanted you to hear this man's story from his own lips."

"Does it matter? Did you think I wouldn't trust you? Since he can't, you tell me."

With an abruptness marked with annoyance, Lanther rolled the body back onto its stomach. "He claimed the Tarmaks have moved the dragon eggs back into the labyrinth. He didn't know why, and he was hazy about where. Apparently he wasn't supposed to be down in the tunnels—none of them are because some of Iyesta's guardians are still loose down there. But he said they—meaning the mercenaries—went down there often through Iyesta's throne room to look for more treasure."

"I can believe that. They were not happy when the Tarmaks cleared out the treasure during our attack."

"No," Lanther agreed.

"So he stumbled on the nest?"

"No. He overheard a large party of Tarmaks moving through the tunnels. He told me he followed them for a short way because they were carrying large baskets."

Linsha lifted the owl back to her shoulder and walked with Lanther out of the cell. "How did he know they had the eggs?" she questioned, continuing their conversation as he left the door open and replaced the torch in its bracket.

"He wanted to get close enough to see if they were carrying treasure, but when he heard them discussing eggs, he hightailed it out of there."

"So who beat him?"

They walked into a small adjoining room.

"His captain," Lanther answered. "He didn't say why."

Her arms crossed, Linsha gazed silently at the wall of the small guardroom that served the men who kept watch on the cells. It was empty at that moment and very quiet. The news of the eggs rolled around and around her head. As questionable as it was, this was the first clue she had of the eggs that was more solid than the hints, hopes, and rumors she had heard before. Was it worth checking?

"You're not thinking of going, are you?" Lanther said with no sign of alarm. He poured a cup of weak wine from a small supply that had been set aside for the officers. He gave it to her.

She pulled her mouth into a wry grin and lifted the cup in a mock salute. "You knew I would. You wouldn't have told me any of this if you had been deeply concerned about the truth of the matter. You would have let him die in silence."

"True." He poured another cup of wine and saluted her in turn. "Your sense of honor is something I admire and can depend on."

"Will you go with me?" she asked, knowing he would. His sense of honor was equally as predictable, and despite his limp, he was an excellent companion to have on a clandestine quest.

"Of course."

"This could be a trap. The Tarmaks know we want the eggs. They could have planted that man out in the Rough for us to find."

"Agreed. We should take some centaurs with us in case we find the eggs. If we find them, we can bring them back here."

"Good idea. Leonidas wouldn't want to be left out."

Linsha felt that old feeling of subdued excitement steal back into her thoughts. It was a tense, exhilarating anticipation that she used to feel often when she was faced with a mission that would test her wits, skills, and courage. It was a feeling she had been too tired to experience lately.

"Nor do I," Varia spoke up again. Although she did not like to talk around other people, she had talked to Lanther before and included him in her small circle of acceptable humans. "How do you plan to get inside the labyrinth? The mercenaries found your door in the garden and guard it day and night."

"They didn't find the pool entrance," Linsha suggested.

Lanther abruptly scowled and set his cup rather heavily on a table. "Isn't that the one with the water weird guarding the stairs?"

Linsha smothered a smile. Lanther and the water weird Iyesta had placed to guard the pool stairs had not met in the friendliest circumstances. The odd water creature had tried to attack the man before Crucible called her off.

"Yes, but the entrance is unguarded outside, and it is out of sight of the palace. All we'd have to do is avoid patrols and slip in after dark."

"What about the weird? How do we get past her?"

Linsha's hand started to reach for the chain and the scales around her neck, then she changed her mind and resisted the temptation to show him. She moved her hand up instead to scratch her chin. Lanther had seen them once, but she preferred not to flash them about. They were a secret, a pact of friendship between herself and the dragons, and something she wasn't ready to share. They were also a safeguard from some of Iyesta's guardian creatures.

"I'll think of something," she said.

He gestured to the doorway. "Then let's not wait. We'll broach this to Falaius and go tonight."

Falaius proved easier to convince than General Dockett or even Sir Remmik. The Legion commander trusted Lanther to be a good judge of his own information and a competent leader of missions. He also respected Linsha's abilities, and if the two of them chose to go into the labyrinth again to look for Iyesta's eggs, he agreed to help. When he asked for volunteers among the sentries and guards coming off duty, seven Legionnaires stepped forward. It was something they all owed to the memory of Iyesta.

General Dockett had some worries about the validity of the information, but in the end he agreed with Falaius and assigned a patrol of eight centaurs and Leonidas to accompany them.

The centaurs, all of them grays or dark browns, looked pleased to be chosen for such an assignment. They hurried off to find baskets large enough to carry dragon eggs but not so large as to interfere with their movements in the tunnels.

Only Sir Remmik voiced strong objections to the "ridiculous and dangerous scheme based on the words of a dead man." He didn't argue for Linsha's sake. She suspected he'd be quite pleased if she got herself killed. But he hated to endanger eight perfectly healthy centaurs and the Legionnaires who could be put to better use. At last he threw up his hands and stalked off to check the guard changes at the posts around the canyon.

Falaius watched him go, a wry look on his weathered face. "It's a shame such a talented Knight has so many burrs stuck up his armor."

By the time a late half moon lifted above the eastern hills, the party was ready to go. The centaurs slipped out of the Wadi in a single file, each one carrying one of the humans and a set of panniers strapped to their sides. They broke into a smooth, ground-eating jog and

39

headed south and east toward the faint glow of the city eight miles away.

The land slept silently around them. The night was too cold for insects, and the small rodents, birds, and reptiles that lived in the sparse grass and scrub stayed snug in their holes and nests. Even the wind was still. Only the faint howl of a distant wild dog broke the silence. Overhead, against the frosty stars, Varia the owl flew on silent wings. Almost as soundless, the centaurs moved like shadows through the darkness. They had padded their harnesses and weapons, so the only sounds that gave them away were the click of hooves on rocks and the dry rustle of disturbed grass.

They were nearing the edge of the known limit of the mercenary patrols when Linsha saw the leading centaur raise his hand and make a motion in a noiseless signal. Every centaur slowed to a walk and spread out in a line across the faint path.

"What is it?" Linsha whispered to Leonidas.

The buckskin, the lightest-coated centaur in the patrol, shifted over to a bare patch of sand and windswept rock where he would not be as noticeable. "There is someone up ahead," he answered softly.

The eerie cry of a hunting owl floated overhead. Wings braked softly by Linsha's head, and she heard Varia say, "It is Mariana."

Leonidas heard her, too, and quickly trotted forward. "Tanefer," he called to the black stallion who served as the leader. "It is the captain's patrol."

There were a few other officers in the dragonlord's militia who held the rank of captain, but only the half-elf Mariana Calanbriar was referred to as "the captain" with automatic recognition and full respect. She materialized out of the darkness, three militia fighters behind her, and trod softly across the grass to meet the centaurs. Seeing Leonidas and Linsha, she raised a slim hand and laughed. "Of course, you are here. Nine centaurs with baskets, in the middle of the night, and the Rose Knight is with them. Are you off to collect berries?"

"No," Linsha said. "Eggs."

Mariana's humor vanished. She and Linsha had been the ones who found Iyesta's body in the great chambers under the palace. She despised the Tarmaks with all her heart for their part in the death of her overlord and had vowed to do anything within her means to help retrieve the brass eggs.

"You found the eggs?" she asked.

"There is a possibility the Tarmaks have moved the eggs back into the labyrinth," Lanther said from Tanefer's back.

A flash of paler white on Mariana's oval face revealed a quick smile. "Good. Then you are probably going in through the pool entrance. I'd like to come with you, but we have three more outposts to check. One of them," she added, her voice grim in the darkness, "was wiped out."

Lanther swore something under his breath. The centaurs and their riders stirred, muttering angrily to each other.

"That is the third watchers' post we've lost," Linsha said. "It makes me wonder if someone is telling the Brutes where they are."

The half-elf made a slight shrug. "Maybe. Or maybe they just have an excellent tracker."

"Have you seen any activity along the ruin's edge?"

"We were there along the outskirts and we saw no sign of the Tarmaks. There are a few mercenary patrols out, but they are slow and not particularly determined.

If you slip in quickly along that low line of hills, you shouldn't be spotted. Good luck!"

She waved to her men, and they moved on, shadows casting shadows on the ground. In a moment, they were gone.

Linsha tossed a salute in the direction of her friend. "Be safe," she murmured.

The centaurs continued at a walk, moving carefully and as noiselessly as possible. They angled down along the slope of hills Mariana pointed out and followed the western foot of the rising land where their tall profiles could not be silhouetted against the night sky.

The small moon was nearly to its zenith when the party came to the farthest flung edges of the ancient city. The humans dismounted. With a signal to Tanefer, Lanther and Linsha crept forward to the brow of a small rise and looked down on Missing City.

Five hundred years ago, the land they looked upon had been vastly different. Instead of desert, large estates and magnificent gardens had filled the desolate land with beauty and provided the region with bountiful harvests. Sparkling fountains, pools, and delightful streams watered the gardens and lawns and provided tranquil settings for the Silvanesti elves who'd built the city and labored for its well-being. Beyond the estates to the south lay the vast gardens and palace of an elf prince, and bordering it were the four districts of the ancient port city of Gal Tra'kalas.

Once a thriving urban center on the southern Courrain Ocean, the fair elven city had prospered until the First Cataclysm shook the world with catastrophic changes. At some time during the shattering event, the city of Gal Tra'kalas was utterly destroyed from the breakwater that stood in the harbor to the last lovely outlying estate, leaving nothing but a barren plain of crumbling ruins. Yet the city and its inhabitants did not disappear completely. Strangely, Gal Tra'kalas remained as a phantom image, inhabited by spectral figures who continued to live their lives totally unaware of the monumental change in the world around them.

Griffin-riding elves from Silvanesti who flew over the ghostly city were appalled and reported that Gal Tra'kalas was cast down and inhabited by fiends. The elves immediately abandoned the ruin. Over the years the site came to be called the Missing City, and for centuries it hung only as an empty mirage on the edge of forgotten tales. It wasn't until nearly four hundred years later that a Second Cataclysm occurred that once again changed the destiny of the city. Out of the empty reaches of the Plains of Dust came the Legion of Steel, who saw the potential of a shadow city, and swiftly on their heels flew a magnificent brass dragon with the strength and the desire to shape a new realm on the ruins of an ancient one. Together the Legion and the dragonlord Iyesta dwelt among the images of Gal Tra'kalas and rebuilt the city into a detailed copy of the mirage, and for years the people who flocked to the Missing City lived in peace with their ghostly neighbors.

Until nearly three months ago. On the eve of midsummer, an odd storm of ferocious intensity swept over the Missing City. When the sun rose the next day, the spectral city of the elves had vanished, obliterated once and for all. Since then, nothing had remained the same.

On this frosty night months after the storm, the old city still looked strangely forlorn and vulnerable to Linsha. In the distance, she could see the dark clusters of the real buildings that comprised the rebuilt districts and the new port. A faint light from a few torches and lamps glowed like a chain of dying embers in the darkness.

In her immediate vicinity there was nothing but sand, scrub, a few cold-hardy cacti, and some eroded piles of rock that hunkered down in the pale moonlight. One large mass of rock in particular held her interest. She concentrated on the area around the rocks but saw nothing that moved, human or otherwise.

Pursing her lips, she blew the soft cry of a night shrike, a small bird that inhabited the grassland.

Varia swooped overhead. "The way is clear," she called in a whispery voice that only Linsha and Lanther could hear.

Lanther gestured to the others, and they hurried forward to the large heap of rock. In the dark the tall heap looked like an outcropping or a natural part of the landscape. It wasn't until a closer inspection was made that the pile proved to be a collapsed heap of quarried stone so weathered and worn it seemed to be melded together.

"What is this?" Tanefer said sharply, for he had no experience with the labyrinth or its hidden entrances.

"Centuries ago it used to be a well until someone got the idea to turn it into a bath house," Linsha said as she peered closely at the cracks and crannies in the rocks. She walked slowly around the old ruin. The entrance was here somewhere.

Then she remembered. The old door faced the west and was hidden behind a large rock that looked like a collapsed lintel stone. "Here," she said and pointed to the wall.

It took three of the strongest centaurs to shove aside the slab of rock that Iyesta had once moved effortlessly. When it was done, the three stood aside, panting and sweating in the chilly air. They all looked into the black entrance that yawned before them.

"There is a short flight of stairs leading down," Linsha told them. "It's broad, but it's in bad shape, so be careful. Don't light the torches until you've moved the stone back."

"Where are you going?" Lanther demanded.

"To talk to the water weird."

The centaurs froze. "Wait," Tanefer said. "No one said anything about a water elementalkin. Where did it come from?"

"Iyesta summoned it to protect this entrance. But I think we can get past it. Just give me a minute."

Linsha ignored Lanther's sharp stare and settled Varia once more on her shoulder. Moving out of the way of the group, she felt her way down the stairs to the chamber that had once been a bathing room. Behind her she heard thumps and grinding noises, the sounds of hooves on stone, and low voices muttering in annoyance. Putting the stone back in place was not as easy as moving it aside. She reached the last step and pressed back against the wall to stay out of the reach of the water weird.

"She's not here," Varia whispered.

Linsha blinked. "What?"

"She's gone. The pool is empty."

Linsha strained to see in the intense darkness, but there wasn't even a beam of moonlight leaking through a crack to lessen her blindness. Frustrated, she pulled from a small pack a tiny lamp and the clay pot that held a precious coal. Breathing gently on the faint orange glow, she was able to light her lamp and cast just enough light in the chamber to see the pool.

Varia was right. The pool had once brimmed with clear water deep enough to swim in. Now it lay still and lifeless. Much of its water had drained or evaporated away, and what was left was muddy and covered with a stagnant scum of dust, dead insects, and old algae. The ancient floor tiles she remembered seeing on her first visit were now covered with dirt and piles of rock that had fallen from the ceiling.

The voices grew louder and hooves clattered down the stairs. The centaurs and the Legionnaires crowded into the chamber with Linsha. They stared at the pool.

"Is it here?" Lanther breathed near her ear.

"She's gone. Probably back to her own elemental plane."

"Really?" He sounded skeptical.

"Iyesta commanded her here. Perhaps when the dragon died, her hold over the water weird disappeared, allowing her to escape."

"Good. Then let's not dawdle."

"Sir!" one of the Legionnaires called to Lanther. "Look here. Someone has been in here before us."

He pointed to the edge of the pool and toward the ground at the furthest reaches of the small lamp. Several sets of tracks were barely visible in the dirt.

Linsha looked and recognized them. She chuckled, with slight undertone of sadness. "Those are our tracks from three months ago. Iyesta's and mine, then mine and several other groups. We brought some of the militia out this way when the city fell."

She led the way past the pool and down another set of stone stairs to a chamber on a lower level. Once there, underground where lights could not be seen above, they brought out torches and lit them from Linsha's lamp. Holding their torches to light the way, the party tramped down another, longer, flight of stairs and moved into a high corridor.

The labyrinth beneath Missing City was as old as Gal Tra'kalas itself. Deep beneath the city it formed a massive maze of chambers, interconnecting corridors, and puzzling dead ends. Its purpose was long forgotten, but its lofty tunnels still bore evidence of the skill and aesthetic taste of its creators. The tunnels were arched, and in many places the graceful lines of fan vaulting helped retain the strength and beauty of ceilings that were centuries old. At the intersections of major corridors, the lintels were carved to resemble tree trunks that rose and burst into leaf in stone relief over the doors.

Only Lanther, Linsha, and a few of the Legionnaires had been in the tunnels before. Anxious for the eggs, they pressed on, following their own faint trail. Whenever they came to a turn or an intersection that gave them doubts, Varia whispered directions in Linsha's ear. The owl had a phenomenal memory for dark places.

The rest of the Legionnaires and centaurs hurried behind, their eyes wide with wonder and surprise. They had heard of Iyesta's death in the labyrinth near her palace, of the midnight escape of a few trapped pockets of militia and Legionnaires out of the city through the tunnels, and of the battle with Thunder in the egg chamber. But they never imagined anything as spacious and well-crafted as these tunnels, nor a space so well preserved after hundreds years of neglect and abandonment.

In silence the party walked deeper and deeper into the maze, making turns to the left and right that Linsha never would have remembered on her own. As they penetrated farther into the labyrinth, they began to pay less attention to the walls around them and more to the floor and to the heavy darkness that pressed close. They were far in now and had seen only the traces of the earlier small groups. If the Tarmaks had truly carried the eggs into the great chamber in the center of the maze, there should have been some evidence of their passing.

True, Linsha thought, there were other entrances to the labyrinth and other tunnels that led toward the chamber, but she worried nonetheless and kept a close eye on the dusty floors of each tunnel they passed or entered.

She was so busy looking for tracks that she did not realize they were nearing the chamber until she heard someone behind her whisper, "What is that light?"

Linsha's head jerked up. A pale gold light glowed through the pitch darkness from a turn in the tunnel ahead. It was still there!

But it looked different, and something else was gone. When she came the first time to the cave with Iyesta, she'd found the air in the egg chamber was rich and moist like the air in the woods around Solace. Now it was like the rest of the labyrinth—cool and dry and smelling just slightly of decay. The hair on her neck rose, and a warning went off in her head.

"They're not there." She said it so sharply that the centaurs jerked to a stop.

Linsha ran forward, nearly unseating the owl on her shoulder. She ignored the pain of Varia's talons on her skin. She ignored Lanther's shout of warning and the exclamations of the others. She charged toward the light with her heart in her throat. At the turn of the tunnel she raced into a chamber as grand and enormous as befitting a nest of dragon eggs, and she came to a skidding halt.

Her eyes took it all in—the withered corpse of the mother brass dragon against the far wall, the mound where they had buried Azurale, the decayed, beetle-chewed carcass of the blue dragonlord, Thunder, and finally, the ruined, trampled nest of sand where the eggs had once lain. Varia flew from her shoulder and flapped in a circle over the nest, her voice sadly keening.

Linsha's body stilled. Her nostrils flared. The warning in her head turned into a klaxon, and she knew without a doubt. Linsha wheeled.

"Go back!" she shouted to the others coming up behind her. "We've got to get out! It's a trap!"

Lanther grabbed her arm and pulled her to a stop. "What do you mean? How do you know?"

"Look!" she said. Her hand pointed to the empty nest. "There are no eggs! They were just used to lure us down here. We've got to go!"

Tanefer trotted to her side, his bearded face locked in a frown. "Are you sure? Couldn't the Tarmaks have placed the eggs somewhere else? This labyrinth is huge."

Linsha didn't want to argue. Every part of her mind screamed at her to leave as quickly as possible. But the centaurs and the Legionnaires milled around in confusion, staring at the dead dragons and talking among themselves.

"There is no other place in this labyrinth suitable for incubation," Linsha said. "Iyesta and Purestian altered this cavern with magic to give it light and warmth and the proper conditions for the eggs' development. There is nothing left here but the light, and even that is failing. No, there are no eggs down here. Now get rid of those baskets and run!"

She was relieved to see her urgency finally sink in. Young Leonidas was the first to accept her word. With a swift cut of his dagger, he loosed the ropes holding the baskets on his back, dumped them on the floor, and gave her his hand. He hauled her onto his back. Lanther and Tanefer exchanged alarmed glances before they too urged the others to move. Baskets fell to the floor, swords were drawn, and the Legionnaires were quickly mounted on the backs of the centaurs.

Suddenly Varia's feathered "ears" popped up. Her eyes grew enormous. She screeched an alarm everyone understood and flew out the tunnel entrance.

Linsha and Leonidas did not need another warning. The buckskin centaur cantered for the tunnel, the others close on his heels. With their torches held high, they hurried back the way they had come, hoping to reach the faraway pool entrance before anyone else in the labyrinth knew they were there.

But they had not gone far when Varia returned, winging up the passage they had just entered. The centaurs stopped, and in the sudden silence that fell among them, they all heard what the owl had heard in the cavern—voices and the sounds of a large troop moving at a quick march through the tunnels. In the twists and turns of the labyrinth, it was difficult to tell exactly where and how far away a sound originated, but no one doubted the creators of the noises that echoed up the tunnel were not far away. Surely they were even now on their trail of hoofprints in the layer of dirt on the tunnel floors.

Linsha thought fast. Although she had spent more time down there than anyone else in the group, she had always had a guide to help her find her way in the lightless maze. She did not know it well, nor was she familiar with more than four or five doors. Two of those doors were out of their reach in the old foundations of the city, one was the way they had come through the pool house, and one was guarded by the mercenaries on the palace grounds.

She raised an arm for Varia. When the owl landed on her wrist, she whispered, "Who is there?"

The owl clacked her beak in anger. "Tarmaks. Many of them. They are in the tunnel that you must take to reach the pool door."

"How convenient," Linsha snapped.

Several well-chosen curses ran through her mind, all aimed at herself. She had been so sure. She wanted to be so sure! She wanted those eggs back so much that instead of doing something sensible like coming down alone to scout out the situation, she had brought along seventeen others to share in her heedless stupidity. Now they were trapped in this maze without a safe door out.

"Where do we go?" Leonidas asked. His hooves shifted nervously beneath him.

There was only one place she could think of, only one door that they might be able to break through. "The palace. We'll have to go to the door in the palace gardens."

"Isn't that one guarded by the mercenaries?" Lanther reminded her. She wished he hadn't, but the others may as well be prepared.

"Yes. Who would you rather fight, the Tarmaks or the mercenaries?"

No one bothered to answer. In one motion, they wheeled around and hurried back toward the egg chamber. They passed the chamber and plunged into a different tunnel, one leading away from the abandoned nest. From that point Varia helped direct Linsha on the route to the western side of the labyrinth and the chambers that lay under the vast palace of Iyesta's old lair. The centaurs jogged as fast as they dared, and for a little while Linsha hoped the Tarmaks would turn into the egg chamber, that they didn't know the militia group was down there. But that faint hope soon died. Their small troop could not seem to escape. Every time they paused and allowed the sound of their hooves to die into silence, they heard the noises of pursuit echoing behind them. Their pursuers moved surprisingly fast and had no trouble tracking them through the settled dust and dirt on the floor.

"Is there another way to reach this door?" Tanefer asked Linsha. "Or could we work our way around and lose them in the maze? Then we could go back to the pool door."

Linsha had wondered the same thing. Although she did not know the tunnels well enough to find an exact route, it just might be possible to hide their tracks, wander around long enough to lose their hunters, and find another way out of the maze. But Lanther didn't give her time to speculate.

"No," he shot back. "We can't afford to run aimlessly around down here. We have no water or food, and the Tarmaks will put guards on every entrance they've found—if they haven't already. It would be better to make a fast break out and try to get past the mercenaries before they know we're there."

Not a word of dissent was spoken. Everyone wanted to escape the heavy, brooding darkness and the threat that closed in on their heels. They hurried on.

Before long they reached a section of the labyrinth Linsha remembered well. She had been here several times with Mariana and Crucible. The chamber where Iyesta had died was only a turn or two away. As much as she would have liked to stop to pay her respects to the dead dragonlord and be sure the body had not be disturbed, she knew there was no time.

"We're almost to the palace," she warned Leonidas.

The young horse-man nodded once. He pulled his short hunting bow off his shoulder, strung it, and settled the quiver of arrows at his side where he could easily reach it. The other centaurs followed suit.

They reached the high, wide passages that criss-crossed beneath the grounds of the old elven palace, and to their relief, found them empty. The treasure-hunting mercenaries seemed to be busy elsewhere. Hurrying faster, they passed the arched entrances to the tunnels and the vast stairs leading to the palace and took the corridor that sloped up to the surface. At the foot of another flight of stairs, Leonidas and Tanefer stopped the others. They gathered close, grim and silent, their weapons ready.

"The entrance is up those stairs and through a short hall," Linsha told them. "The last time I saw it, the doorway was hidden behind vines and overgrown bushes, but it was open and wide enough for us to pass through one at a time."

The centaurs and the Legionnaires did not look happy at that news. A small doorway made it too easy for an enemy to pick off departing opponents one by one. Warily they walked up the steps. At the end of the hall they saw a glimmer of daylight and realized night had passed and the sun was beginning to rise. So much for the cover of darkness.

Tanefer set three centaurs and their riders to watch the top of the stairs, then he and Leonidas led the rest down the hallway toward the light. A clatter and a loud outcry from outside suddenly broke the quiet of the dawn. A horn's blast echoed into the corridor. The centaurs and the humans looked one another in alarm.

They recognized those sounds all too well. It was the noise of armed conflict.

"Oh, gods, now what?" Tanefer growled, voicing the frustration of all. Their group wasn't outside yet. Who would the mercenaries be fighting?

Linsha slid off Leonidas's back and hurried to the entrance. The door was smaller than the arches and corridors below and opened into a spacious courtyard that was part of the large, overgrown gardens connected to the palace where Iyesta had once made her lair. The doorway was as she remembered, its wooden door long rotted away, its opening cloaked in vines and disguised by the roots and branches of shrubs and young trees. Keeping to the shadows, she pushed aside some vines and peered carefully out, squinting in the early morning light.

The signal horn sounded again, loud and fierce, and this time it was accompanied by shouts and screams from several directions. Weapons clashed somewhere out of sight.

There was nothing Linsha could see in her immediate vicinity, so she held out her arm for the owl and waited as Varia stepped to her wrist and launched herself out into the rising morning wind.

Lanther crowded in beside her and together they watched the owl wing silently into a copse of nearby trees. "Where are they?" he muttered in Linsha's ear. "Do you see anything?"

She stared into the trees and gave her head a brief shake. "No. But judging by the horns, the mercenaries are under attack. Did Falaius have something planned I didn't know about?"

"Not that he told me. Maybe this was meant to be a distraction?"

Any thought of that abruptly ended when a dozen or so mercenaries burst through the grove of trees where

Varia hid. They ran as if all the denizens of the Abyss were after them. The mercenaries scrambled over a collapsed wall and ran through the overgrowth toward the distant palace. A flight of arrows ripped through leaves behind them and fell in their midst. Several men fell and lay still. Another fell screaming but fought his way to his feet and staggered after his companions, none of whom stopped to help him.

More figures, their bare skin stained blue, crashed through the undergrowth into the courtyard and loped after the mercenaries. They caught up with the wounded man, slit his throat, and moved on without a pause. They disappeared into the trees and brush just behind the fleeing mercenaries.

Linsha stood transfixed.

Lanther's eyes smoldered with anger while he watched; the scar on his face burned a dull red against his weathered skin. "The Tarmaks are finally moving," he said as if pronouncing a doom.

Linsha knew he was. She had suspected for some time that the Tarmaks were biding their time, allowing Thunder's hired mercenaries to grow lazy and complacent in the dragon's lair before they disposed of them. Today of all days they had launched a surprise attack against the soldiers, and Linsha and her militia had rushed into the thick of it.

"We can't go out there," she said. "We'll be caught in the middle."

Shouts suddenly rang through the passageway behind them. Hoofbeats pounded on stone.

"We already are," Lanther said as the centaurs crowded into the hall.

"What are you waiting for?" Tanefer bellowed from the back. "The Tarmaks are coming up the stairs. Two of ours have already fallen."

"The Tarmaks are in front of us, too!" Linsha replied. She glanced back at the centaurs and Legionnaires crowded into the dimly lit corridor. She saw concern and some anxiety on their faces, but there was determination as well. They had fought together for so long, they had no need to question one another or seek advice. They knew what needed to be done.

Linsha hauled aside a clump of vines to clear the door. "Go!" she snapped.

The first centaur sprang out, his rider ducking low and hanging on with all his strength. They did not run though. Both man and centaur drew their bows and took a position to the right of the door to cover the courtyard. The second centaur drew up beside them, then a third.

Four centaurs waited outside the entrance when an owl's cry shattered the air. Ten more Tarmaks erupted from the dense stand of trees and raced over the ruined wall. Both foes saw one another and released their arrows at the same time. A howl rose from the Brute warriors, and without waiting to see how their arrows fell, they plunged in with swords and battle-axes. Two Legionnaires and a centaur fell, mortally wounded. Two more centaurs charged out the doorway.

Linsha had no time left to watch. Leonidas came up beside her, hauled her onto his back, and barged out of the door before she could see if Tanefer and Lanther were behind her.

War cries rang out in the passage, and a bevy of crossbow bolts whirred out behind her. She felt a stinging blow to the back of her left arm, and when she reached around, she felt a bolt protruding from the fleshy part of her upper arm. It was only a flesh wound, but it hurt like fury down to her fingers, and she had no time to work the bolt loose. Warm blood stained her sleeve and seeped down her skin.

Meanwhile the Tarmaks had pressed their attack with a cold ferocity, in spite of the fact that they were attacking a superior force of men and centaurs. Their swords brought down two more centaurs and badly wounded a Legionnaire before Leonidas reached the fray.

The young stallion fired his crossbow pointblank into the neck of the Brute attacking the wounded Legionnaire. Blood spattered over his chest and Linsha's legs. Linsha tried to help the wounded man onto Leonidas's back, but another Brute whirled and threw a small axe into the man's back, severing his spinal cord. The Legionnaire, a man Linsha respected and knew well, gave a grunt of pain and shock and sagged out of her arms. His face went slack as his body struck the ground. Leonidas sidestepped away from the body and drew his sword.

"Linsha, we've got to get out of this!" he yelled. He blocked a blow from another warrior and kicked a hind hoof into the knee of a third. Linsha forced herself to hold on. Her head felt heavy and dizzy from the loss of blood.

"Where are Tanefer and Lanther?" she cried. She looked around wildly and saw nothing of the man or the black stallion. Forms moved in the doorway, but when she looked that way she saw only Tarmaks hacking aside the vines and pouring out of the dark exit. Her heart sank.

"Go! Go! Go!" she shouted.

There was nothing else to do. If Tanefer and Lanther had not left the passageway by now, they had probably given their lives holding the door against the enemy.

The centaurs still standing upright heard her call and obeyed. Including Leonidas, there were only four centaurs, three Legionnaires, and Linsha able to flee. They took what wounded they could and broke away from the Tarmaks. The footing was treacherous for horse hooves among the tumbled stones, fallen trees, and tangled roots of the ancient ruin, but they tried to increase their speed away from the bows and throwing axes of the enemy.

The Tarmaks jeered loudly and moved to follow at a determined pace. One pulled out a small horn and blew two quick blasts and a longer one.

Linsha stiffened. Those horn blasts sounded too much like a signal. But a signal for what? She was also alarmed to see that her small group was moving toward the palace instead of north to the edges of the ruined city and the open plains beyond. If the Tarmaks were attacking the mercenaries' headquarters in the dragon's palace as she suspected, the last place she wanted to be was caught in the middle of *that* fight. Just what did that signal portend?

The centaurs reached a strip of open grassland where a few cattle stood huddled in a frightened group. Bodies of mercenaries lay scattered across the grass in cooling pools of blood. Just beyond a line of tall pines, the crumbled buildings of the huge palace thrust up through centuries of wild growth. The tall, elegant hall of the dragonlord still stood proud and gleaming above the ruins. Its missing roof was the only visible sign of the damage inflicted by Thunder during his brief possession of the lair a few months ago.

In the open areas of grassland and park around the outskirts of the palace, Linsha saw groups of mercenaries locked in desperate struggle. Sunlight gleamed off weapons and polished helms. The wind, blowing warm from the plains, pulled at wisps of smoke rising from the palace's main gate in the encircling wall. Not far from the gates a Tarmak siege engine hurled another fireball at the walls, and more warriors released a thick hail of arrows at the defenders.

Leonidas did not need prompting. He saw the fighting and veered to the right away from the palace and toward the outskirts of the city that led to the open plains. Out on the flatter grasslands, the centaurs could run and not even a Tarmak on horseback could catch them.

But the small group of survivors never had the chance to reach the open plains. They were nearing the edge of the meadow when Linsha saw Varia flying overhead. The owl winged by them, reached a grove of trees, and all at once veered on a wingtip. To Linsha's horror, several arrows flew from the trees after the owl. She saw Varia lurch in flight then vanish into the tree canopy.

"Archers ahead!" she screamed. "There are Tarmaks in the trees!"

The centaurs dug in their hooves, slid to a stop, and tried to turn another direction.

Too late.

Tarmaks approached from the gardens at a swift run, while others came from the east where the battle raged around the palace. More blue-skinned warriors emerged in a line from the grove of trees, their bows drawn and arrows nocked, effectively cutting off any hope of escape.

The centaurs milled frantically then drew in a tight circle, rump to rump, back to back, their weapons drawn and ready to make a last stand. The humans did likewise.

Swiftly the Tarmaks came after them, as fierce and hungry as a pack of wolves. With a shout in their strange language, they encircled the beleaguered militia and drew the trap closed.

Silence measured a long, terrifying minute. The centaurs panted for breath and waited, their expressions grim. The larger number of Tarmaks crouched, bows and a dozen spears ready to kill.

"Surrender!" one Tarmak said in clear Common. "Surrender at once or we kill all of you!"

Linsha sagged against Leonidas, numb with defeat.

Ambush

6

By the time the fire burned through the flimsy barricade erected by the defenders, the remaining mercenaries caught outside the palace had been eliminated and those trapped inside had been demoralized. As soon as the gate fell, the Tarmaks charged in and captured the throne room. It took most of the day to track down and slaughter the entire garrison of slightly more than four hundred mercenaries, for the old ruin had warrens of tunnels, numerous rooms, and more hiding holes than anyone could count. The mercenaries put up more of a struggle than expected, but in the late afternoon the Tarmak warriors gathered in the forecourt of the palace, confident they had the palace to themselves. Beyond the gates, in the grassy meadow, a huge pyre took care of the final mercenary problem.

An *ekwegul*, the leader of a Tarmak hundred (or *ekwul*), that had been assigned to this job, wiped his hands in satisfaction and watched the black smoke rise from the pyre in the nearby field. His warriors moved confidently around him, picking up weapons, kicking dirt over pools of blood, and looking for anything of interest. Their general would be coming soon to inspect the dragon's lair, and while no one was squeamish about pools of blood and bits of bodies lying around, the mess did tend to draw flies and those vicious ants even the Tarmaks had grown to hate.

A human man, wearing filthy bloodstained clothes, emerged from the open doors of the throne room and strode across the courtyard toward the *ekwegul*. None of the Tarmaks made a move to stop him. In fact many tilted their heads or touched their chests in gestures of respect when they saw him. The *ekwegul* watched him come, a lazy smile on his face.

"So, they fell into our trap," he said when the man stopped beside him.

"We had the right bait."

The *ekwegul* looked down at the man. The Tarmak officer was over seven feet tall, a normal height for his people. The human barely reached six feet and did not have the elegantly pointed ears the Tarmaks prized. Yet he was a cunning warrior, an astute military planner, and the adopted son of the Tarmak king's beloved younger brother. The Tarmaks had long ago forgotten the man's minor physical deformities.

"Where are they now?" the *ekwegul* asked.

"The centaurs have been sent to the slave pens. I separated the woman from the buckskin stallion. He is very loyal to her. The lady knight and men are in the cells under the palace."

The Tarmak nodded. "Good. I've seen those cells. A rat could not escape from one."

The human gave a brief laugh. "Don't underestimate the talents of that woman. I want a guard on her day and night. Did the owl get away?"

"Mathurra told me it was nicked by an arrow, but it escaped. Into the trees he thinks."

The man's mouth and eyes narrowed in displeasure. "Send someone out to scour the grounds under the trees. Be certain. The owl must be undamaged."

"It will be done."

They stood for a moment in thoughtful silence, watching the smoke rise into the afternoon sky, before the man said, "The attack is still set for tonight. The 2nd and 4th *ekwul* will lead the way, but you will be needed to watch the paths and escape routes. Will your warriors be ready?"

The Tarmak did not hesitate. "Of course. We had light casualties. I will see they are fed and rested, and they will be ready to serve."

"The goddess be with you tonight," the man replied.

They exchanged salutes, and the man walked back toward the throne room.

Linsha was still awake when the Tarmaks brought down another prisoner. She heard the creak of the door at the top of the stairs and the plod of feet coming down the stone steps into the circular room that had once been an interrogation chamber of sorts. Five stone cells set in the wall opened into the room and could be watched by one man. Several torches in brackets on the walls lit the room and cast some illumination on a bare table, several stools, and the rusted remains of a few chains dangling from the ceiling. Two Tarmaks sat at the table and did nothing but watch the cell doors.

A dim light from the torches lit the cells as well through the barred doors. The bars were in remarkable shape in spite of their age and the dampness in the room, prompting Linsha to test one when the Tarmak guards were not looking her way. As she suspected, the bars had been forged with elven spells and still carried vestiges of that power. There would be no bending or crumbling or snapping of a rusty bar in these cells, even if any of the humans could wield enough magic to try it.

Feigning disinterest, she leaned back against the damp wall of her cell and watched through half-closed lids as two new Tarmaks appeared at the foot of the stairs carrying a litter. The two guards rose to greet them, and one pointed to Linsha's cell. Linsha tensed. She dropped her pretense of inattention and opened her eyes as the Tarmaks unlocked her cell door.

Linsha made no effort to move. She did not even entertain the notion of rushing these warriors and trying to battle her way out. Besides being skilled warriors, the Tarmaks were all six feet or taller, well muscled, and as graceful in their movements as hunting cats. Up close, without their blue skin paint, they were a handsome people with dark hair usually worn long, fair skin, and eyes of earth colors that often burned with a fanatical zeal. She would have as much luck fighting four Tarmaks barehanded as she would facing four minotaurs.

Her own eyes wary, Linsha watched while the Tarmaks dumped the occupant of the litter to a pallet of straw on the floor and left. One Brute said something to the guards in their guttural language, then the two left. She waited until the door creaked shut at the top of the stairs before she slipped over to the pallet and rolled the man over onto his back. He groaned and opened a pair of vivid blue eyes.

"Lanther." Linsha couldn't help but smile. "I thought you were dead."

He rubbed a hand over his battered face and winced when he hit a large bruise on his temple.

"So did I." With her help he managed to sit up and prop his back against the stone wall of the cell. "Is there any water in here?"

She brought the small bucket the Tarmaks had left in her cell and gave him a few sips of water. She was bursting with questions, but she waited for him to gather his wits and find the strength to speak. Pale and dirty and splattered with blood, he looked terrible in the half-light of the cell. She could not see any obvious wounds leaking blood onto his clothes, but she could not tell yet if he had any broken bones or internal injuries.

"What happened to your arm?" he asked, staring blearily at the crude wrapping on her upper arm.

"Crossbow. The Tarmaks were kind enough to pull it out. They slathered some of that odd smelling blue paint of theirs on it." She twisted her arm around to look at it. "When they put it on, the wound started to tingle and the pain eased. I would not be surprised if that paint had some healing properties to it."

"Maybe that's why they don't wear armor." His eyes crinkled in a slight grimace, and he shifted to get more comfortable. "Where are we?"

"Under the palace. In those prisoner cells Iyesta did not like."

"Of course not. She couldn't get to them," he said with a grunt. "Where are the centaurs?"

Linsha sat down beside him and let her breath out in a long sigh. "I don't know. They were led away while we were still out in the palace courtyard. There were only four left."

He took her hand in his and held it, their fingers intertwined. "It's not your fault," he said quietly. "Or mine. We acted on good evidence."

"We were deliberately trapped like wild dogs," she said forcefully. "They led us in and slammed every door. I wouldn't be surprised if they watched the pool entrance and timed our capture with the attack on the palace. Neat, efficient, and successful."

Lanther leaned his head back and closed his eyes. "You may be right." After awhile he added, "Gods of all, I hate prisoner cells."

Linsha took several long moments to gather her courage, then asked, "Lanther, what happened to Tanefer?"

"He's dead. Two arrows to the chest. When he fell, I hit my head on the wall. The Tarmaks took me for dead, too, until later. Now I'm here." He spoke his short narrative with spare words and little emotion, and when he finished, his words faded into steady breathing.

With gentle hands Linsha laid his shoulders and head down on the pallet and straightened his body. While she moved him, she carefully checked him for broken bones and unseen wounds, and when she was satisfied that he was basically unhurt, she made him as comfortable as possible on the lumpy pallet. She wished she had a cloak or a blanket for him, for the underground cells were chilly and damp, but he would have to be content in his ragged, dirty clothes.

"Lady," a soft voice hissed from the next cell.

The Tarmak guards watched the two cells with avid eyes, but they did not try to stop the speaker.

Linsha responded quietly, "Yes?"

One of the Legionnaires in the neighboring cell asked, "Is Lanther injured?"

"He seems well enough. He is asleep now."

A sword blade slammed on the table indicating the Tarmaks had heard enough talk. The prisoners retreated to the back of their cells.

Returning to her own pallet, Linsha lay down and tried to sleep. She didn't know what time of day it was, but it felt like evening, and her body, deprived of a night's sleep, was aching with exhaustion. She wanted to sleep, to slip into the forgetfulness of slumber and let her thoughts rest, but her mind wouldn't let her. Too many worries, concerns, and feelings of guilt and recrimination played through her head.

Where were the centaurs? Had the Tarmaks killed them or just imprisoned them somewhere else?

Where was Varia? She had seen the owl falter in flight. Was Varia dead? Wounded? Was she slowly bleeding to death somewhere out in those trees? Or was she all right? What would she do? Surely she wouldn't try to get Crucible again. That fearful thought led to another that repeated over and over in her head as if Varia could hear. *Don't tell Crucible. Don't bring him back here. He must stay in Sanction. He must stay with Lord Bight. Don't risk yourself.*

Linsha put an arm over her face and groaned. By Kiri-Jolith, she had caused enough death and defeat for one night. She couldn't bear it if the owl or the dragon died too.

How could she have been so careless? She had taken the word of a dead man—second-hand information!—and had not checked it out. Instead of following the basic rules for a good clandestine operation, she'd followed her desires and led good men and centaurs to their deaths or captivity. And Lanther had gone along with her! She hated to admit it, but the only one who had guessed it right was Sir Remmik. She could just imagine him lifting his long aristocratic nose, raising one eyebrow, and silently radiating "I told you so" from every line of his lean posture.

Thinking of Sir Remmik put her on a different path—the Tarmaks. They had effectively destroyed the mercenaries. Why hadn't they tried to bribe or pay off the soldiers? If the Tarmaks were truly building a new army, why hadn't they tried to hire the mercenaries? Why kill them all? And who had the dragon's treasure now? Where was Iyesta's hoard? Where were those damnable eggs? It seemed to her that the Tarmaks now had everything the Missing City had to offer—the city, the harbor, the lands, the palace, the dragon's eggs, and the dragonlord's treasure. What was left?

Knight Commander Jamis uth Remmik slapped irritably at the flea on his neck and shoved his blanket aside in disgust. This sleeping place was just too crowded. Between the sand fleas, the bed mites, and the occasional scorpion that crawled in for warmth, there wasn't a peaceful scrap of material on the entire bed. He rubbed his neck again and crawled to his feet. There was no need to put on boots or a tunic. Like everyone else in the Wadi, he slept fully dressed.

Stretching his aching back, he walked out of the cave and into the cold night air. How he longed for his comfortable bed and warm fire in his room in the Citadel. That room had been built exactly to his specifications and needs and had been kept scrupulously clean. Everything had been in its place—his armor, his uniforms, his books of Solamnic law, his razor and toiletries. Now his magnificent Citadel was a pile of rubble and he was reduced to one tattered uniform, a pallet full of fleas, and a cold, stinking cave he had to share with twenty other people.

He drew in a deep breath of cold air, let it out in a cloudy exhalation, then walked over to the small fire still burning in one of the cooking hearths. A pot of hot water was always kept on the hearth for the night sentries who wanted hot tea or kefre. The ale and beer were long gone.

For a long while Remmik stood and stared at the small flames dancing in the hearth. He let the silence of the night fill his troubled mind. The presence of nearly six hundred people in the narrow, twisting canyon rarely made for long periods of stillness, but this late at night a semblance of peace had settled over the camp. Most of the inhabitants were asleep. Some were on guard duty scattered through the canyon, and some were on patrol or manning the lookout posts. One guard walked by the fire on his rounds and nodded once to the Solamnic commander. Sir Remmik noted the man's signal horn, his bow strung and hanging ready from his back, and his sword loose in his sheath. He nodded back in approval.

He was reaching for the pot of kefre, a powerful concoction favored by the Khurs, when a small sound reached him. He jerked his head up and stared in the direction of the guard. The young man had just reached the edge of the firelight and could barely be seen against the intense darkness of the canyon. A second person appeared to be with him, although they were so close together it was hard to tell. Then Sir Remmik abruptly straightened, the hot pot still in his hand. The young guard made an odd gurgling sound and slumped to the ground. The second person stood over him, dark and indistinct, a long slim knife in his hand.

Sir Remmik fumbled for his sword and realized with a start of horror that he had come out of the cave without his weapons. He stared in disbelief as the dark figure leaped toward him. For a moment everything seemed to move slowly while his mind absorbed the shock of what had just happened. A heartbeat later his Solamnic training jolted him out of his astonishment, and he hurled the pot of hot kefre at the figure and bolted for the cave. He forced out one shout of warning before a tremendous pain slammed him on the back of his head and sent him crashing to the ground. In that instant of woozy consciousness, he felt himself waiting on the edge of eternity. In a blink, he knew the warrior with the knife would be on his back, the blade would be at his throat, and then his blood would spill on the ground and he would die. He was so sure of it that he could only stare at the earth inches away from his eyes. He felt the weight of a man press a knee into his back.

Then someone said something quiet in a strange tongue to the warrior on his back, and a different figure moved over to Sir Remmik's head. By lifting his head, he was able to see bare blue feet. The Brutes. A cold fear for himself, for the camp, and for the Solamnic Knights he had brought here filled Remmik until his head throbbed with pain. He stifled a groan and waited for death.

But death did not come. The Brute on his back complained—quietly—for a moment, then stuffed a gag in Remmik's mouth and tied his hands and feet. Sir Remmik found himself lying by the fire totally helpless to stop what happened next. The Tarmaks were joined by three more, and together they dashed into the cave. Ten minutes later they emerged with four prisoners and blood on their hands and knives. There had not been a single scream. After binding their captives, they dumped the two men—both Solamnic Knights—and two women beside Sir Remmik and moved on to the next cave. More Tarmaks slid by in the darkness. Shouts and screams suddenly rang through the camp. Somewhere down the canyon a guard sounded a belated warning that was answered by several other horns. But Sir Remmik knew it was already too late.

The Tarmaks had somehow slipped past the pickets

and infiltrated the canyon. All of the fortifications and preparations the militia had made had been with the one belief that the Tarmaks or mercenaries would attack up the canyon in a full frontal assault. The back of the canyon was too steep and rugged to bring troops down in large numbers, and the walls of the canyon were too sheer. No one imagined the Tarmaks would try something so audacious as to slip in small numbers that would slaughter the inhabitants of the Wadi while they slept. Perhaps he and Falaius and Dockett had relied too much on the daunting presence of the bronze dragon to keep the enemy at bay. They should have set more sentries, done something constructive after he left.

Remmik's vision began to swim into slow, dizzying waves. The terrified faces of his fellow prisoners blurred out of focus, and Sir Remmik found himself slipping inexorably out of consciousness. Briefly his mind thought of the others, of Falaius and Dockett, the other Knights, and even of Linsha away on her useless quest. The party had still not returned, and Sir Remmik suspected he knew why. As his vision dimmed to black and his thoughts slowly receded, one stray flash of curiosity surfaced in his mind. Was this how the Rose Knight had felt that night of storm when the honor guard was attacked and she had been knocked unconscious? Could there possibly have been some truth to her story? But as soon as it took shape, the idea faded and the Knight Commander slid into a black sleep.

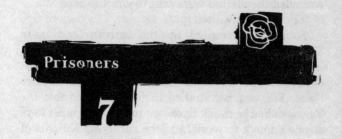

Prisoners

7

The destruction of the Wadi camp took less time than the slaughter in the dragonlord's palace. Unlike the mercenaries who had daylight and a slight warning before the Tarmaks were upon them, the people in the camp were caught asleep, trapped in their caves, fighting a foe in the dark that took them totally by surprise. By the time the defenders came awake and were able to mount some meager self-defense it was already beyond hope. The Tarmaks swept over the camp and moved in behind to attack the fortified barricades and guard positions. The last to fall was the Post where General Dockett led a bitter resistance. By dawn even that vain attempt was gone. In the small rooms of the roughhewn headquarters General Dockett fell with ten of his militia.

In a small niche halfway up the canyon wall, a small observer watched with wide eyes and a grief-laden heart as the Tarmaks dragged the bodies out of the Post and off the walls and heaped them in a pile near the entrance. With practiced efficiency the warriors chopped off the heads of the corpses and placed them on tall stakes in a row in front of the Post. The remaining dead were left to the carrion eaters and the sun. The few wounded they found were sent to join the dead.

The watcher waited.

Soon smoke curled up the canyon, and more Tarmaks appeared. Some led the camp's few horses—including Linsha's favorite mount—on lead lines. Others drove a miserable collection of prisoners before them. The watcher studied the captives and saw the Tarmaks had been selective—young women, older boys strong enough to work, and the surviving Knights of Solamnia. There were no Legionnaires, no militia, no centaurs; they had died fighting.

In the midst of the group, Sir Remmik stumbled by, his arms tightly bound and blood clotting on the back of his head. He looked ill and older than his years. Behind him staggered the other Knights—bloodied, bruised, and stunned. Only a few of the eighteen Knights were missing—Linsha, Sir Hugh Bronan, the young Knight who had once stood up for Linsha at her trial, Sir Fellion, and perhaps two others. The Tarmaks had obviously wanted the Solamnics alive.

Voices shouted through the canyon. Horns blew, and more Tarmaks jogged down the trails to join the gathering force by the entrance. About a dozen Tarmaks with large ropes coiled around their shoulders came in through the opening.

The watcher eyed the ropes and began to understand.

A horn blared again, an officer shouted a command, and the Tarmaks fell into a column of fours with the prisoners confined tightly in the middle. Giving a roar of conquest that echoed down the Wadi, the Tarmaks moved out at a quick trot. The dust kicked up by their tramping feet rose like a storm behind them.

The watcher stared at the lingering cloud of dust long after the enemy had left and the sound of the wailing women and the pounding of feet had passed away.

The sun rose on its accustomed path and eventually cast its rays into the Wadi. The heat increased, and the warm air rose above the walls of stone. Moved by a fitful wind, a faint odor became detectable to the carrion feeders in the vicinity. The first to appear was a magpie, its black and white feathers a stark flash of color amid the dusty browns and reds of the Wadi. A moment later a winged shadow drifted silently across the canyon floor and circled over the pile of corpses.

The observer knew it was time to go. Where there was one vulture, there soon would be dozens. Though they usually did not bother to attack owls, they could be vicious in the defense of a meal. Besides, Varia hated vultures. She stepped out of her shadowy niche, spread her wings, and dropped soundlessly into the air. She caught a rising heat wave and use it to glide through the open spaces of the canyon.

The first thing she noticed was the silence. A narrow place like the Wadi collected sounds and sent them bouncing back and forth. When the militia was active, the canyon filled with the voices of men, women, and children, the cries of stock animals, the ring of axes or hammers, the clatter of hooves, and the clash of weapons used in training. Now the only sounds the owl's sharp ears heard were the buzz of gathering flies and the lonely rustle of the wind through the scraggly trees that grew in the shelter of the rocks.

She saw several bodies sprawled at the base of the rocks—the sentries who had once stood at the top of the canyon walls. The Tarmaks had knifed them in the dark and tossed their bodies over the precipice. Beyond the barricades, she spotted more corpses—

some beheaded and dismembered, some merely killed as quickly and silently as possible. Only a few looked as if they had had time to fight back. There were no dead Tarmaks.

Gliding on, she dipped a little lower to go below the rising smoke and flew over the camp, knowing what she would find.

There were no shelters, tents, huts, workouts, or sheds left standing. Everything made by the hands of the camp inhabitants had been hacked down, trampled, burned, and rendered useless. A few pitiful dogs and goats had been slaughtered. Several clusters of centaurs lay on the trail sprawled in their own blood. More bodies were scattered across the camp's grounds where people had tried to flee or fight. They had been felled by arrows or hacked by swords. Varia guessed many of the people still lay in the caves, murdered in their sleep by the stealthy assassins.

She swung around a few columns of smoke rising from the burning camp and flew farther up the canyon into cleaner air. But there was little more to find here. The guards who were supposed to watch the Wadi's back ways lay dead at their posts. It was as if someone had told the Tarmaks exactly where to find each guard and sentry. There was one other thing she found that confirmed another suspicion. On four different places along the sheer tops of the canyon walls, she spotted scuff marks, metal stakes pounded into the rock, and rub marks on the crumbling edges as if ropes had dug into the earth. She studied the signs carefully from her height then flew to the end of the canyon. There was no one left alive that she could see. The camp and the city's last defenders were dead.

At least Linsha had not been here. The Tarmaks held her for now, but she was alive, and Varia was a firm believer that where there was life, there was hope. She did not believe the Tarmaks were going to kill Linsha. Not right away. There still might be time to fly north and find Crucible again. If she could, somehow, persuade him to return, he could free Linsha and the others.

He should never have left in the first place, the owl thought peevishly, unsettled by the massacre she had been unable to prevent.

Dispirited, she rose above the Wadi and left the vultures to their meal. Somewhere out on the plains were other militia patrols and Mariana. Varia hadn't seen Falaius Taneek in the canyon either. If he wasn't among the dead in the caves, perhaps he was safe with a troop somewhere. They would have to be warned and sent on to their rendezvous place. Then she would return to the palace and see how Linsha fared before she decided whether or not to risk the long, dangerous trip to Sanction a second time.

***

Linsha squinted against the bright light of day as she stepped outside. She would have appreciated a moment to let her eyes adjust to the stronger light, but a Tarmak pushed the butt of his spear into her back and shoved her forward. She banged into Lanther and exited the dragon's palace by staggering sideways to avoid hurting him, losing her balance, and falling on her side.

Rough hands hauled her to her feet, and the guard cursed her in his own tongue. Linsha filed that phrase away for later with every other fragment and remark of the Tarmak language she had been able to pick up. She had always had a knack for learning languages. This one, she sensed with deep bitterness, had become important.

She shrugged away from the guard and walked blinking after the rest of the prisoners into a stone paved court she had never seen before. From the placement and appearance of the crumbling buildings, she guessed they were behind the spacious throne room and great hall in the maze of stables, outbuildings, storehouses, barracks, and craft halls that once comprised the working quarters of the huge palace. The court they were in was formed by a large storehouse at the north end, what may have been a carriage house at the east, and the palace wing on the south. To the west, the remains of a toppled wall formed the fourth side of the courtyard. Everywhere she looked, she saw Tarmaks either standing guard or working industriously among the ruins.

She and the prisoners halted in a group in the center of the courtyard where they were forced to stand and wait. After a long, uncomfortable night in the underground dungeon, they were all exhausted. They had been given no food or water and had been rousted out of their cells and marched outside, no reasons given. Were they to be executed? Tortured? Linsha glanced sideways at the men with her and saw varying degrees of dread in all their faces. She couldn't fault them. She had to fight to keep her own composure calm and to still the trembling in her hands.

Lifting her eyes, she scanned the roof lines and walls of the ruin around her, looking for a familiar shape or the glint of owlish eyes. But if Varia was in the courtyard, she had carefully hidden herself. There was no sign of her. Linsha sighed and steeled her mind to wait whatever came. She feared that whatever it was, none of them were going to like it.

The wait took longer than she anticipated. The sun rose higher in the clear sky, and the heat in the stone courtyard became stifling. The faint breeze gave a few last fitful gusts and died completely. Soon Linsha felt sweat gather on her forehead and trickle down her face. She would have liked to move to wipe it off, but the Tarmaks watched them closely, and any time one of the prisoners moved, a guard snapped a harsh word and cracked a short whip across the offender's shoulders.

Yet the Brutes did little else to the captives. They were obviously holding them there in anticipation of something. But what?

Linsha's head was beginning to pound from an intense headache when loud voices and the tramp of feet alerted the guards. The prisoners shifted imperceptibly closer together and straightened weary backs and legs. Linsha and Lanther shared a quick look.

A group of ten Tarmaks with swords, daggers, battle axes, and round shields marched into the court through an entrance in the fallen wall and bore down on the small group of alarmed prisoners. Linsha glanced again at the Legion men beside her and felt a faint glow of pride. Not one of them cowered as the tall, powerful warriors halted in front of them and snapped to attention.

By the absent gods, Linsha mused, these Brutes were imposing specimens. Each one was over seven feet, had the muscular shoulders and chest of a trained fighter, and wore little more than bronze studded battle harnesses for their weapons, a lightweight cloak of dark red, and a flap of leather that passed for a loin cloth. Their skin was painted the dark blue they were infamous for, and graceful white feathers were braided into their long, dark hair. In spite of their barbaric appearance, the Tarmaks reminded Linsha of elves somehow. It was not just their pointed ears but something more subtle, an athletic prowess in their movement, a powerful sense of racial pride and dignity, and a self-assurance that equaled that of most dragons.

An eleventh man walked out from behind his honor guards and approached the group of prisoners. Her headache took a turn for the worse and her mouth went dry.

"Oh, no," she whispered. "Not him."

A golden mask hid his face and marked his status as leader of the Tarmak invaders. Linsha didn't know what the Tarmaks called their commander, so for lack of a better word, she knew him as the General. She had never seen his face and had no notion of what he looked like or how old he was, but she was all too aware of what he was capable of doing. He wore a pleated kilt of fine linen and golden armbands, and like his followers, his skin was painted blue. His dark eyes pierced through the holes of the mask. He came to a stop in front of her and stared down at her.

"The Rose Knight." His voice rumbled deep in his chest. "The exiled Solamnic who slays dragons. Once again we are pleased to see you."

Across his chest hung a necklace Linsha had not seen before. It was made with dragon's teeth curved like Khurish scimitars. Her eyes narrowed. Which dragon? She dragged her eyes from the teeth to his masked face and bowed her head ever so slightly—a gesture that just bordered on insolence. She said nothing.

The general continued to observe her from the dirty bandage on her arm to her stained clothes and worn boots. "I have not had an opportunity to thank you for ridding us of that troublesome dragon."

Linsha tried to be casual. She lifted an arched eyebrow and forced the fear out of her voice. "I have not thanked you for leaving that lance lying about so conveniently. Tell me why you wanted us to kill him. He should have been a valuable ally."

"Should have been. But was not. You knew him. Thunder was too vindictive, greedy, and cruel."

"Even for you?"

He chuckled, a hollow sound behind the mask. "Even for us. We have our own plans that did not include Thunder."

"Which are?"

"In good time, Lady Linsha. For today, we have other things to do. There are more prisoners coming in. We have to move all of you out here."

Linsha felt a chill slide down her spine. More prisoners from where?

The general swiveled away from her and stalked down the line of prisoners, studying each one like a wizard eyes his next experiment, then he turned and came back to stop in front of Lanther.

"Ah, yes. You. You have been a thorn in my foot for some time. You'll do."

Two guards came forward at his word and grasped the Legionnaire's arms.

Lanther's eyes met Linsha's, and she thought she saw a flash of something in his bright blue eyes, but before she could understand what it was, he was forced to walk to the wall behind them. Linsha and the Legionnaires turned and saw for the first time a narrow metal cage made of heavy woven wire strips lying on the paving near a tall wooden gibbet.

The Tarmaks opened the cage, shoved Lanther inside, and locked the door. With little effort they lifted the cage upright and hung it about three feet off the ground. It was barely big enough for Lanther to stand upright and too narrow for him to turn around. He couldn't even lift his arms. He looked as if he had been bound in a metal coffin. Much worse, the cage hung in the full sun.

A few hours in that cage would be misery, Linsha knew. Half a day would leave him badly weakened, and a full day with no water in the hot sun added to the complications of his head injury would probably kill him. She took a step toward him.

A forceful blow from a whip sent a sharp pain across her back and caused her to stagger. Furious, she turned to face her tormentor then caught herself before she leaped to attack him. The Brute guard grinned and lashed her again, this time across the wound on her arm. Linsha cried out in pain and outrage.

She knew better than to attack the guard. He was a head taller, many pounds heavier, and he was goading her. Yet she couldn't help taking one short step in his direction, her hands raised, her eyes hot as green fire.

The Tarmak general stepped in front of her. His hand gripped her shoulder and jerked her closer. Before she could stop him, he reached beneath her tunic, grasped the gold chain, wrenched the dragon scales off her neck, then clamped his hand to her face, the thumb and middle fingers pressing in on her temples.

Linsha had only a moment to remember that one night in his tent when he had bound her to a tent pole and burst into her mind with a power she could not resist. A scream rose in her throat. Before the sound reached her lips, the general pressed his fingers into her face, and an agony of pain exploded in her head. Her breath failed her; her scream exploded in her chest. The power he used took the pain of her headache, expanded it into a white-hot dagger, and stabbed it into her brain just behind her eyes.

Linsha fell to her knees, clutching her throbbing skull and sobbing. Somewhere, from far away, she thought she heard someone shouting her name, but she could not respond. Her strength was gone; her body was beyond her control. There was only the excruciating pain that thundered in her head to the exclusion of all else. She sagged forward to the dust-covered stone pavings and banged her head on the stone. Anything to end this agony.

"The other prisoners are coming," someone said above her. "As soon as they're here, put them all in the cells."

The words meant nothing. The only thing she realized was the hand had gone from her face, and the brutal pain was slowly ebbing. Gentler hands gripped her arms and lifted her to her feet. She felt her body moving, but she could do nothing to help. She could find no strength left in her muscles. Her aching head lolled forward, and she watched as a line of filthy, pathetic looking men were led into the court. She could not see well enough to recognize any of them.

The Tarmaks shouted an order, and the two groups of prisoners were herded into the ancient storehouse.

Linsha staggered as best she could between the two Legionnaires who helped her, but as soon as they reached the shade of their prison, her legs buckled and she could not stand. Dizziness overwhelmed her. She had a vague feeling she was being laid down on cold stone, but she didn't care. She was lying down and didn't have to move.

The pain and dizziness eased just a little. Someone put a folded cloth under her head, and she to rolled her side, curled into a ball, and wept.

By the time night returned to Scorpion Wadi, the silence had been replaced by the sounds of scavengers. Vultures, magpies, crows, wild dogs, jackals, and an old lion too lame to kill his own food had found their way to the Wadi and the ample supply of decaying bodies. When darkness came, the birds settled on nearby roosts to wait for the sun and another chance to feed, while the ants, the carrion beetles, the lion, and the wild dogs helped themselves. Their snarls, yaps, and growls jarred the quiet of the canyon.

A particularly loud ruckus between the aged lion and a small pack of dogs erupted near midnight near the smoldering ruins of the camp. The noise bounced from the canyon walls and reverberated into the caves where many of the dead lay. Faint echoes of the barking and roaring reached deep into several caves and finally found the ears of a small girl. Shaking with fear, she reached out in the intense darkness and clutched the arm of her companion.

He came awake with a start, his hand automatically fumbling for his sword. Only when his fingers touched the empty space at his side where his belt usually hung did his memories come back of the nightmare. The slaughter. The pain in his side.

"Oh, dear gods," he groaned. He pushed his back up against the rock wall until he was sitting up, then he gathered the small girl close. "What is it? What's wrong, Amania?"

She whimpered something and pushed herself deeper into his arms. "Sir Hugh," she whispered. "There's things out there."

He listened to the distant sounds long enough to recognize them and realized it was time to go. Still holding the girl, he leaned over and felt for the third person in the crevice. "Fellion, wake up," he hissed.

The Knight he called moaned and sagged toward him. "Hugh, fetch me an ale. There's a good fellow."

Sir Hugh wished he could oblige. He couldn't think of anything that sounded better to his parched throat. But they'd have to settle for water, if they could find it.

"Let's go."

"Go?" Sir Fellion boomed. "Go where? I want an ale."

His voice rang in the narrow space and startled the girl. She cowered back, her small body trembling in fear.

Sir Hugh held her close as he reached his hand out in the blackness and found his friend's arm. He touched the sling that supported the broken arm close to Fellion's body and the bandages that covered the skin torn by the bad break. That break worried him. A mystic healer in the camp had tried to mend the bone, but his power failed him, and he had been forced to use the crudest poultices and rough splints. Sir Fellion had been healing well enough the past few days, until he'd taken a heavy fall on his arm during their frantic escape into the depths of the cave. There was no telling what further damage had been done. Hugh's fingers traveled up Fellion's shoulder and found the man's bare neck. He winced when the heat of Fellion's skin registered on his fingertips. The young man was burning with a fever.

Hugh knew he could not leave the girl or the man alone in the cave. The girl was too terrified, and Fellion was delirious. Mindful of his own wound, he climbed over Fellion's legs and, with Amania's help, he hefted the Knight to his feet and led him out of the crevice where they had sought refuge. Taking both by the hand, he guided them through the narrow, twisting passage that returned to the main cavern. He had to feel his way out with his feet and his elbows, and twice he slammed his shins against sharp protrusions of rock.

When they reached the front cave that opened out to the Wadi, Hugh halted to listen and to catch his breath. The animal sounds of fighting had ended, and now all he heard was the rustle of carrion beetles and an occasional distant yap. About thirty feet away he could just make out the cave entrance, filled with a misty moonlight. He wanted to light a lamp, a candle, a torch, something that would help him find his way through. The sleepers in this cave had been awakened by the sounds of fighting in the camp and put up a ferocious defense when the Tarmaks slipped in to attack them. There were numerous bodies stretched over the stony floor amid scattered blankets and belongings.

Yes, a light would be handy, but somewhere in this bloody carnage lay Amania's mother and brother, and Hugh could not subject the little girl to that scene. He lifted the girl into his arms, gripped Fellion's elbow, and began a slow, careful shuffle toward the faint light that glimmered through the cave opening. Amania buried her face in his shoulder. Fellion muttered feverishly to himself and stumbled alongside.

They managed to make it outside without falling over a corpse or stepping on body parts, and Hugh breathed a sigh when they finally left the cave behind. After the intense darkness of the underground passages, the pale moonlight seemed as bright as day. He cast a wary look around at the busy scavengers and at the empty camp in case the Tarmaks had left a guard. At last he helped Fellion to a seat on a nearby rock. He paused a moment himself to get his strength back. Sir Hugh was a compact man, athletic and well-muscled, but he was wounded and thirsty and already exhausted from his exertions.

"I've got to find some water," he said softly to Amania. "Will you stay with Sir Fellion and watch him until I come back?"

In earlier days, Amania would have obeyed and done her best to help her friend, Sir Hugh. But not this night. She was only seven, and she had suffered through a horrendous nightmare. She would not let go of the one familiar and living person she had left. She wrapped her arms tighter around his neck and whimpered.

Hugh knew how she felt. In spite of the pain in his side, he continued to hold her, and taking Fellion's sound arm again, he led the feverish Knight down the trail to one of the camp's wells.

There were only two wells in the big camp, both dug into the lowest depressions of the ancient river bed. They tended to be muddy and yielded barely enough water to supply the basic needs of the population. But they were certainly better than nothing.

As soon as Hugh reached the closest well, he let go of Fellion, pulled off the cover, and reached for the bucket to lower into the well shaft.

"The well's been poisoned," a voice said out of the darkness.

Both Knights jerked at the unexpected words. Hugh whirled into the shadows, putting the cliff wall to his back. His eyes searched the path and the rocks around him.

Fellion laughed. "Fill 'em up again, boys!" he shouted, and he waved an imaginary mug. "Hugh! Dammit, where's that ale?"

There was a long silence, then, "Sir Hugh? Is that you?" the strange voice called.

This time, Hugh thought he recognized the speaker. Her voice was lower than normal and husky, affected no doubt by shock, caution, or grief.

"Mariana?" he called and stepped out into the moonlight again.

Five forms clambered out of the rocks and surrounded the three survivors. Hugh heard familiar voices talking and questioning. The newcomers touched him as if to reassure themselves and him that he was all right. Others took Fellion and gave him water from a skin.

A tall, lean figure came to Hugh. She pulled off her helmet, revealing a head of pale silvery hair cut short. The long braids she had worn before the war were gone, hacked off in a gesture of defiance and grief.

He grinned a weak semblance of a smile. "Captain, glad I am to see you."

The half-elf nodded once, and Hugh thought he saw moonlight glitter on a rivulet of tears on her cheeks. She helped him sit and pressed a waterskin into his hands. Using the lure of water, she encouraged Amania to let go of his neck and sit beside him.

The militia captain studied them both in the dim light and shook her pale head. "I have seen this camp. How did you three survive?"

Hugh could only shrug. He tried to explain. "I still

don't know. I was sitting up with Fellion when I heard Sir Remmik yell something. I thought he was shouting at a guard or a dog or something. A few moments passed, then all chaos broke loose. It was dark in the cave." He shuddered, remembering the shrieks and the panic in the darkness. "Amania came to me. She couldn't stop screaming. Fellion tried to help me. A Tarmak attacked us. He drove us back . . . his sword slashed me. . . Fellion and I killed . . . Amania pulled us back into a passage. We fled. . . . " His voice faltered and failed to silence. He could feel tears running down his cheeks and could do nothing to stop them. He buried his face in his hands.

Mariana sat and watched wordlessly to allow him time to regain his composure.

Fiercely he wiped his eyes on his sleeve and took another long swallow of water. "Thanks," he said with a thick voice. "How did you know we were here?"

"We didn't. Varia found us and told us about the massacre. We came to see for ourselves. Some of my men—" she gestured to the militia men helping Fellion— "have friends and family here."

"Is anyone else still alive?"

"None but you so far. We found General Dockett by the Post." Her voice remained cool and contained—too much so, Hugh thought—as she said, "We found his head jammed on a stake. Vultures have been at it."

"What about Knight Commander Remmik? Or Falaius?"

She repeated everything Varia had told her about the Solamnic prisoners and the absence of the Legion commander. Thus far her patrol had not found Falaius either.

"That's odd," Sir Hugh murmured.

Mariana left him by the well with Amania, Sir

Fellion, and one of her men with strict orders not to touch the water from the well. The Tarmaks, in their efforts to destroy everything useable to the defenders, had poisoned both wells. While the men tended Fellion and treated Sir Hugh's slash wound, the rest of the patrol finished their search of the caves and the canyon.

They came back tightlipped and silent. No one else was with them

"We will have to come back and bury them," one soldier said in a voice wracked with pain. He clutched a light-colored hair scarf often worn by women.

Sir Hugh shook his head. "Seal them in the caves," he suggested. "There aren't enough of us left to bury them all."

"We were lucky to get in here tonight," snapped the captain. "The Tarmaks may decide to post a watch to catch a burial detail. We'll have to leave them for now."

A misty hint of light edged the eastern horizon, and the late moon dropped toward its rest. Mariana eyed the sky and ordered her charges to move. The militia, what was left of it, was gathering at Sinking Wells miles to the east. She wanted her patrol out of the canyon and out of sight of any Tarmak hunters.

Reluctantly they gathered what little they could of anything salvageable and constructed a litter for Fellion. They left the Wadi at the mouth's entrance. As soon as they were gone, the wild dogs and the old lion slunk out of their hiding places and resumed their feeding.

insha came awake abruptly. From only a few feet away a bony face stared down its aristocratic nose at her. Shadows cast from the torchlight outside their prison lay in sharp relief along the edges of its features. The steely gray eyes stared at a point somewhere beyond her left cheek as if their owner could not bear to look her in the eye.

"Your friend is back," Sir Remmik said in a curt tone. "You may want to take a look at him."

Having done what he felt was necessary, Remmik withdrew, leaving her lying in confusion.

Her mind, still drugged with sleep, did not grasp his meaning right away. Her friend? Which friend? She opened her mouth and tasted the acrid aftertaste of the general's magic. Gods, how did he do that? Even worse she felt a stinging sensation on her neck where the gold chain had cut into her skin. Her hand flew unbidden to her throat. She touched the empty space where the scales had hung and felt the bloody weal on the back of her neck. The scales were gone.

She felt as though the Tarmak had ripped away the

only connection she had left with both dragons. What was left felt like a gaping raw hole in her heart. She would have curled back into a ball and tried to escape back into sleep again, except Sir Remmik's words resurfaced in her groggy memory. Her friend was back. What friend? Then another bit of memory returned, and she sat up and looked around.

Lanther lay close to the barred doors where the guards had dumped him, sprawled on his back and still as death. No one else moved to help him because most were sleeping the sleep of the mentally and physically exhausted, and apparently Sir Remmik did not want to be bothered any further.

Careful of her aching head, Linsha rolled to her hands and knees and crawled to the Legionnaire's side. He didn't move when she checked his pulse, but she felt his heartbeat slow and steady under his jaw. The man had a constitution of steel. She fetched water from a bucket the Tarmaks had left and bathed his face until he regained consciousness enough to drink some water.

For the next hour or so, she gave him water a little at a time and fed him crumbs of the dry bread their captors had given them as supper. Eventually he fell asleep with his head in her lap. She didn't mind. The night was quite chilly, and her body needed what little warmth he could share.

She sat with her back against the old wall and listened to him breathe. At least he was still alive and here with her, not lying in the blood-drenched caves or out in the garden with arrows in his back. That was something.

For a while she watched him sleep. When sleep did not return to her, she watched the Tarmak guards pass by the doors of the prison on their rounds. She timed them as they walked by the doors, and she paid close attention when they changed the guards sometime around midnight. But soon that palled, too, and it wasn't long after the guards resumed their stations that her mind began to wander. Although she wanted to shy away from it, she finally let her thoughts pick through the tales the Knights had told her of the massacre in Scorpion Wadi. Sir Remmik had said nothing of the catastrophe, but several of the younger ones, Sir Johand and Sir Pieter, had talked with the horror still fresh on their faces.

She asked about Sir Hugh, General Dockett, Falaius and others, but the only death they knew for certain was the general's, for they had seen his head on the stake staring down on them as they marched past.

The entire camp.

Even now Linsha could hardly comprehend it. The Tarmaks had barely waited for the dust of Crucible's departure to settle before they attacked. They had probably had the attack planned and the warriors ready to go. They'd only waited for the dragon to leave. Someone must have told them, Linsha decided. Unless the Tarmaks had a spy in the camp, they would not have known so quickly that Crucible had left the Plains. Certainly they could have seen him flying the evening he departed, but without better information, they would not realize he had returned to Sanction.

The idea of a spy in their midst burned in Linsha's mind. She had suspected it before, during the battle for the city, and the Tarmak general had admitted as much to her in his tent the night before the fight with Thunder. She had told Falaius and General Dockett about her suspicions, but they had been unable to ferret out any possible suspects. She wondered if the spy had lain low while Crucible was in the south and immediately reported to the Tarmaks the moment the dragon disappeared. Or perhaps this informer was very clever. Perhaps he or she had been able to pass on information about the militia, the Wadi, the leaders, the gods knew what else, and still avoid detection. That would help explain the number of watching posts that had been wiped out and the ease with which the Tarmaks were able to find the sentries around the Wadi and slip in undetected. Simply put, the defenders had been betrayed.

A sound came from the prison doors— a sound so small and insignificant only a person awake and listening could have heard it, a noise that would hardly excite attention in a ruin overrun with lizards and rats. Linsha's breath stilled. Her eyes sought the source of the sound.

Near the floor where the door met the wall, she spotted a small, round form slip furtively through the bars and come sidling into the dark room. It turned its head as it slowly studied the recumbent forms on the floor, and as the creature looked toward her, Linsha saw round creamy eye circles catch the light from the torch just outside.

Linsha and Varia recognized each other at the same moment. The owl's "ear" feathers popped up, and she scurried over on her stubby legs to where Linsha extended her arm in greeting. Varia joyfully climbed up to Linsha's shoulder. Murmuring softly, the two friends shared a quiet and delighted reunion.

"You are hurt," Varia whispered. "There are clouds of blue and purple in your aura."

Like some human mystics, Varia had the ability to translate the invisible aura radiated by most living beings. Linsha could also read auras, but she had to focus her mystic power of the heart in order to do so, and that magic had almost failed her.

She grimaced and leaned her head back against the wall. "The Tarmak general took my scales," she said softly, voicing her greatest personal hurt.

The owl bobbed her head. "He used sorcery, too. I can sense it."

Linsha nodded. Her mind was so tired that her thoughts slowly surfaced like random bubbles in a muddy swamp. "I don't know where he gets his power. It is strong and seems unaffected by the problems our sorcerers are having. I didn't think the Tarmaks had magic-wielders."

The owl's round eyes narrowed to slits and her beak clacked in anger. She peered over the woman's shoulder to the sleeping Legionnaire. "What did they do to Lanther?"

"Hung him in a cage out in the sun."

Varia hissed. "We need Crucible."

"No!" Linsha didn't intend to be so loud, but the word came out sharp and emphatic. She glanced guiltily down at Lanther, but he seemed to be still sleeping in spite of her outburst. "No," she repeated in a whisper. "He should stay with Lord Bight."

"He would come to you."

"Why should he? He came here for Iyesta and stayed because his wing was injured."

Linsha heard the petulant tone in her voice, but she was too weary, too sore, and too downhearted to summon the strength to change it.

The owl swiveled her head around and regarded the woman with widened eyes. "You have suffered much. You are not interpreting your feelings correctly."

"Probably not," Linsha said with a sigh. She was really too tired to argue. "I fear for him. I don't want his blood on my hands . . . or yours."

Varia said nothing. She understood much and saw

many things Linsha did not. Humans were sometimes an enigma to her, but this time she thought she knew why Linsha had said no. Well, she would see what Crucible had to say. The big bronze had the right to make his own decisions.

The bird crept a little closer to Linsha's head and pressed her warm feathers against the lady knight's cheek. Ever so quietly she began to hum a slow, wordless tune as soft as down, as soothing as a lullaby.

Linsha propped her eyes open. "You can't sing me to sleep like an obstinate owlet," she whispered.

Varia continued to hum her song, her body gently vibrating against Linsha's face. In spite of herself, Linsha's eyes drooped. Her strained features relaxed. Three breaths later she was asleep, her head lolled back against the wall, her lips slighted parted.

Satisfied, Varia eased away and hopped to the floor. Moments later her small form scurried out into the shadows of the ruin. As soon as she was out of sight of the Tarmak guards, she thrust off with wing and taloned feet and beat upwards into the night sky. Silent and determined, the owl turned north and went to find a bronze dragon.

The sun rose in a tawny dawn and banished the night's chill. A haze hung over the ocean, but the plains came to light sharp, clear, golden in the morning light. Even before the sun lifted clear of the sea, the people of the Missing City stirred and prepared for another day of work. No matter who ruled the city, there was still the business of survival to attend to. The crops that looked so promising in midsummer had ripened and needed to be harvested to feed the hungry Tarmak army. Livestock scattered across the grasslands had to be rounded up and brought in before winter. Hay had to be cut, grapes gathered and crushed for wine, sheep and goats sheared one last time. In the city market a limited trade of sorts still existed. While there were no foreign merchants, the local craftspeople, farmers, merchants, and fishermen still had wares to trade or sell. The Tarmaks had stripped the city of its militia and the government and had transported many of its young, strong inhabitants to the gods knew where, but they had left the remaining population alive and in place to maintain the city.

To perform the hard labor required for the maintenance and construction needed in their new domain, the Tarmaks also kept a large group of slaves drawn from the city population, the defeated defenders, and any person they happened to capture on their frequent patrols of the surrounding plains. These slaves were kept in pens scattered around the city, and they worked hard to repair the damage of battle and to prepare the city for its new rulers.

One such group was imprisoned at the dragon's palace, in the old slave pens once used by Thunder. As the sun rose and the day advanced, Linsha and the other prisoners sat in their makeshift prison and listened to the distant sounds of many slave voices shouting and groaning, of rocks crashing into other rocks, of odd grinding noises, and the ring of tools on stone. They wondered what was happening and if their turn would come to join the ranks of the slaves. Although slavery seemed a dreadful prospect to these Knights and Legionnaires, pondering the possibility of becoming a slave seemed preferable to dwelling on the fear that their small group was being held for something worse.

At midmorning they received an answer of sorts.

The Tarmak general arrived at the palace with his personal guard, and once again the prisoners were ordered outside and lined up in the courtyard. This time the general stood aside and watched as his men separated the prisoners into two groups.

"Those," he ordered pointing to one group of Knights and Legionnaires. "Put them to work on the palace." He turned his masked face to Linsha's group. "Put her in the cage. Bring him to my tent."

Hard hands gripped Linsha's arms and hustled her to the oblong metal cage. She whipped her head around in time to see the Tarmaks force Lanther after the Tarmak general, then she was slammed into the cage and the door closed. The cage was hoisted on its frame, and all too quickly, Linsha found herself alone, left to hang in the morning sun. The workers were marched away while the remaining men, including Sir Remmik, were returned to the prison. A tense quiet descended on the open yard.

The first few hours were not too unbearable. The morning breeze played among the palace ruins until nearly noon before it skipped away and left the land to the mercies of the hot sun. Linsha tried to keep her limbs limber by shifting her weight from foot to foot, by tensing and relaxing her muscles, and by flexing the few joints she could bend. She tried to distract her mind by studying the Tarmaks she could see. She studied the guards, she observed their gestures and body movements and listened to the snatches of conversation she could hear. She watched the procession of prisoners, one by one from the storehouse to some place she could not see.

Sir Remmik was the first to go, and he left between his guards, his back stiff and his expression severe. He came back staggering between his guards, his face gray and deeply lined. The other men left looking apprehensive and defiant and returned barely able to walk. Several had to be carried. Linsha worried for them and feared for Lanther who had not yet come back. She had a fairly good idea what was happening to them.

With plenty of time to think, she wondered, too, about her other friends—Hugh, Mariana, Falaius, and others in the camp. Where were they? Had any of them survived? Where was Leonidas? And where had Varia gone?

Linsha scanned the trees and ruins around the courtyard and saw no sign of the owl, but if Varia did not want to be seen, even a sharp-eyed elf would have trouble spotting her. Was the owl still here, or had she left on some errand?

As the morning passed and Linsha's mind slogged over a long trail of thoughts, the breeze died and the sun's heat collected in the old stone. Linsha's body, cramped in the iron cage, grew sore and stiff in some places and numb in others. She ached to move. Her clothes itched abominably, yet she could reach nothing to scratch. Her stomach raged at her, her head hurt, and her mouth felt as dry as parched stone.

An hour or so past noon, the Tarmak general in his golden mask returned to the ruined court, escorted by his guards. He walked to Linsha's cage, crossed his arms, and stared up at her like a statue of a god.

"Where is the owl?" he demanded, his voice as hard as granite.

Linsha glared back. "She's dead." She forced the words past her parched throat.

He snapped his fingers and at his command, a wine flask was brought with two stemmed cups. A white wine, shining and fruity, was poured into the two cups. Linsha's entire body longed for a drink of that pale, cool liquid.

The Tarmak held one cup up toward her and raised the other to his mask. He tossed the contents into his mouth without spilling more than a drop or two. "Where is the rendezvous point for the surviving militia?"

"A little pub on the south side of Palanthas."

He nodded as if he expected such an answer and spilled the contents of the second cup on the ground. "Later," he said. "We will talk."

He left Linsha alone again to stare at the puddle of the wine as it slowly sank down into the cracks between the stones and disappeared. She wanted to cry, she wanted to shriek, but she had no strength left nor moisture in her eyes to form tears. Instead, she forced her eyes closed and turned her mind away from external distractions and focused on the reserves of strength she had left in her heart. She put aside the discomforts of her hunger and her headache, her aching limbs and her thirsty mouth, and she looked deep inside to the inner tranquility she kept hidden for times of great need. Gradually she slowed her heartbeat and soothed the pain in her head. Her muscles relaxed. The world receded into a silence that bore nothing but peace. Sooner than she would have liked, she felt the ephemeral tickle on her face and neck and sensed the power of her heart drain from her like the wine from the cup. It was a feeling she hated and could do nothing to stop. But the mystic power Goldmoon had taught her to use had eased her long enough to serve its purpose. She fell into a deep sleep and left the pain and fear of her confinement behind.

The Akkad-Ur

10

A tremendous buffet on the cage jerked Linsha abruptly awake. Confused, she stared blearily. Warriors stood before her, and above was a darkening sky. The Tarmaks lowered the cage until it touched the ground, unlocked the door, and hauled her out. Her numb feet and aching knees would not support her, so the guards had to carry her out of the prison yard, through the great hall, and to the large front courtyard where Iyesta used to meet with her human guests.

Linsha stared around the courtyard in amazement. At last she could see what all the noise had been about. Slave gangs had spent the day demolishing the front entrance to the dragon's throne room. The great double doors where the brass triplets used to stand guard were gone—as was most of the front wall that supported the door frame. Two huge piles of stone and rubble had been heaped near the gate, and more had been dumped within the throne room. Although she had accepted the reality of Iyesta's death, she could not help but be sick at heart at the destruction of her lair.

Just outside the broken walls, a large, spacious

tent had been set up for the Tarmak officers. Several of its walls had been rolled up to allow a breeze, and guards stood impassively around the perimeter. Torches burned at all four corners, and plain oil lamps cast a yellow glow in the interior.

Linsha saw the tent and realized what was coming. Her stomach twisted into knots. She pulled fiercely away from her guards and snapped, "Put me down!"

They must have understood enough Common or understood her desire to walk unaided, for they lowered her feet to the ground and allowed her to walk between them. She staggered a little on her wobbly legs then hauled herself upright as she was escorted into the tent and brought before the Tarmak general. She stood straight, her head up, and watched him warily as the guards bowed to their lord.

One guard beside her jabbed the butt of his spear into the back of her knee. Her leg buckled and she fell sideways to the rugged floor.

"You will kneel in the presence of the Akkad-Ur," the guard growled.

"Akkad-Ur," the second guard said, and he launched into a long speech in the rough, guttural tongue of the Tarmaks.

Linsha pushed herself to her knees and sat upright on her heels. Kneel she might. Grovel she would not. Casting a quick look around, she realized this tent was the same—or at least a copy—to the one she had been in before when the Tarmaks had left her to find the Abyssal Lance. The general sat in the same carved couch padded with pelts. A low table sat to his left—still covered with writing implements, scrolls, and what looked like building plans. The ornate banner decorated with the lion and the geometric designs still hung in its accustomed place behind him.

The general had not changed much in the past few months. He was still a magnificent specimen of a Tarmak, statuesque and dangerous. The war paint was absent this night, revealing his fair skin and numerous scars, and his kilted skirt had been replaced with a linen cuirass decorated with small disks of brass that looked suspiciously like brass dragon scales. The general gestured his warriors to leave and silently watched Linsha in front of him.

"You are called Akkad-Ur?" she said before he could address her.

The golden mask stared down at her. "Akkad is a rank, Lady Knight. It is similar to your rank of general. Ur is part of my name." He continued to study her for a few moments, then he called out something.

Immediately two women entered the tent carrying several basins, jugs, and towels. Linsha stared in astonishment at one she recognized—a lovely buxom blond with flexible legs and a talent for turning a profit with her body. It was the courtesan Callista, the favorite of the captain of the city watch and òne of Linsha's informers. After Linsha's flight from the Somanic citadel, Callista had loaned her some clothes to escape detection. Since then Linsha had neither seen nor heard from the woman. She lifted her eyebrows in a silent question, but Callista shot a furtive glance at the Akkad-Ur and gave her head a quick shake.

She and her companion laid their burdens down in front of Linsha, helped her to her feet, and to her utter mortification, stripped off her clothes. Not that the clothes were in excellent repair or that Linsha was sentimentally attached to them. They were filthy and little more than rags. But now she stood naked in front of the Akkad-Ur. Her embarrassment burned in her face. Silently, while the Tarmak watched, the women washed Linsha with water and soap from the basins. They cleaned off days of sweat, blood, dirt, and grime. They washed her hair and rubbed her muscles with a sweet oil. Callista's eyes widened at the number of scars and the half-healed wound on Linsha's body, yet she said nothing.

If Linsha hadn't been so unnerved by the sight of the Tarmak general sitting only a few feet away, she would have enjoyed this first cleaning she had had in days and the attention of someone other than smelly, grumpy men. She wanted to talk to Callista, to ask her a dozen questions, to inquire if she was all right and why she was in the service of the general. And more than anything she wanted a drink of water!

But for Callista's sake, she gritted her teeth and said nothing until the ladies gathered their jugs and basins and prepared to leave. Only then did Linsha realize they had not brought extra clothes with them, and they were picking hers up to carry them away. She held out her hand in entreaty, and Callista could only shrug a bit and hurry after her companion, leaving Linsha alone with the Akkad-Ur.

The general chuckled, a rumbling sound behind his mask. "My informant was right. You do clean up well. You should not feel embarrassed by your nakedness. In our world, the body is a utensil to care for and use well. You have the body of a warrior—a thing that would bring you much respect in my city."

Linsha wasn't sure whether she should feel complimented or threatened. She stood still, trying to feel at ease, and waited for him to make a move. When he did nothing but continue to study her, she lost patience. She did not believe she was particularly desirable. Compared to someone like Callista, she was too thin, too old. Her breasts were small, and her hair was a curly disaster.

Yet who knew what the Tarmak males desired? She had heard that a number of young women had been taken and shipped out of the city by the Tarmaks, and she knew the warriors had enjoyed the pleasures of the flesh among many of the women. Was the general any different?

"So now what?" she demanded. "You left me hanging in a cage all day, and now you clean me up just so you can stare at me?"

He lifted a hand and waved away her questions. "I was satisfying my curiosity. Nothing else." Reaching down beside his chair, he picked up a tunic and some pants and held them up. "Where is the bronze dragon?"

She crossed her arms over her breasts and glared at him.

"All right. I will tell you. He returned to his lair in Sanction. Not a wise move. I have heard the Knights of Neraka desire that city for their own. They will get it eventually, I believe."

He sat back in his chair and regarded her for a moment, then he tossed her the tunic. Linsha caught it.

"I know, too, your owl has left the city to seek the dragon. I believe he will come to your aid."

Linsha was so surprised by his words that she simply stared at him, the tunic dangling from her hand. "I told her not to," she whispered.

"The owl has a mind of her own. As does the dragon. I am told he cares for you. He stayed longer than he needed to because he worried about you. If it wasn't for the lord governor of Sanction, he would never have left."

"How do you know this?" Linsha snapped.

But she knew. Gods, she thought miserably, the informant had been a busy little spy. Only someone who lived in the Wadi and observed her and Crucible day by day would have known these details.

The Akkad-Ur held up the pants. "Our spies are numerous. And quite good. I asked you today where the militia would rendezvous. However, I have already learned where they are."

The cold threat of his words stung her. "If you already know everything," she said nastily, "why do you bother asking me?"

"It is your spirit of cooperation I wish to test. Just because you are a prisoner does not mean you are entirely without choice. You may choose to help us or you may accept to suffer our displeasure."

He tossed the pants to her and stood.

"No boots?" she said, her hands tightening around the clothes.

He stepped away from the couch. "Bare feet will make it more difficult for you to run away."

Linsha wasted no more time. She pulled on the clothes and stepped back to keep some distance between herself and the Akkad-Ur. Apprehension and anger shared equal parts of her thoughts.

"You have already wiped out the militia. Just like the mercenaries. What difference does it make where a few pitiful stragglers go?" She hoped to steer him away from the subject of escape and keep him talking about something else. If he was distracted by discussing his plans and ambitions, perhaps he would not touch her or use his magic. It hadn't worked the last time she'd tried it, but at least she had gained some very useful information. Her eyes flicked up to the ceiling of the tent, but the Abyssal Lance was not there. Had the Tarmaks been the ones who retrieved it from the cavern?

"There are a few survivors we missed." The Akkad-Ur crossed his arms over his muscular chest, and his piercing eyes glared out the eyeholes of the mask. "I dislike leaving loose ends. I had planned to wipe out the militia earlier, to use the eggs to lure them out and slaughter them on the field. But we changed our plans when you took the Abyssal Lance and organized such a neat plan to rid us of Thunder. If it soothes your mind to know, your militia has proven more tenacious and useful than we expected. We have been impressed with your resistance."

Linsha edged a little farther away and skimmed her mind for something else to say, anything to keep him talking. "Why did you massacre your mercenaries?"

"They were like Thunder. Useful for time before they grew too lazy and greedy. They would not be of help on our next campaign, and we could not afford to leave them behind. Their slaughter also served as an excellent lesson to the inhabitants of the city and as a distraction for your troop. Their deaths allowed us to, as you say, kill two birds with one stone."

Linsha kept her face impassive, but her heart began a heavy pound. Several thoughts impressed her mind at the same time: the Tarmaks knew where the militia was hiding, and the army planned to march soon. By all that was sacred, she had to get out of this place and warn the survivors. Sinking Wells was not a fortress. It was simply an old sinkhole, a place of well-worn campgrounds, scattered trees, and old dunes. Anyone who made it safely there could not mount a successful defense against the likes of the Tarmak. They would have to flee, perhaps north to the King's Road or north-west to Duntollik. They had to be warned.

Linsha's eyes narrowed, and she stared hard at the Akkad-Ur with a suspicious new thought. The last time he brought her into his tent and turned chatty, he'd manipulated her into stealing the Lance. What was he trying to accomplish now?

"Speaking of eggs, where are they?" she asked, trying to sound casual. She turned slowly to keep him in view while he walked over to his work table.

"They are safe. The ones that are left. We find them very useful." He picked up something from the table, then turned and approached her.

Linsha almost ran. Only the thought of the guards just outside the tent and the strength of her own pride kept her standing in place. What would be the point of trying to run and making a fool of herself? Her eyes remained fixed on his golden mask, and her hands clenched into fists.

"Then what are you doing to Iyesta's lair?" she asked, hoping to gain a little more time.

"Tearing it down so it will not be a temptation to other dragons or treasure-seekers. The tunnel entrance will be buried, the throne room destroyed."

He stopped only a few inches away from her and looked down at her through the holes of the mask. "Your courage is almost equal to ours. It is a pity you are not a Tarmak."

His hand lifted to her head, but he did not touch her body or lay his fingers on her face. Something gold slid over her head and slipped by her eyes. A thin, strong chain with two dragon scales fell neatly across her neck and into their familiar place on her chest.

She glanced down in surprise. "Why—"

The Akkad-Ur cut her off with a sharp command. Two guards entered the tent and took her by the arms. Before she could receive a reply, they hurried her out and returned her to the prison.

She stood bemused in the darkness of the old store-house while the guards closed and barred the door behind her. Her hand went to the scales on the chain and touched them carefully. They felt the same with their familiar bumps and lines and smooth places, but who knew what the Tarmak might have done to them? When daylight came, she would try to examine them more carefully.

After a few minutes she became aware that the men in the prison were staring at her. The light from the torch just outside the door fell across her, setting her in a glow that made her very visible to men already accustomed to the dark. She glanced down at her clean clothes, and her heart sank. It didn't take a wise man to know what they were thinking. She silently cursed the general into several generations.

Sir Remmik was the first to move. He walked over to her and studied her different clothes, the cleanliness of her skin, the glint of gold light on the dragon scales. His thin lips curled in a sneer.

"You have obviously been cooperative," he remarked acidly. "That is another transgression to add to your record." He picked up the dragon scales and turned them over in his fingers. "Were you trying to preserve your safety by trading favors with the Tarmak?"

For the first time in her life, Linsha struck a superior officer. The humiliation and apprehension she had felt in the Akkad-Ur's tent, the frustration and misery she had endured in the cage, and the hatred she had felt for Sir Remmik since her arrival in the Missing City erupted like one of Sanction's volcanoes. At the spurious insult to her honor, she pulled back a fist and punched him in the face.

The blow was so unexpected that the Knight Commander stumbled backward and fell to the ground, stunned. Linsha stepped over him. She leveled a glare at the rest of the Knights and the Legionnaires.

"Does anyone else have anything to say?" she snarled.

They eyed her warily like cattle eye an approaching lioness. No one said a word.

Only Lanther laughed. He climbed to his feet, stiff and dusty, and limped to greet her.

"Is this a new form of torture?" he called out. "Baths and clean clothes? Bring it here! Torture me!"

Her frown lightened. "You could even suffer the exquisite agony of Callista performing your torture."

His eyebrows disappeared into his hairline. He took her elbow and led her aside. "Did she really?"

The others chuckled halfheartedly and let the matter slide for now. They were really too tired to deal with a furious woman. Lanther would get to the truth of the matter.

Linsha looked at his hollow eyes and thin face, at the livid scar on his cheek, and at the indomitable spirit she saw in his blue eyes, and she forced her cracked lips into a grin of sorts. She had forgotten Lanther had been one of Callista's admirers.

"Yes," she replied wearily. "It's an old form of humiliation and division. I didn't tell him anything, Lanther. He already knew the answers he wanted. And no—" she added quickly when his eyebrows drew together in a silent question— "I did not give him anything else."

She went to an empty place by the wall and sagged down into a sitting position, her legs stretched out.

He fetched water for her and a few crumbs of bread he had saved from their meager dinner, and they talked softly for several hours, comparing information and questions and conjectures about the Tarmaks. They tried to decide who the spy in their midst could be, but they came no closer to identifying a suspect.

"I would like to think it is Sir Remmik," Linsha said with a grimace. Her hand still hurt from the punch she had given the Knight Commander, and her pride still hurt from his insult. "He would do almost anything to preserve his reputation and the Circle."

"Including betray the militia?" Lanther asked with interest. He didn't like the Knight anymore than Linsha did. "He was questioned rather extensively today."

She sighed. "I know he doesn't truly care about the militia. But he lives for the letter of the law. His entire set of beliefs rest solely in the Oath and the Measure. And the Oath and the Measure do not allow for betraying one's allies. Besides," she said with a tired chuckle, "if he had been feeding the Tarmaks information from the beginning, he would have worked a deal to save his beloved citadel."

Lanther grunted. "I suppose you're right. Being a traitor does seem beneath his dignity. Perhaps it is someone outside the militia, one of the townspeople who came to the Wadi? Perhaps this person is already dead."

Linsha slipped down until she was lying on her back. "Perhaps. Whoever it is knows a great deal about me and Varia and Crucible. I think the Tarmaks are hoping Crucible comes back."

The Legionnaire looked at her, interested by her statement. "Why do you say that?"

"The general thinks Varia went to get him."

"Did she?"

"I don't know. But I think they still have the Abyssal Lance somewhere, and Crucible is the only dragon likely to give them trouble right now. All the others seem to be busy with their own problems or are missing . . . or dead. Now that the mercenaries, the militia, Thunder, Iyesta, and her companions are gone, there is no one left but Crucible who can stop them from spreading across the Plains."

"What if Crucible stays in Sanction?"

Memories of a tall, blond lord governor teased Linsha's mind. "I hope he does," she replied. "Lord Bight needs him more."

She closed her eyes and allowed her thoughts to dwell in Sanction for a time. She had faced many difficulties and disasters in Sanction, but there had been a few joys as well. Her unexpected friendship with Lord Bight had been one of those. He was not an easy man to know, prone to arrogance and temper and hidden secrets. Nevertheless, she respected him and liked him in spite of his erratic moods, and she liked to think he cared for her too.

After a while, when she said nothing more, Lanther leaned over her and realized she had fallen asleep. He studied her face for a short time, noticing the new lines and shadows on her lovely features. Hesitantly he reached out and traced a finger along her cheekbone and jaw. He did not think he would ever forget the memory of her standing over the prone Knight with her fist clenched and her green eyes alight with fury. She was a woman worthy of much more than a prison cell and slavery. With a slight grin on his face, he lay down beside her and joined her in sleep.

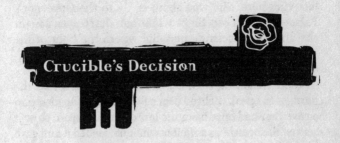

Crucible's Decision

1 t took Varia six days to fly from Missing City to Sanction. During that time she passed over the noxious swamp of the black dragon, Sable, and was chased by a foul winged creature with no feathers, leathery wings, and the head of a lizard. She found herself over Blöde the fourth day and was shot at by ogres. On the fifth and sixth days she flew through the passes and valleys of the southern Khalkist Mountains until at last she saw the smoking peaks of the Lords of Doom. Weary and wingsore she flew past Mount Ashkir and circled warily over the city of Sanction. She was relieved to see little had changed since her brief visit three months ago. Many of the ships in the harbor still flew the Solamnic flag. The city walls were still standing; the moat of lava still flowed like a fiery necklace around the city, and the Knights of Neraka still camped outside the city walls in the mouths of the two passes to the east and the north. There were no signs of heavy damage to the city buildings and no apparent indication of imminent disaster. The population moved freely about the city streets and harbor, making the best of another day in a long, bitter siege.

Varia cooed a sound of relief. The sight of the city reassured her that things had changed little since her last visit here. She was about to fly to the Governor's Palace to find Lord Bight when her sharp eyes caught the glint of something metallic where the light of the setting sun gleamed on the steep side of Mount Thunderhorn. Tipping a wing, she flew toward it.

The dragon sat on a broad ledge that cut across the flank of the peak. Behind him a large crevice opened into a cave that had once been the lair of a red dragon. Now it served the bronze as a shelter when he needed it and gave him a vantage point that looked out over the entire city. Above him, the massive crown of the volcano spewed lava into the air and sent smoke boiling into the sky.

Varia glanced nervously up at the peak before she came to a landing on the dragon's long wing. He didn't seem to notice she was there, so she hopped across to his crossed front legs and rested on his forearm. Still he said nothing while he gazed silently across the panorama of the city below him. His long face looked pensive, and his golden eyes seemed lost in some ancient memory. She turned her head to look down at Sanction. Shadows of evening slowly filled the streets, and twinkling lights were starting to appear like fireflies along the buildings and the harbor. The golden rivers of lava glowed a deep yellow-orange in the gathering dusk. In the east pass near the base of Mount Thunderhorn, she could see the watchfires of the Dark Knights burning.

"I am losing the city," Crucible said, his deep voice resonant with sadness.

Varia swiveled her head up to look at him then looked at the city again. It appeared no different to her. There were no Dark Knights in the streets. No fires burned out of control. No warriors swept up to the walls to kill the city.

"I can hear her voice," he said so softly that the owl had to concentrate to hear him. "She is out there, calling. The chromatic dragons are answering her call. The dead listen and obey her. I can feel her will bending toward Sanction, and I can do nothing about it. She will take it from me."

The owl stared up at the big dragon in amazement. Who was he talking about? Linsha? She flipped her wings and hooted a question.

The dragon's big head tilted down toward her. "I thought she was gone, but now I know she has been here all along. I heard her voice in the great storm, and now I hear it again. She is coming."

"Who?" The owl screeched.

"Takhisis."

Varia nearly slipped off his scaly leg in surprise. What was he talking about?

"The dark goddess left with the others after the Chaos War."

Crucible tilted his head as if he was still listening to a faraway voice. "I don't think so. I think she is still on Krynn, in hiding maybe. She wants Sanction back."

Varia's eyes grew to round globes. She did not doubt the validity of the dragon's belief. She, too, remembered that horrible storm and the terrifying voices in its winds. Although she had no feeling yet of the goddess's presence in the world, if Crucible insisted it was true, she would not argue with his feelings. "What will you do?" she asked.

He glanced up the fiery display of the volcano above them. "I thought of loosening my control of the Lords of Doom and letting the mountains take back what I fought to save. There would be little left of the city to leave for the Dark Queen."

Varia hooted softly. "You cannot. You are not like her."

"No," he agreed. "I cannot." A silence settled over him, and he stared again down at the city he worked so hard to build.

He said nothing for a long while, and Varia let him be, knowing he would speak in his own good time. Beneath him, the ground trembled from the violent energies of the volcano and the roar of its voice filled the evening with a steady rumble of distant thunder.

"Since you are here, I must assume things are not going well in Missing City," he said at last.

Varia agreed that no, things were not, and she told him of the massacre and Linsha's capture by the Tarmaks. "She told me not to come. She worried for you. But they are torturing her. I fear if they do not kill her, they will enslave her—or worse, ship her away."

Crucible's large eyes blinked slowly as he pondered what the owl had said. "Stupid to fall for a trap like that. She cares so much for those eggs." He fell silent again then went on. "So I must choose between a city and a woman."

"A city you said was already doomed," Varia pointed out.

She knew how much the dragon cared for both and how the loss of either would wound him deeply, but she also knew Sanction had a larger voice, a longer history, a deeper hold on the dragon's soul. This was his home, his lair, his territory. No dragon would give up a lair without a fight for anything less than a very powerful reason. Linsha, on the other side, had only one small owl to speak for her, and Varia was not going to leave without her best effort of persuasion.

"If what you fear is true," she forced herself to go on, "if the Dark Queen is back in our world, then nothing you can do will save Sanction. Her temple was here years ago, and to this place she is naturally drawn. She will come here, her Knights will take the city, and they will kill you."

He snorted a jet of agitated steam. "I will not abandon my city just to save my life. I do not know with a certainty that Takhisis will come here."

"I don't suppose you have heard the voices of any of the other gods?" Varia asked hopefully.

"No. She is alone . . . gathering her armies."

Varia clacked her beak in anger. She despised the dark goddess Takhisis with all her being. She hoped that the dragon was wrong, that he was just suffering from a difficult day or depression or loneliness. On top of everything else this long-suffering world dealt with, the goddess was the last thing they needed. She tried one more time.

"Linsha needs you, Crucible. You don't have to stay. On your wings you can fly to Iyesta's lair, free Linsha, and be back in Sanction before the Dark Knights miss you. Give your life to that evil bitch if you must, but help your friend first."

He climbed to his feet, causing the owl to flutter off his leg. "I will think about it. There is much to decide. Go to the palace and wait there."

Varia knew better than to argue. She flew off the ledge and angled down the mountain. She glanced back once in time to see the bronze's tail disappear into the darkness of his cave.

The palace was in an uproar. Doors slammed and booted feet ran up and down the halls. Men shouted orders, and servants scurried everywhere. Outside, the governor's guards locked and sealed the doors and gates and positioned themselves along the walls and the roof.

In an embrasure of a window in Lord Bight's room Varia sat and listened to the noises. Something was obviously happening. The governor's palace was not usually so chaotic. She stared out the leaded glass window to the courts below and watched the guards in their red tunics. They were all fully armed, and those who were not manning the walls seemed to be searching the grounds for something. What was going on?

A small noise drew her attention away from the window in time to see a panel slide open in the wall close to Lord Bight's large bed. The Lord Governor stepped through and, holding the panel open behind him, gestured to the bird.

Curious, Varia flew to his arm and sat quietly while Lord Bight stepped back into a narrow passage and closed the panel. Without speaking, he carried her down narrow stairs and down dim and musty passages until they reached the lowest level of the palace cut deep into the bedrock of the hill. They came to another stone wall that slid aside under Lord Bight's hand, and proceeding with caution, he stepped out into a dark tunnel.

"What is happening?" Varia said at last.

"I had to make a few arrangements," Lord Bright replied, his voice curt.

"Where are we going?"

"Mount Thunderhorn. Crucible will go to Missing City."

He said nothing more, but Varia was satisfied. She gripped his arm and rode quietly while he carried her down deeper into the maze of tunnels and passages that cut underneath the city of Sanction. Here in the realm of the Shadowpeople, he slipped silently through, unseen by his people above, and came at last to the tunnel that linked the lower levels with the cavern that was Crucible's lair.

"The dragon cannot stay long on the Plains," Lord Bight said as he climbed the long stairs. "You understand that. Much is happening. I fear a greater war than our small siege is about to descend on Ansalon. Crucible must come back."

Varia hooted her agreement.

They reached the back entrance to the cavern close to a deep cleft that dropped down into a stream of lava. The cave was deadly hot and reeked of molten rock. A deep rumbling noise vibrated the rocks around them. The noxious fumes and the heat did not seem to bother Lord Bight, but Varia was forced to fly out of the cave and wait. Moments later, the bronze dragon emerged, stretching his stout legs and unfurling his long wings. He looked like he had just awakened from a nap.

He waited until the owl found a safe perch on his back, then he leaped off the ledge. He rose high above Mount Thunderhorn, his wings outstretched to catch the hot air boiling off the volcano. With a flip of his tail, he turned south and soon left Sanction behind.

One Last Survivor

12

To the people who lived in the region of Missing City and to those travelers who crossed the Plains, Sinking Wells was an oasis, a resting place, and a source for tales. Called a well, it was actually an old sinkhole created thousands of years before when an underground cavern collapsed. Through the centuries it slowly filled with sand, dirt, dead animals, and wind-blown debris until it dropped only thirty feet at its deepest end. The only thing that sank was the water level that rose or fell acccording to the rainfall and the underground water table. During some years the water would brim near the banks of the oval-shaped hole, and other times the water dropped out of sight below ground, forcing visitors to trek down a slippery path to an old well shaft that pierced down into the earth at the bottom of the sinkhole.

As Linsha well knew, Sinking Wells was not a fortress. It was a gathering place. It had no fortified walls, protective landmarks, or even heavy brush where people could hide. All it had was water and a central location in the region around Missing City. Now, a few days after the massacre at Scorpion Wadi, it also had twenty-six survivors, scouts, messengers, and outpost guards—the last remnant of the city's proud defenders.

A search party found Falaius Taneek four days after the massacre at Scorpion Wadi. The small party of humans and centaurs had worked tirelessly the past nights to search every known watchpost, hiding place, campsite, and trail known to the militia to find any stragglers, survivors, and patrols that had not received news of the massacre or of the rendezvous at Sinking Wells.

On their way back to the Wells, they passed one of several stock ponds along their route. The pond, a depression dug by farmers to catch rainwater for stock, was nearly dry, but a sharp-eyed centaur noticed a body lying in the thick grass and trotted over to investigate. His call brought everyone else running.

The old Plainsman was feverish, dehydrated, and bore several wounds. But he was a man of the Plains, tempered by heat, strengthened by barren wastes, empowered by storms, and toughened by years of hard labor. He needed only water and the joy of seeing familiar faces again to find the strength to rise. The centaurs vied to offer him a ride, and two Legionnaires, who had accompanied the troop, walked beside him, their wan faces smiling for the first time in days.

A large group greeted the party when they returned to Sinking Wells shortly after dawn. Cheering the return of the Plainsman, they followed the search party to three crude tents that had been set up in the shelter of a copse of trees. The tents served as a headquarters for the militia leaders and a healing place for the sick and wounded. Mariana, accompanied by two elves, walked out of the headquarters tent to meet the Legionnaire.

The half-elf smiled and extended a hand to help Falaius to the ground. "Old Man, it is a joy to see you!"

A grin of sorts spread across his weathered face at her nickname for him. "Young woman, the pleasure is all mine."

He refused to go in the healer's tent until he had talked to General Dockett or Knight Commander Remmik, so Mariana ordered a healer to come to him. They brought him soup and a pallet and made a couch for him under the trees. A fire was built, and while the Legion commander ate his soup, the Captain told him of General Dockett's death, the slaughter in the Wadi, and the capture of the Solamnic Knights.

Falaius ran his gaze around the faces of the people who had gathered to listen, and his heart grieved. There were too many faces missing, too few here beside him. Of those he saw and recognized, most were people who had been out on patrol or stationed out in the watch posts. There were a few messengers, one child, one Solamnic Knight, and some new arrivals he did not know. Of the guards he had been with the night of the attack and the people he knew to be in the Wadi, there were none.

"Falaius," Mariana said when he had finished his soup. "We looked for you in the canyon. We spent three days searching the gullies and caves for you. We gave you up for lost. How did you survive?"

A grimace passed over the Plainsman's features. "If our gods had not left us, I would have said the hand of a god passed over me and held me in grace. I was checking the outlying pickets along the top of the Wadi when we were ambushed by Tarmak assassins. One of our guards managed to give a warning before he was killed, and a moment later, we were attacked. I was struck by several arrows, and Tomarick, the Legionnaire who accompanied me, took two in the back. Even so he had enough strength left to help me kill two attackers." He paused, his deep-set eyes staring into the past. "He had enough strength, too, to push me into a crevice and hide my body with his. I shall honor Tomarick's name for the rest of my time in this life."

His listeners leaned forward to better hear his tale. When he did not continue right away, someone from the back of the crowd said, "Then what happened, Falaius?"

Mariana passed him a cup filled with deep red wine, part of a small stash one of the centaurs had found in an abandoned farm. He inhaled the aroma with pleasure and sampled it before he continued.

"I don't know what happened after that. The Tarmaks must have passed me by, because the next things I remember seeing are daylight and hearing the sounds of vultures. It was almost midday."

Mariana nodded. That explained why Varia hadn't seen him. She'd left the canyon about midmorning.

The centaur who had carried him back asked, "How did you get to the stock pond? That is almost seven miles away."

Falaius pointed to his bandaged leg and bloodstained boots. "One step at a time. I moved at night and was planning to make my way here. I am very grateful you spotted me."

"We are grateful, more than you know, that you are here," replied Mariana.

The Legionnaire's expression folded into a frown. "But many are not. Tell me what else has been happening? Have you heard news of Lanther or Linsha?"

With the help of various comments and additions from others, Mariana told him the rest of the news of the battered militia, of the scattered and grief-stricken survivors that came trickling in to the Wells, of the stunned patrols who returned to find their families dead, of the search party that found him, and of their struggle to regroup and find more help. She reported Varia's news of the prisoners, and the remarkable survival of Sir Hugh, Sir Fellion, and little Amania.

"I see Sir Hugh," Falaius said, giving the young Knight a nod. "Where is your companion, Sir Fellion?"

Sir Hugh looked down at his hands. "I buried him this afternoon. The healers could not stop the infection."

"I am truly sorry." Falaius's face grew more troubled. "Too many have joined the ranks of the dead," he murmured. "Too many souls."

He said nothing more of what he knew to the younger people around him, for few would understand and none would be comforted. Only to Linsha had he once voiced his suspicion that the souls of the dead were not leaving this world. Something held them here, some great power that kept them in thrall for reasons Falaius could only guess. It galled him to think that the gallant spirits of Tomarick, Sir Fellion, and hundreds of his friends, acquaintances, and members of his fighting forces had met their deaths only to be trapped in a place where they no longer belonged.

"There is other news as well." Mariana's voice broke into his thoughts and drew him back to the camp. "These elves—" she indicated the two who had sat silent by her side for whole telling of the tales— "are kirath from Silvanesti. They bring their own news."

Falaius sat up. "Friends, it is a pleasure to welcome you, but from your expressions, I fear your news is no better than ours."

The oldest of the two bowed to the Legion commander, "This has been a summer of disasters for us both. We came hoping to ask for help only to discover you are in as dire shape as the Silvanesti."

Falaius suddenly remembered what the kirath were. These elves who looked so wan and haggard were members of the band of elves who guarded the borders of the elf realm, Silvanesti. His understanding made a leap forward and he exclaimed, "Your shield has fallen!"

Exclamations and sounds of surprise came from the crowd all around him. Obviously, no one else had heard this. The two elves nodded.

The oldest continued, "We were telling Mariana when you were brought in. To make a long tale shorter, a Dark Knight named Mina found a way through the shield. She exposed one of our trusted ministers as Cyan Bloodbane, the green dragon of our nightmares. We killed him, and our King Silvanoshei tore down the shield tree and destroyed the shield."

"That's wonderful news!" someone cried.

The others took up the excitement.

"The elves could help us!"

"Silvanesti is free! It's about time!"

Voices spoke with happiness and relief until Falaius held up a hand to silence them. He had been watching Mariana and the two elves and could see as plain as daylight that the fall of the elven shield was not wonderful news. "What happened?"

The younger elf answered, "The Dark Knight Mina had an army just outside our borders. As soon as the shield came down, they marched in. The Knights of Neraka now control Silvanost."

A cold and empty silence dropped over the ring of listeners. Dappled sunlight danced around them and a warm breeze whisked through the camp, yet a chill of despair settled down around the huddled survivors as they pondered the scope of the disaster. There would be no help from their neighbors, no elven army to rescue the city. Now there were Dark Knights to the east and a nation in trouble.

"We had hoped to call on Iyesta and her militia for aid," the older elf said sadly. "We did not know she was dead. I am truly sorry to hear this."

Falaius had a number of questions he still wanted to ask the elves, but his renewed strength seemed to be quickly fading. "Stay another day or two," he offered. "I wish to talk to you further about your new king, the green dragon, and this Knight named Mina."

The elves exchanged glances and then agreed. Another day or two was not going to make much difference now.

"Mariana," the Plainsman said. His eyes were drooping, and his voice was growing heavy with drowsiness. "What did you put in the wine?" He lay back on his couch.

The half-elf gave him a crooked smile. "What you needed. Rest."

His eyes closed and his body relaxed, but he wasn't finished with the questions yet. "What are the chances of freeing Lanther and Linsha? We need them."

"I will look into it," she answered. She pulled away the wine cup and the empty bowl and nodded to two Legionnaires. They took positions at their commander's head and feet while everyone else stood and moved quietly away.

"Come," she said to the elves. "Come to the big tent and we will talk more. I must know more about these Dark Knights."

Return of the Dragon

13

Morning came too quickly for Linsha.

The sun had barely tinted the horizon when the Tarmak guards barged into the prison, shouting and prodding people to their feet. They dropped two large kettles and an armload of rounds of unleavened bread on the ground and departed. The hungry prisoners made an orderly rush for the food. One kettle contained a soup of sorts that might have had a few vegetables or scraps of meat if they were lucky. The other kettle held water, the only water they would have until nightfall. There were no cups or plates or utensils, so the prisoners had to dip their bread into the soup and take turns drinking from the kettle. The first time or two they were given this fare, the frantic men tipped the kettles over and wasted a day's ration of water. Since then, Sir Remmik had taken control of the prisoners and organized an orderly procession past the food and water so each person received a fair share. Linsha feared at first that he would deprive her of her share in retaliation for her punch. But as petty and obsessive as the Knight Commander could be sometimes, he proved to be ruthlessly fair about the food and water.

Feeling sore in every bone of her body, Linsha took her place in line behind Lanther and claimed her round of bread. It was hard and unappetizing as usual, but if she dipped it in the soup she could force it down her throat. She submerged the bread for a moment in the greasy-looking broth, took a long drink of water from the second kettle, and returned to her place by the wall. For a moment she stared at the pale brown loaf dripping in her hand. Her mind rebelled at the thought of eating it, but her stomach insisted. This was the only food she would get until night, and there was no telling what the Tarmaks would force her to do today. Since her capture, she had been interrogated, hung in the cage several times, beaten, and forced to work with the slave gangs on the destruction of the palace. She had found no chance to escape and no way to get word to the remaining militia at Sinking Wells. She could only hope the survivors were on their guard and would see the danger before it destroyed them.

Daylight gleamed through the bars of the prison doors when the guards returned. For once, no one was chosen to hang in the cage and no one was dragged away for questioning.

"They must have all the answers," Linsha whispered to Lanther as the prisoners were herded out of the courtyard.

They were taken around to the front of the palace and put to work removing the rock and rubble from the second wall of the throne room that had been pulled down the day before. Centaurs had been brought this morning to pull sledges of rock to the city wall, and they stood, their faces thunderous, waiting for the sledges to be loaded.

One centaur stood out from the rest, not only for his apparent youth and smaller stature but for the color of his light hide. Even the dark stains of sweat and the coating of dust could not hide the yellowish sand color of the buckskin. Linsha saw him and felt a burst of joy. Leonidas! He made no move toward her nor any overt indication that he had seen her, but his face turned her way and one eye dropped in a quick wink of acknowledgment.

A towering Tarmak of minotauran proportions was the overseer that day, and he divided the slaves into several groups. The smallest and the youngest were given baskets and sent to clear out the broken rocks and chunks of mortar that lay piled over the collapsed wall. A second, much smaller group was chosen to sort the stones from the palace walls, and a third group, the largest and strongest of the men, was ordered to the load the rock onto the sledges.

Linsha found herself in the sorters, a group she quickly found out required a certain degree of intelligence. The overseer explained exactly, in excellent Common, how he wanted the rocks sorted. The large quarried stones with no flaws were to be marked with red chalk and sent to the centaurs to be loaded on the sledges. These stones were being used to repair the city wall. Stone blocks of smaller dimensions but good condition were to be marked with yellow chalk and set aside for buildings in the city. Any block that was cracked or badly damaged had to be marked with black and thrown into the treasure room below the stairs. Anyone miss-marking a stone swiftly learned the mistake when the overseer's lash slashed across his or her back.

Linsha only took two lashes before she began to see exactly what the Tarmaks were looking for. With a careful eye she scrambled barefoot over the heaps of collapsed stone, marking the stones for removal and indicating each one to the slaves in charge of the other groups. She tried very hard to block out her memories of this place and concentrate on her work. These were just stones, cut centuries ago by elven hands. There was nothing left of the great dragon overlord that had resided here. Occasionally she would find a shard of bone, a broken bottle, or a scrap of clothing under the mounds of dust and rock, but these were just bits of trash left by the mercenaries from their time here.

She worked her way to the back of the throne room near the north wall that still remained standing. It was to be brought down the next day. After checking to be sure the overseer had his back to her, she paused for a moment in the shade of the wall and wiped her sweating face. The washing she had been given by the two courtesans was a memory now, erased by six days of sweat, dirt, and hard labor. Her pants and tunic were almost as dirty as the previous ones.

She sighed. It was barely noon and she was already very tired. Her back ached and stung where the lash had cut her skin. A headache was building behind her eyes. She stretched her arms and shoulders then twisted her head to stretch her neck.

Something odd caught her eye. Something so out of place and so unexpected that she nearly lost her balance trying to twist around to see it. Just beyond the ruin of the throne room, on the remains of an ancient foundation, sat a cat. An orange-striped tomcat. He did not move or blink or twitch his tail. He merely sat and stared at her. Linsha's eyes widened. Her heart raced. It couldn't be.

She heard a heavy step behind her, and the cat whisked out of sight. A Tarmak guard grabbed her arm and swung her around. He raised a club over his head to strike her, but she spat a word at him and raised the chalk up so he could see it in her hand. She pointed angrily at the stones she had already marked.

The guard dropped his club, bemused that the woman had used one of the better-known Tarmak swear words at him. He laughed and shoved her out of the shade to a place where he could see her better, then he took her place in the shelter of the wall.

Linsha risked a quick glance back at the place where the cat had been, but he was gone. There was no sign of him anywhere. A fleeting smile lifted her lips, and her hand slid to the two scales tucked carefully under her shirt. She gave them a grateful rub for good luck. She knew that cat. She would know him anywhere, in any street, in any city or farm. That cat meant Crucible had returned, and with him some hope. While it was true she had told Varia not to ask him to come, and it was also true she worried deeply for his safety, she was immeasurably glad to see him. She kept the image of the cat in her mind for the rest of the day like a secret gift and told no one. The dragon would make his move when he was ready, and until then she would have to be patient and bide her time.

The red star was rising in the east when the Tarmaks finally sent the slaves back to their quarters for the night. Linsha, Lanther, and their group were herded together and taken back to their prison in the old storehouse. Linsha wondered again why she and the others were kept separate from the rest of the slaves. Maybe it was just a lack of room, or maybe the Tarmaks had kept them apart for interrogation. That onerous pastime seemed to be over, so maybe the Tarmaks would soon move them to the bigger slave pens. Linsha hoped so. She had caught glimpses of the big slave pens to the east of the palace in the old stables and knew it would be easier to escape from those than this old stone prison.

"Why do you look like you just swallowed the cream?" Lanther said, leaning over her shoulder. He looked hot, sweaty, tired, and very irritable.

His words startled her so much she flinched and stared at him in surprise. "What did you say?" she exclaimed.

"You look like a cat that just drank the cream," he said softly. "You aren't exactly grinning, but you radiate pleasure. What has happened?"

She made certain none of the other prisoners or guards were close enough to hear, then she whispered, "Crucible is back."

"What?" he hissed. "How do you know?"

"I saw him this morning."

Lanther's eyebrows rose to his hairline, but he made no other remark. Neither of them said another word until they were back in the prison and the meager supper had been doled out under Sir Remmik's stern eye. As soon as she picked up her bread and drank her water, Linsha hurried to a place near the door where she could see out into the court. Lanther sat with her.

"Your eyes must be better than mine," he said irritably. "I didn't see a bronze dragon sneaking around the premises." He held up his bread and waved it like a fan. The bread was still so hard it did not even wobble.

"He was in his cat shape," Linsha murmured. "He was watching us."

"Are you sure it wasn't just an orange cat? There are a few cats around this city."

She shook her head. "I know this cat."

"Well, it would be nice if he would assume his

dragon shape and come blow the doors off this place. I've just about had enough. Look at this!" He flapped his bread at her. "Disgusting. Why can't they give us some decent food?" Lanther flipped the bread at the bars of the door.

His aim was so precise that Linsha chuckled to see it pass cleanly between the bars and out of the cell.

But as luck would have it, a Tarmak guard walked by the door at the precise instant the flat bread flew between the bars. It struck his leg with a splatting noise and fell to bits over his sandalled foot. The guard growled something harsh in his own language and glared through the bars of the door. The first person he saw was Linsha, a smile still on her face. Furious, he unbolted the door, charged inside, and wrenched her upright. She was so astounded to be accosted like this that she did not react fast enough. Her bread fell from her hands.

Lanther and the other men leaped to their feet. The guard shouted at them and swung Linsha toward the door. Although she was trained in several martial defense arts, she did not have the chance to use them on the tall Tarmak. She lost her balance in the impetous of his swing, fell forward, and cracked her head on the heavy wooden frame. Pain exploded into sparks that danced in her eyes, and her muscles turned to jelly. When Lanther tried to intervene, the Tarmak slammed a fist into his jaw and knocked him senseless into the wall.

Other Tarmaks ran to the guard's aid. Linsha struggled, but the blue-skinned warriors hauled her out of the prison cell and dragged her to the metal cage.

"Sit in here and laugh," the guard ordered. He pushed her inside and locked the door.

Linsha felt the cage being hauled into the air. The angry guard slammed a shield into the side of cage in spite, then the Tarmaks left her gently swinging at the end of a rope. She sagged against the bars while her head threatened to explode. A number of well-chosen words in several languages told the Tarmaks exactly what she thought of them and where they could put their swords, but the warriors ignored her and went back to their posts.

After a while Linsha wriggled her arm up high enough to touch her forehead. A large lump and a sticky rivulet down the side of her face confirmed her suspicions. She would have a bangup of a bruise the next morning. Blasted Tarmaks. She hadn't even been able to eat her dinner. She was hungry and thirsty and tired and thoroughly annoyed, and she had a headache reminiscent of a dwarf spirits hangover. Now she was hung out like a bird in a cage, and there was nothing she could do about it except try to conserve her strength until the guards decided to let her out.

Taking a deep breath, she relaxed and stared upward. The night was fully dark by this time and the stars shone bright in a flawless sky. There would probably be frost tonight, she thought unhappily—and she was without her cloak.

The hours dragged by. She tried to sleep and found that sleep was impossible, for she was too cold and cramped in the metal box. When she sought to relieve her boredom and frustration by singing bawdy tavern songs at the top of her lungs, both the prisoners and the guards yelled at her. The threat of arrows being loosed at her finally convinced her to be quiet.

Shortly after midnight, new guards came out to take the place of the old, and for a brief moment Linsha hoped they would release her. But none of them looked her way or made any move toward the cage. She watched them stride around the yard and along the walls until they were all in their places, then the ruins fell quiet again, and she had to resign herself to enduring the cage until dawn. Surely they would free her at sunrise to work with the rest of the prisoners.

Late into the night, a waning crescent moon slowly lifted its horns above the line of hills to the east. Linsha watched it wearily. She was too uncomfortable to sleep and too tired to think. Her entire mind and body felt numb from cold and exhaustion. She was so distracted by the moon and her own misery that she did not see the small, dark shape slink noiselessly along a wall toward her.

Somewhere out in the ruins, the hunting cry of an owl cut through the frosty night.

Linsha suddenly grew alert.

Linsha.

Her name rang in her head, sent by a worried and powerful mind. If she'd had any space to move, she would have jumped out of her skin. Shaking, she jerked her head down and saw the cat standing close to the posts that held the cage upright.

Linsha. One moment and I will have you free.

A bright glow suffused the small cat. Golden, shimmering light covered its body and hid it from view in a ball of dazzling power that rapidly expanded outward like a small nova into a brilliant haze that glimmered with sparks of orange, yellow, and white. Within the haze, a shape began to form with a long neck and nebulous wings of fire.

In that instant between light and shape, Linsha heard shouts and the unmistakable snap of a large crossbow. The dragon within the cloud of light screamed in pain and surprise.

Linsha's voice rose to join the cry with her own scream of terror and denial. *"No!"*

135

The golden light vanished, leaving Linsha blinking in the dark. She could not see well, but she could hear the dragon thrashing on the ground, and she heard the unmistakable voice of the Akkad-Ur coming from somewhere close by. She twisted her head and spotted several black silhouettes on the roofline of the storehouse.

"Be still, dragon!" thundered the Tarmak general. "Be still or both you and the woman shall die."

A sudden understanding glowed in Linsha's mind like the light of the dragon's power. They had been waiting for him. Damn! She berated herself. How could she not have seen it? She had said herself she thought the Tarmaks wanted the dragon to return. Having listened to the Akkad-Ur discuss Crucible and Varia, how could she not have guessed what they would do? She was not out here as punishment, she was hanging here as bait. Somehow the Tarmaks had known the dragon had returned, or perhaps they just calculated the number of days it would take for one small owl to fly to Sanction and one large dragon to fly back. Whatever they knew, they had put her in the cage in plain view and waited for Crucible to come. Would they have hung her out for the next seven days? Maybe so. And maybe she would have seen through this in another night or two. But it was Crucible's bad luck that he came this night.

Gods above, what had they done to him? What sort of crossbow did they have that was large enough to wound a dragon?

She locked her fingers around the bars and shook the cage in a rage, angry at her own stupidity and terrified for his safety. He was still writhing in pain on the ground. She was able to see he was trying to reach something between his shoulder blades at the base of his neck. His eyes glowed with a fiery edge of scarlet, and his nostrils blew jets of steam in the cold night air. His talons scraped sparks from the stone flagging.

"I said be still, Crucible!" the Akkad-Ur shouted. "There are arrows aimed at your lady and at your neck. If you wish both of you to die, continue with this struggle."

The sound of his name seemed to reach through his frantic struggles, for he stopped snapping at his back and crouched, his tail lashing across the yard. His large head lifted to spot his tormentors.

Inside the storehouse, the prisoners crowded up to the doors and stared horrified at the bronze. None of the Tarmak guards were visible.

Linsha froze in place and forced herself to be calm. She could not do anything to help Crucible.

"Do not try to sear us with your breath," the Tarmak went on in a reasonable tone of voice. "You cannot reach all of us, and by the time you shot one beam, the lady knight would be dead."

"Crucible, don't listen," Linsha pleaded. "Just go. Get away! Shapeshift, if you can, and go!"

"That would not be wise," said the Akkad-Ur. "If he tries to shapeshift now, the barb in his back will kill him."

Crucible chose to ignore him. Clamping his wings tight to his sides, he peered into Linsha's cage.

"I smell blood," he said. "Are you hurt?"

Linsha felt her heart contract. He was in pain and trapped by a dangerous enemy, yet his first question was for her. More than anything she wanted to reach through the bars to touch him, but she could barely move her arms from her body. Her eyes ached with unshed tears.

"Crucible," she said. "Why did you come?"

An arrow ricocheted off the cage with a jarring

clang. Crucible's head snapped up, and a thunderous growl rumbled from his throat. He shrugged his shoulders and squirmed again with pain.

"What is this weapon you have used against me?" he roared at the Tarmaks. "What have you done?"

"It is very simple," Linsha heard the Akkad-Ur shout from the roof. "We are planning a campaign to complete our conquest of the brass dragon's realm. We no longer have our mercenaries or the blue dragon to help us. What we do have is you. Metallics, I am told, are much more reasonable than chromatics."

Linsha felt her mouth fall open. She hadn't expected anything like this.

I will not help you!" Crucible roared. "You slaughtered my friends. You killed a great dragon. You destroyed this city."

"And I will kill this friend if you do not obey me."

"I'll take my chances, Crucible," Linsha implored. "Get out of here!"

"If he leaves, he will die as well," the Akkad-Ur warned.

Torches flared on the roof, illuminating the Akkad-Ur in his golden mask. Behind him stood three guards. One held a large crossbow, and the others carried a long, slim, black lance with a barbed tip and a heavy cowl for the hand. Linsha saw the lance and gasped. A tremor ran through her.

"You see we did retrieve the Abyssal Lance that you so helpfully left behind. However, we have changed it somewhat. In case you can't tell from where you are, the lance is now about ten inches shorter." He took the crossbow from his guard and held it high so both Crucible and Linsha could see it had been fired. "The bolt that is now lodged between your shoulders is a barbed dart crafted from this lance. Think about that.

You knew the evil spells that were imbued in this wood. It will kill whatever it penetrates. Fortunately for you, the dart is a smaller piece. It does not work as quickly as the larger lance. Unless I say—"

He spat a word in his own tongue and pointed to the dragon. Crucible screamed a frantic sound of agony and rage. Twisting and curving his sinuous neck, he tried desperately to snatch the bolt that burned into his neck. He scratched at it with a hind leg and stretched his forelegs around to reach it, but it was placed in such a way that nothing he tried could pull it free. His wings flapped loose and whipped the air around him in agitation. Dust rose up in a thick, choking cloud.

Linsha's fingers tightened around the bars. A gut-wrenching terror exploded in her mind, dissolving her will and sucking away her strength. If the cage had not held her upright, she would have collapsed, groveling and shrieking on the ground. Although she had never felt Crucible use the powerful sense of awe and fear that dragons could exude, she had enough experience with dragonfear to recognize it.

Massive and paralyzing, the dragonfear rolled outward from the dragon and swept over those nearby. The prisoners in the cell fell to the ground, overcome by the fear, and the guards nearest the dragon dropped their weapons and clutched their heads. Upon the roof, only the Akkad-Ur remained on his feet. He shook in every limb, but he looked over the wall at the dragon and choked out an order.

Linsha heard his voice and forced herself to look up. What was the Akkad-Ur doing to Crucible? How could one small bolt cause such pain? Then out of the shadowed corners of the ruin, she saw tall figures moving toward the writhing bronze. Terror for him rose up within her and overcame the dragonfear. Her voice burst out in a frantic scream— "Crucible! Behind you!"

Mad with pain, he barely heard her. His reactions were dazed, confused, and too slow. He forced his body around to face this new danger. His tail caught one of the warriors and slammed the Tarmak into the store-house wall, but three others reached his side.

Linsha saw torchlight flash on sword blades in the swirling dust, then Crucible roared again. His head dropped into the curtain of dust and his teeth snapped loudly in the dark, but the Tarmaks dashed away from him, and as they fled his wrath, the Akkad-Ur shouted another command over the uproar.

Abruptly Crucible fell still. The dragonfear faded around him, but Linsha stared in growing panic at the big bronze. It was difficult to see him in the dark and the clouds of dust.

"Crucible?" she called.

There was a rustling noise, a stamp of heavy feet, and a vicious string of words in the ancient tongue of the dragons. No one needed a translation. Linsha stared hard at the dark shape before her, and as the dust began to settle, she saw the dragon more clearly. Thank the absent gods he was still alive.

He crouched between her cage and the prison, his head raised to glare at the Tarmaks on the roof. His wings were partially open, but they looked wrong. Linsha bit back a cry. She realized the torchlight from the prison door was still burning despite the uproar in the yard, and its light gleamed through places in Crucible's wings that should not show light. The Tarmaks with the swords had not tried to kill, only to maim. Their heavy two-handed blades had sliced through the leathery vanes of his wings, crippling him again and trapping him on the ground. Crucible would not be returning to Sanction any time soon.

"Now, perhaps you understand," the Akkad-Ur said into the heavy silence. "You cannot fly. If you leave, even on foot, I will torture this woman to death and leave you with the bolt embedded in your neck. In a few days, maybe a week, it will work its way into your body, pierce your heart, and kill you. There is nothing that can remove it. However, if you stay, if you obey my commands and serve this army, I will keep the bolt in its place, allowing you to live, and I will not harm the woman. It is your choice."

Linsha shivered in a cold that bit deeper than the night's frost. "Go, Crucible!" she whispered. "Go. Surely there are mages who can help you. Go north and find my father."

"I will not leave you," the dragon hissed. "I had hoped to return to Sanction, but our destiny seems to lie here in the south. We will see it through together."

"It is done then," said the Akkad-Ur. "Remember, dragon. I have but to speak one word and the bolt will begin to bore into your back. One word and this woman is dead. You will go to my tent and wait for me there."

Linsha watched Crucible leave the yard. Conflicting emotions swirled around her like the winds of a cyclone—relief that he was still alive, worry that he could still be hurt, fear that the Tarmaks would use him against the people of the plains, but the worst was the guilt. Guilt, like a huge ache, settled into her mind. He had come back because of her, and now he was enslaved because of her. His rationalization of destiny might keep him satisfied for a few days, but in time he would come to resent her, perhaps hate her, for her part in his capture. And what about Lord Bight? The lord governor would not be happy that Sanction's guardian was now trapped in Missing City. What would Lord Bight do now?

She heard footsteps approach her, and she looked down to see the Akkad-Ur standing by the foot of the suspended cage. "Thusly our plans fall into place. Do not do anything to jeopardize *his* well-being. You have seen what I can do to him."

Linsha said nothing. She could think of nothing to say.

When the Tarmak turned on his heel and left, she pressed her aching head back against the cage and let the tears fall.

If only Crucible had stayed in Sanction . . .

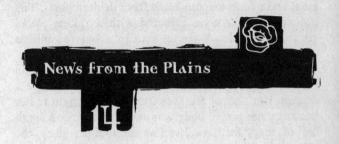

Varia returned to the camp at Sinking Wells just before dawn with the news Crucible had been captured. At first no one would believe her. She had just returned from her journey to Sanction only the day before and told Mariana and Falaius that Crucible had come back and that he would rescue Linsha—and perhaps some of the others—that night. How could he have failed? How could the Tarmaks have captured a large bronze dragon? It didn't seem possible.

Captain Calanbriar observed the small owl for a short while and tactfully suggested she come into the tent and tell her tale again in the quiet of the shelter. The half-elf could see the owl was terribly upset—so upset, in fact, that she had forgotten her usual reticent shyness and was blurting her news out in front of a dozen startled and staring people. Quickly, Mariana took the owl into the command tent and invited Falaius, Sir Hugh, and the two kirath elves to join them.

The tent, set up under a small cluster of trees, was an airy tribal design that swept over their heads like a

143

canopy. Inside was a low rough table on a tattered rug. A blanket hung in the back to curtain off the small sleeping area, and a few weapons hung from the tent posts. The humans and the elves gathered within, taking places around the table. A young man in a tattered militia uniform brought them cups of water.

Varia sat on the small rough table and told them exactly how the Tarmaks had managed to enslave a dragon. Her "horn" feathers were clamped tight to her head and her entire body was compressed into a small ball of angry feathers. Even as she told her story, she trembled with emotion and outrage.

"I found a perch high on the standing wall of the old throne room where I could look down into the court where the Tarmaks are holding the Solamnic Knights. They had put Linsha in a small cage and left her hanging out in plain view."

Falaius's deeply line face turned down into a frown. "Could they have known he was coming?"

"I don't know," Varia said. "We have feared for some time that there is a spy in the militia, but how could someone like that know so quickly that we were back? Crucible shapeshifted into a cat *miles* away from the city. No one saw him fly in."

"Perhaps they were guessing," Mariana suggested, "or just hoping the dragon would come. Maybe they've been hanging Linsha up in that cage for nights now." She stifled a shudder at the thought of being trapped in a tight metal box for so long.

The owl shifted her weight from foot to foot. She could understand how skeptical these people felt. She had seen what happened to the dragon, and she still could barely believe it. She described the Abyssal Lance to them, the wicked black weapon with the rust colored barbs enchanted to kill whatever it penetrated. She told them about the crossbow and the bolt made from the tip of the lance.

Falaius slammed a hand on the table, causing Varia to jump. "How does this Tarmak control it? That's what I don't understand. This is a weapon created in a war long past by men far different from the Brutes."

"The Brutes fought in that war," Mariana reminded him. "The weapon was given to them by the Dark Knights. The Knights probably gave them the spells to control it as well."

"So why do their spells work, while our mystics are relegated to poultices and herbal teas for healing?" Sir Hugh said. He sat sullenly at the table, the sole representative of the Solamnic Knights. Exhaustion colored his square face with gray and tainted his voice with impatience.

"I do not know," Varia said. "I have seen the Tarmak general in daylight, and I know he wears a necklace made of dragon's teeth." She saw Mariana's fair face darken with anger. "But maybe there is something else. Maybe he has some artifacts from Istar or a power from his own land we know nothing about."

"Where is Crucible now?" asked the Legion Commander.

Varia hissed a little sound of displeasure. "The Tarmaks have chained him to a tree beside their headquarters in the city square. They are making a spectacle of him."

The half-elf shook her fair head. "Where is Linsha?"

"She was put back with men. I counted three Legionnaires and fourteen Knights, including Sir Remmik and Lady Linsha."

"They are in the dragon's lair?" asked Falaius.

"In the old complex of ruins behind the throne room," Varia said.

Sir Hugh sat up a little straighter. Falaius and the captain were looking very thoughtful. "What are you thinking?"

Mariana paused before she answered. Her eyes, one of blue and one of green, stared thoughtfully into the distance. "If we could free Linsha—"

"And the others," Falaius put in.

"And the others. We need her. And it might weaken the Tarmaks' hold over Crucible." She looked to Varia. "Do you think this is so?"

The owl slowly blinked her round eyes. She thought about what she knew of Crucible and bobbed her head. "It is possible."

Some of the despair lifted from Sir Hugh's face and his expression grew lighter. "If Linsha is free, then all we'd have to do is figure out how to remove that bolt from Crucible's neck."

"Will the Tarmaks not kill him if she escapes?" said one of the elves.

Varia stepped around to look at the newcomers. She had noticed them the day before, and she was pleased to see them again, for she had finally learned the truth of the disappearance of the Shield over Silvanesti. "As long that dart is in his neck, I do not think Crucible will try to leave. We must find a way to remove it without killing him."

A loud shout rang out outside, drawing everyone's attention. They leaped to their feet just as a scout pushed into the tent. Dirty and sweaty, he saluted both commanders and said, "A rider coming. Fast. From the north. A tribesman, I think."

Mariana extended an arm to Varia and settled the owl on her shoulder before she followed the others outside. They could see a horseman coming along a trail that lay between two low hills. A reddish plume of dust flew from the horse's hooves.

The older elf shaded his eyes to better see the rider. "It is a young man, a tribesman," he said. "His horse is lathered and weary."

With surprising speed, the militia reached for their weapons and ran to their posts. The few women and older folk in the camp immediately disappeared from sight, hiding out in the dunes and outcroppings. A dozen or so militia grouped around Mariana, Falaius, and the others and set arrows to their bows. A tense silence fell over the Wells.

The hoofbeats grew louder. Along the dusty road the rider came as if all the forces of Neraka were on his heels. Wisely, he reined his mount to a stop just out of arrow range and raised his arms to show he had no weapon in his hands.

"I bring word from my chieftain to the forces of Iyesta!" he called. "Do you know where I can find Scorpion Wadi?"

Mariana sighed before she called, "The Wadi is nothing more than a graveyard! We are all that is left of the dragonlord's forces!"

The rider slid off his steaming horse and gratefully handed the reins to a soldier.

"I bring news." His face glowed with a light of importance even the news of another disaster could not dampen. "The green dragon, Beryl, is dead. She died during the fall of Qualinesti. The elves' city is destroyed, but the king saved many of his people by evacuating them through underground tunnels. They are making their way across the Plains even now."

The young rider, lost in the import of his news, suddenly became aware that people were staring at him in a silent state of shock. No one moved. No sound was made. He cleared his throat to continue when he saw the two Silvanesti elves standing close by. Their pale, elegant faces were rigid with horror.

The eldest elf seemed to shake himself and he laid a hand on his companion's shoulder for support. "Why are the Qualinesti crossing the Plains?" he asked.

"I . . . I don't know exactly," the rider stammered. "They have been driven from their lands by the Knights of Neraka and the forces of the green dragon. I guess they hope to seek shelter with your people."

The two elves exchanged a look of dread. "We must leave," the elder said to Mariana. "We must see for ourselves."

Without a further word, they retrieved their horses from the picket line, saddled them, and were away in less time than it took for Falaius to salute the tribesman and draw him into the commander's tent.

"Come, boy. Tell us again, and this time fill in some details."

The same news arrived in Missing City the next night, brought by one of the Tarmak long-range patrols. The patrol, sent out to gather information about the lands north of the city, had come across another messenger heading for City of Morning Dew. After capturing him and extracting his news, they felt it was important enough to bring it themselves to the Akkad-Ur. They found him in his headquarters in the city square where the city's lord mayor and his council used to meet. Outside, they were astonished to see a bronze dragon crouched balefully under the shade of a large yew.

The Akkad-Ur was not pleased to see them so soon, but he listened to their news and interrogated their prisoner. When he was satisfied he gave each warrior a coveted steel dagger from the treasury of the dead dragonlord.

"Throw him in the slave pens," he ordered, indicating the cowering tribesman. Then he paused and a slight smile eased across his face. "Better still, take him to the old palace and put him in with the Knights. We'll let the woman brood a little further on disaster. And summon the *dekegul*."

He leaned both hands on his work table and studied his latest map while the warriors bowed and left to obey his orders. Quickly his hand snatched another map from a stack and another and another until he had most of the Plains of Dust as far west as the Kharolis Mountains and Thorbardin spread out before him. He pondered the maps for a long time. There it was spread out before him. A land ready for the taking.

It was too good to keep to himself. Gloating, he went outside, past his guards, and across the street to the yew where the bronze dragon sat chained and waiting for his command. For once the Akkad-Ur did not bother to don his ceremonial mask, and his long face and aquiline nose were exposed to the bronze dragon's sullen view. Crucible glanced at him briefly then turned his head away and glared into the darkness that had fallen over the city.

Too energized to stand still, the Akkad-Ur paced in front of Crucible only a few steps away from the limit of the short chain that bound the dragon.

"This seems to be a disastrous year for dragons," he said, knowing full well that Crucible was listening to him. "I have heard from my scouts that Thunder and Iyesta were not the only dragons to fall this summer. The dragon Beryllinthranox has also died."

In spite of his efforts to appear disinterested, Crucible's

ears swiveled around to hear the Tarmak better.

The Akkad-Ur continued to pace back and forth. "She invaded the Qualinesti Forest and destroyed the city of Qualinost. But in the course of the invasion, she was killed. It's a shame really. All those elves displaced and wandering. But there you are. The fortunes of war." He stopped in front of Crucible and crossed his arms. "You certainly know what that means. The deaths of these three dragons leaves the entire Plains of Dust now available to the first conqueror strong and daring enough to take it."

Crucible's head swung around until he was staring down at the Tarmak, his golden eyes as cold as a winter dawn.

The Akkad-Ur gave the dragon a short, derisive bow and turned on his sandalled heel. He made it nearly ten paces back toward his headquarters when the *dekegul*, the Akkad-Ur's commanders of the army, came running at his command. They saluted and waited eagerly for his news.

"Tomorrow the next shipment of reinforcements and supplies arrives. In three days we march. We will take the army north and west to consolidate our hold on Iyesta's realm as planned and take the remaining lands of the Plains of Dust. In the name of our emperor, we shall establish a new realm where the Tarmak nation will grow strong."

The *dekegul* cheered.

Distracted by his plans and visions of conquest, the Akkad-Ur paid no heed to the dragon behind him. Gesturing to his officers to follow, he strode back to his office to make further plans.

The dragon watched him go. *Did you hear that?* He sent his thought to a creamy white and brown owl sitting motionless in the depths of the yew tree.

Yes. If he goes north and west, he will soon reach Duntollik, the owl replied in his mind. *And if he takes that the rest of the northern Plains will fall.*

He may decide to finish off the militia before he goes. He has ignored them thus far, but he is known to rid himself of loose ends.

That is very likely. He knows where they are.

Take the news to Linsha. And to Mariana. Perhaps the militia should flee north and warn Duntollik.

I will tell them. Be careful, Crucible. The owl dropped from her branch and drifted silently away on the night wind.

You, too, small one.

The first storm of autumn came early that year in a chilly, blustery wall of clouds that moved in from the southwest and blew over the city. That night the fleet of Tarmak ships arrived. In the lashing rain and pounding waves, the ships staggered into the harbor and signaled for help. Every available Tarmak was pulled out of the city and sent to the harbor to help the warriors disembark, to unload the shipment of Damjatt horses, and to batten down the ships. They made no attempt to unload the supplies and stacks of weapons that lay within the holds. Those could wait until the sea calmed. But the horses were exhausted, and the warriors were seasick and thoroughly tired of the cramped conditions on the ships. Tarmaks and horses alike wanted off, and the Akkad-Ur wanted them to have time to recover before they marched north. Unfortunately, the docks and the harbor facilities were only primitive makeshift structures set up after the huge storm in the early summer had destroyed the entire waterfront. Only one ship at a time could be brought to the one long pier, and it had to be carefully roped at the bow and stern to prevent the ship from being smashed to splinters in the heavy surf. The difficult process of unloading the Tarmaks and their horses from each ship took most of the night.

The storm also caused some minor damage and flooding in the town. The wind ripped off some roofs and blew down a few trees. The rain flooded cellars, dripped through old ceilings and ran gurgling through the streets. But it filled rain barrels in town and filled the stock ponds and dry creeks for miles around the city. The storm also offered one service to the beleaguered militia they had not looked for. It offered them excellent cover when they raided the slave pens just outside the dragon's palace.

Using a few tricks they learned from the Tarmaks, a small group of Legionnaires led by Falaius eased through the driving rain to the rear of one of the high makeshift fences that formed the complex of pens and waited for the guards to make their rounds.

They killed three without a sound and moved the bodies out of sight in the ruins. While the Legionnaires protected their flanks, a party of militia went to work on the stockade fence. The fence was crafted of pointed upright poles woven together with strips of green wood tied with stout rope. It was strong enough to hold unarmed people within, flexible enough to prevent a centaur from kicking it over, and high enough to keep the centaurs from jumping over. But it was not impervious to determined soldiers with stout knives and axes. They reduced a section of the wall to collapsed strips of wood and bits of rope in short order.

Mariana and Sir Hugh slipped into the compound. In the dark and rain they went from one huddled group to another and sent them moving silently toward the hole in the fence. The pen they had penetrated held mostly the centaurs from Linsha's captured party, soldiers captured in the field, and a few craftspeople from the city. Every one snatched at the opportunity to escape and followed Mariana's orders without question.

Every one except Leonidas. The young buckskin ambled casually to the back of the pen and ducked quietly through the hole as everyone else did, but the moment he was out he grabbed Sir Hugh's arm.

"Where are the Knights?" he hissed. "We must get Lady Linsha out, too."

Sir Hugh shushed him. "Come with me," he murmured over the wind. "You can help."

He led the stallion out into the darkness to another small group of militia that waited patiently in the storm. At Sir Hugh's nod, they fell in behind him and worked their way through the ruins to the back of the storehouse that served as the Knights' prison. Using hand signals, the Knight sent two men to watch for Tarmak guards and the rest began to hack at the base of the wall with trowels and small shovels.

For a moment Leonidas thought they had lost their minds. The storehouse was built of stone and had survived almost intact for five hundred years. They could not dig underneath this building in anything less than days, and then what would be the point? The Tarmaks would find them long before they made a hole large enough for a human to slip through. Yet as he watched, he began to see some sense in their labor. The old walls were not solid stone. Behind a facade of crumbling sandstone was a thick layer of ancient mud bricks that had gradually deteriorated over the centuries. It easily gave way to the determined efforts of the men with the tools.

Taking turns, the men hacked and chopped until they had made a small hole through the wall. Voices from within called out to them but quickly hushed when Sir Hugh warned them to be quiet.

One of the sentries hurried back to the wall. "Sir Hugh, there are three Tarmaks walking through the yard. They are coming to this end of the building."

Leonidas and the militia melted back into the darkness. Shielding their eyes from the downpour, they watched as the Tarmaks climbed over the ruins of the courtyard wall and walked around the corner of the prison. The warriors stopped and waited, obviously listening and looking out into the rain. Nothing must have excited their attention, for they conversed a moment then went back to the yard and disappeared into the shadows of the palace.

The militiamen went back to work prying and chopping the bricks loose to form a larger hole. They could hear the Knights within working on their side of the wall with their fingers.

"Sir Hugh," a stern voice called through the hole. "Is that you? Did you survive?"

"Sir Remmik, yes, I am here." Hugh said as loudly as he dared. "Let me speak to Lady Linsha."

There was a cold silence on the other side, then Linsha's voice answered him softly.

"If we get you out, will the Tarmak general kill Crucible?" he asked.

She pulled a brick out of the way, and he saw the pale blur of her face in the blackness of the gap. "I don't think so," she replied. "Varia brought me the news of his plans to take the Plains of Dust. I think he wants the dragon more than he wants me."

"I don't agree," Lanther said from behind her. "He knows how much the dragon cares for you. If you are gone—or worse if you are killed—there will be no holding that dragon. The general will be forced to kill him."

Sir Hugh was about to reply when shouts rang out from the slave pens nearby. A horn sounded a warning. The Knight swore under his breath. "Leonidas, here!" He pointed to the wall. "Finish it."

Men scrambled out of the way as the buckskin stallion turned his rump to the wall. His powerful haunches rose and his hooves delivered a resounding kick to the edges of the hole. Sandstone crumbled and bricks flew under the force of his blow. He gathered his legs under him again and slammed another kick into the wall.

More shouting came from the slave pens, and torches appeared in the darkness. Screams followed the shouts as the Tarmaks charged to destroy the raiders. Sir Hugh did not wait any longer. Pushing Leonidas's rump aside, he reached in through the hole in the wall, shoving bricks and pieces of mortar aside. The prisoners helped from their side until a hole perhaps a foot and a half wide had been made. He reached through, grabbed the first arm he felt, and hauled the person out of the storehouse.

Linsha fell flopping in the mud at his feet and grinned at him. "Ouch," she said.

"Leonidas, get her out of here!" Sir Hugh shouted. He reached in again to help the next Knight.

Linsha climbed to her feet and helped Sir Hugh pulled a Knight from the gap. "Lanther! Come on, get out now!" she cried into the prison.

But he ignored her and pushed one of the Legionnaires through. Another Knight followed.

The sounds of shouting orders and clash of weapons could be heard even over the rain. "Please, Lanther! They'll be here any moment!"

She felt a muddy hand grasp her wrist, and Lanther's face peered through the hole. "I can't. They're here already. Don't go, Linsha! It's too dangerous! Let the others go, but if you are killed, they will destroy Crucible. Remember what the general said! 'Don't do anything to jeopardize his well-being.' "

Her eyes wide, she stared at him, her heart torn by his words.

"Please!" he exclaimed. "I don't want to lose you."

Something sliced past her and buried itself in the wall by her shoulder. Another arrow struck the first freed Knight, sending him spinning to the ground. The fletched end of an arrow quivered in his chest. From somewhere inside the prison she heard the loud commands of a Tarmak guard.

"That's it!" Sir Hugh shouted. He wrenched her out. "Leonidas, take her now! The rest of you, get out!"

Linsha hesitated. What if Lanther was right? What if her escape angered the Akkad-Ur so much he killed the bronze? Would he do that? Would Crucible understand why she left and be patient? Gods, what a muddle! And what did Lanther mean in his last plea?

She wasn't given more time to think. More arrows rained down around them, and she could see warriors running around the building to cut them off.

The militia and the two freed prisoners bolted into the darkness, Sir Hugh close on their heels. She felt the centaur's two strong hands on her waist swing her around and throw her up in the air. She landed with a thump on Leonidas's back and scrambled to find her balance just before he wheeled and sprinted into the driving rain.

The night and storm swallowed them, and the old ruins vanished behind.

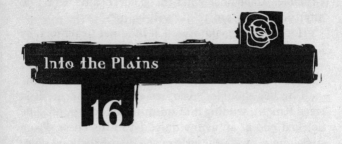

At dawn the *orgwegul*, the officer in charge of the guards at the dragon's palace, presented himself and his second at the Akkad-Ur's headquarters to report the escape of the prisoners. In the proud manner of the Tarmak warrior, he did not cringe, complain, grovel, or make excuses. He explained the facts, including the deaths of five Tarmaks, one Solamnic Knight, a dozen slaves, and three militia raiders. He also reported the escape of the Rose Knight and two companions from the prison, and fifteen centaurs and slaves from the pens. He was standing so stiffly that it took his body several moments before it collapsed on the floor next to his head.

The Akkad-Ur gripped his sword and glared at the *orgwegul's* second officer. The officer threw back his shoulders, lifted his chin, and waited. There was little tolerance for failure in the forces of the Tarmak emperor.

"You," the Akkad-Ur said, stabbing the point of the sword toward the waiting warrior. "You and the rest of the guards in your command will report to the Dog Units

158

until such time as I deem you are worthy to return to the ranks. If one word of this escape leaks to the dragon, I will personally flay you alive."

The warrior bowed, his face stony. Only the tremor in his hands revealed the pent-up feelings he dared not express. The Dog Units were a punishment one step away from death. A position in the emperor's cohorts afforded a Tarmak advancement, honor, and an opportunity to plunder. The Dog Units were little more than servants who served the cooks, the wagon masters, and the gravediggers. It was almost worse than exile. Stepping over the corpse of his dead commander, he bowed again and departed to give the news to the remaining guards.

When the warrior was gone, the Akkad-Ur shoved his sword at a waiting slave and said, "Remove that body and clean the sword." He turned back to his officers. Three men who commanded the *dekul* of thousands and one black-clad Keena priest stood around his table.

"What of the dragon?" asked one of the *dekegul*. "If he learns the woman has fled, he may try to break the spell of the dart."

"We will keep that news from him as long as possible. If he learns the truth and grows intractable, we will remind him of the Abyssal Lance."

The Keena, a slim male with eyes the color of tropical seas, said, "There are the eggs as well. We should have enough left to discourage any thoughts of disobedience."

"Take care of those eggs, Shurnasir," the Akkad-Ur warned. "They are more valuable than the gold and steel of the dragon's treasure."

"They are well packed and warm, my lord. My assistants assure me they are still viable."

"Excellent. Now," he said, bending over the maps, "tell me of the condition of the army."

"According to our spies and to Varia's reports, the Tarmak can field about nine thousand men. That's including foot soldiers, archers, and a small contingent of two-man chariots—gods know where they picked those up—which will leave about two to three thousand here in Missing City."

Mariana's tone of bitter sarcasm was not lost on Linsha. She thought about the dismal numbers of militia that had straggled into Sinking Wells—the escaped slaves, the few reinforcements from the scattered plains tribes, and the refugees that had found their way to the camp—and she wanted to weep. They could field ninety. Maybe. If they were lucky. If the wounded came. If the cooks and camp followers showed up.

"We have no choice," Falaius said. "We must abandon the city."

Leaving Missing City was a difficult choice for them all, but especially, Linsha knew, for Falaius and the Legion. This was their city. Falaius had come with the first group of Legionnaires that set up their tents in the shelter of the ancient ruins and began to rebuild the buildings from the ghostly images that still glowed and reflected the vanished city back to the world. He had stood in the sands and welcomed Iyesta and watched with pride as the lonely outpost turned into a thriving community. He had fought and bled to defend it and had watched his Legionnaires give their lives for it. Now he was being forced to leave it in the hands of the enemy.

"It would be better for us to leave," Linsha said. "The

Akkad-Ur has not bothered with us yet. But he will."
She reached over and squeezed Falaius's arm. "The
Tarmaks are vast compared to us, well-trained, and
disciplined. Their commanders are experts and their
equipment is plentiful."

"They are also ferocious fighters—and brutal,"
Sir Hugh added. He didn't need to mention Scorpion
Wadi. The massacre was still a raw place in all their
thoughts.

"The Dark Knights trained them well," Falaius
said

"And they have a dragon," said Linsha.

She sat back in her saddle, careful not to disturb
Varia perched on her shoulder, and continued to gaze
down toward the distant city. Smoke curled from a
thousand fires and rose to meet an incoming bank of
fog. The storm had finally ended just after dawn, but
the clouds had remained thick and heavy. Now in the
late afternoon, just out to sea a heavy bank of fog slowly
rolled toward shore. On a hill miles away from Missing City the four riders sat quietly on their mounts and
looked over the city they had tried so hard to save.

"Will they kill him?" Sir Hugh asked her again.

Linsha did not answer immediately. Lanther had
seemed so certain the night before.

If she squinted hard enough and looked in just the
right place in the center of the city, she fancied she saw
a faint glint of bronze. "No," she said at last. "I still
don't believe so. The Akkad-Ur wanted a dragon to
help his army defeat the people of the plains. Thunder
was too unreliable. Iyesta was too powerful. Crucible
is just right."

"But he is not an evil dragon," Mariana protested.
"He will not kill at the Tarmak's command."

Linsha shrugged. "Probably not. Not even to save

himself. But I was thinking about that while I was in the prison. The Tarmaks do not need him to fight, they can do that themselves. They just want him to be there. To lure any would be attackers into a false sense of security. Who wouldn't look at a bronze dragon in the midst of a large army and think, 'Oh, they must be on our side. They have a metallic with them.' By the time they get close enough to learn differently, the Tarmaks have moved in for the kill. And if the battle isn't going their way, all they have to do is jab that dart deeper into Crucible's neck, and he radiates dragonfear like an infuriated blue."

And it is my fault he is with them, repeated her persistent guilt.

Another, smaller voice of reason spoke up in her mind. *Don't be so self-centered. This isn't just about you. He could have come back for any number of reasons. And you cannot be blamed for what the Tarmaks did to him.*

But she could hardly hear the voice over the guilt that plagued her. He had come to the prison yard for her. He'd come thinking it would be an easy task, and there she was hanging like a side of beef in plain view—a perfect target from the roof. It was her fault he was there; her fault he was hurt and crippled.

"Does Crucible know you escaped?" Sir Hugh's question cut into her inner debate and pulled her back to the present.

Linsha shook her head fiercely as if to rid herself of the demons in her mind. On her shoulder, Varia turned her head to look at the Knight and answered for her. "I don't think he does. Apparently the Tarmaks haven't told him, and I can't get close to him. They've put archers up on the roofs to shoot at anything larger than a sparrow that comes near him."

"You could try tonight," Mariana suggested.

Linsha rubbed her temples. Her head still ached from the blow two nights before, which only exacerbated her foul mood. "I'm not sure we should tell him yet," she said, reluctance in every word. "Bronzes are straightforward thinkers. If he knows I am free of the Tarmaks, he may try something stupid to get away. We have to try to find a way to remove that dart before we can free him of the Akkad-Ur."

And what if he finds out I've left without telling him? she thought miserably.

The owl swiveled her head around to stare at Linsha, but she said no word of encouragement or rebuke.

"Then we'd better save the militia," Falaius said. "Save those we can and go north to Duntollik. They have the weapons and the warriors to oppose the Tarmak army. And," he said for Linsha's sake, "there are powerful mystics and shamans among the tribes to the north. They may have an answer to your problem."

Sir Hugh scratched the dirty blond stubble on his chin. "What about the rest of the prisoners?"

"They will have to wait," Mariana answered. "We dare not try another raid."

The black mood settled deeper into Linsha's mind. Of course she knew they must leave the others behind, but the words hit her hard. They would have to leave Lanther, the rest of the Knights, and even Sir Remmik. She would miss Lanther very much. As much as she disliked the knight commander, even Remmik did not deserve to be abandoned to the enemy.

The four riders looked at one another and finally agreed with the barest of nods. In unspoken unity, they wheeled their horses back to the faint path that led to Sinking Wells.

Two hours later, as the fog descended on the hills, the last remnants of Iyesta's forces prepared to leave. They sent a small party of women, the child, and a few wounded with an escort to Mem-Thon, the tribal village close to the Silvanesti Forest. Those who remained lit a few fires, left some tents standing among the trees, and mounted their horses to leave the oasis.

At the edge of the deserted camp, Linsha reined her horse to a stop and watched the silent centaurs and riders as they filed past. The greater number of the two-legged militia had scrounged or stolen enough horses to ride and vowed to follow Falaius and Mariana wherever they would lead them. A few had chosen to stay behind and try to work their way back into the city. They had family still trapped in Missing City they did not want to leave behind. Two other Legionnaires had offered to pose as slaves and travel with the Tarmaks to gather what information they could on the army and its plans. Linsha was not sure how successful they would be, but she respected their courage and willingness to try.

The thought of the spies brought another unpleasant thought to mind: The spy in their own midst. Where was he or she now? Had this person been killed in the Wadi? Or left behind in the slave pens? Or worse, were they taking the spy with them into the Plains?

She patted her horse's neck and set the thought aside for now. They all would have to be vigilant in the days ahead. But for now, there was a long ride through the night and into the next day to look forward to. They had to put some distance between themselves and the Tarmaks.

With a whistle to Varia, she urged her horse into the line of riders and soon disappeared into the night and mist.

Under the assumption that the militia leaders would have learned a lesson, the Tarmaks did not attack the oasis of Sinking Wells in the cover of darkness. They kept their distance and waited until dawn. Instead of slinking in to kill the sentries and attack the soldiers in their beds, the *ekwul* charged the camp in a yelling, intimidating horde, swinging their swords and clashing their shields.

All they found were empty tents, dead fires, and a few graves.

Annoyed, the *ekwegul* sent a runner to the Akkad-Ur, who told him to wait.

A wind from the desert blew in and tore away the curtain of sea fog. The clouds shredded and faded away to reveal a sky of cerulean blue. The sun warmed the earth and dried the grass. Sheep drifted out of their shelters and onto the hills, looking like bits of cloud left behind.

Three hours after sunrise the Tarmak warriors at the oasis heard the distant sound of horns. Excitedly they grouped on the top of a nearby slope and watched with pride as the army of their emperor marched along the trail from Missing City. In the vanguard rode the scouts and a unit of chariots pulled by the large, stocky Damjatt horses. Behind them came the Akkad-Ur's personal retainers, accompanying the bronze dragon, who stalked silently among them. Then marched the foot soldiers in rank after rank of blue skins and shining weapons. To the rear rolled the chariots followed by the baggage wagons pulled by massive oxen and the mob of slaves pressed into duty as laborers and pack carriers. In their midst trudged the Knights of Solamnia and the two members of the Legion of Steel.

The watching hundred cheered their companions heartily and jogged down the hill to join them. Battles lay ahead and a land to conquer—without the taskmasters of Neraka looking over their shoulders. This is what they had trained for and what the emperor had sent them to do. Thunder rolled under their feet, and their voices lifted in song. Swinging steadily in a ground-eating jog, the Tarmaks moved into the heart of Iyesta's realm.

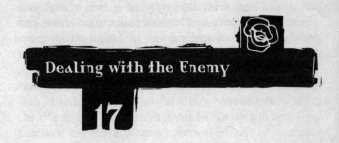

Dealing with the Enemy

17

Before the arrival of the great dragon overlords, the eastern half of the Plains of Dust had been a barren, arid land of sweeping hills open to a vast sky where nomadic tribes followed the seasons north and south. Little had grown on the red lands but tough grasses, indomitable shrubs, and cold-hardy cacti. As far east as the skirts of the sweeping Silvanesti Forest, the dry lands spread and supported little more than snakes, goats, sheep, and a few hardy species of antelope.

Then came Sable, the black dragon, who used her powers of geomancy to transform great stretches of fertile land between the Plains of Dust and Blöde into a swamp. She drowned Blödehelm and New Coast and extended her dismal realm into the New Sea. Huge tracts of land disappeared under stagnant water, twisted trees, moss, and slime.

While this tragedy affected millions of acres and displaced thousands of humans, ogres, and centaurs, it held one small blessing for the Plains of Dust. That much water to the northeast of the Plains, combined with several other minor climactic changes, altered the climate of the eastern plains from cold and arid to temperate and semiarid, changing the barren wastelands on the eastern fringes of Iyesta's realm to savannas and grasslands. The winters north of Missing City grew more tolerable and the warmth of the summers lasted longer. Trees thrived along the riverbanks, old creek beds, and in the depressions of scattered oases. Grass grew in abundance and with it, the herds of wild animals and domesticated stock flourished. Flocks of birds returned to the fields and rivers. Wildflowers bloomed where none had grown before.

Many of the plains tribes, attracted by the more abundant grass and water, drifted eastward out of the desert into Iyesta's realm and flourished in the comparative safety of her peace. Other peoples came too—clans of centaurs, families of humans, traders, explorers, and some others not so desirable.

Although Iyesta and her companion dragons had worked hard to keep the violent element out of her realm, they could not watch every hiding place, every path, every patch of woods. Small bands of brigands or draconians or sometimes both together roamed the edges and byways of the Plains, especially on the northeast borders where Sable's foul swamp offered many places to hide. Like wild dogs they would slink out at night and attack small groups of travelers, isolated farms, or unarmed caravans. Since Iyesta's disappearance and the troubles with the Dark Knights to the east, the bands had grown bolder, and several had joined to together to form larger and more dangerous groups. They roved out, looking for loot and weapons and women, and they rarely took prisoners.

The Tarmak army, however, made them think twice.

Four days after leaving Missing City, the Tarmak scouts lost the trail of the fleeing militia in an area of rough, eroded badlands. In a single night the band seemed to have split apart and melted away into the grass.

The Akkad-Ur looked at the region, at the exposed rock, the crumbling, twisted hills, and the intricate sculpturing of the weathered stone and released his scouts from blame. He doubted even a pack of hounds could have tracked the refugees out of that place. Instead of uselessly venting his anger over the escape of the militia, he looked for other means of tracking Falaius's forces, and very quickly he found one.

Each day the scouts had reported seeing riders or sometimes individuals watching the advancing army from afar. These observers would sit on a distant hill and watch or track the army for miles before fading out of sight. If a Tarmak tried to approach, the watchers vanished. For three days these spies followed the army, until the Akkad-Ur decided it was time to find out who they were. He gave orders to his best trackers, and they, wanting to make amends for their failure in the badlands, obeyed with a vengence. The Akkad-Ur curbed his impatience and sat back to await results.

By late evening the trackers returned with a human and a draconian.

The first indication the Akkad-Ur had of their arrival was a loud, vicious snarl from Crucible, who was chained near his tent. As soon as they entered the shelter, the Akkad-Ur understood why. There were few draconians on the Plains, thanks to Iyesta's efforts, and of the races native to Ansalon, he hadn't anticipated seeing this one.

The man, upon seeing the statuesque Tarmak painted and masked and seated in his black chair, fell

169

promptly to his knees and bowed low. The draconian merely grunted a greeting of sorts.

"How appropriate," said the Akkad-Ur in smooth tones. "A bozak."

The bozaks were the draconians created from the bronze dragon eggs. They were not the brightest, toughest, strongest, or most magical of the five races, but they were *good* at all of those together and possessed their own form of paranoid intelligence. This particular one stood about six feet tall—shorter than the Tarmaks—and had dirty bronze scales, long leathery wings, and a long muzzled face. Although his weapons had been taken away from him, bits of armor were still tied to his arms and broad chest, and his hands had not been bound. He glowered at the general with bulbous, black eyes.

The Akkad-Ur was not one to waste time. He assessed the prisoners for a moment then gestured to his trackers to come close. After he received their report, he rose to his feet and walked slowly around the two spies. "You, or others like you, have been following us for days. Why?"

As he guessed, the man answered. Garbed in rough brown robes and leather pants, the man was short in stature, narrow-faced, and brought to mind the image of a weasel. "We were merely curious, my lord. The sight of such a magnificent army has not been seen on these Plains in generations."

"True," agreed the Tarmak. "But I know you better than you think. You are thieves. Brigands. Probably part of a larger gang of robbers, murderers, and sneaks. And I do not—" he moved swiftly in front of the kneeling man, slid a long, slim dagger smoothly out of its sheath, and rammed it into the man's left eye, killing him instantly. "Tolerate sneaks," he finished while the robber's body sagged to the floor. He turned to the bozak. "Which are you?"

Without blinking an eye, the bozak replied, "The murderer."

"Good." The Akkad-Ur wiped the dagger blade on the dead man's chest and slid the weapon back out of sight. "Perhaps we understand each other. I have heard the bozaks fight their battles with more than bloodlust."

The draconian eyed him without reply. The Akkad-Ur returned to his chair and sat down.

"In the event you have not heard the news out here, the dragonlords Iyesta and Thunder are dead." A widening of the draconian's already bulging eyes was answer enough. "This realm is ours. We have taken Missing City and driven the dragon's forces from the region."

The bozak jerked his head. "We saw their trail," he growled.

"Their complete destruction is a matter of time. However, if you and your fellow brigands do not wish to join them, I have an offer." He picked up a leather bag from among the things on his worktable and tossed it to the bozak. It fell on the floor at his feet with a satisfying clink. "We are marching on Duntollik. With that realm in our grasp, the rest of the Plains will fall like overripe fruit. If you wish to participate in this glorious victory, we would welcome any news your trackers and scouts find interesting—any stray soldier you happen to capture, perhaps information on Duntollik's tribes, the landmarks, or its leaders. Also if your people wish to join us in battle, we would reward you well."

"How well?"

The Akkad-Ur waved a hand at the leather bag and smiled behind his mask. "Very well. There is plenty more where that came from."

The bozak hesitated before he turned his heavy eyes to the necklace of dragon's teeth around the Tarmak's neck. "What will you do with the bronze?"

"Kill him eventually. For now he is useful."

"Give me your word I may have his scales, and I will spread the news of your offer from the Toranth River pirates to the border gangs."

"What makes you think you can trust my word?"

"I'd sooner trust a cobra," snorted the draconian. "But we know many things about these plains you do not. We can be of service."

"Such as?"

"The militia you seek has split up."

"Where have they gone?"

The bozak only grinned a toothy, tightlipped grimace.

"I see," said the Akkad-Ur, his mask glinting in the lamplight. "Very well. You have a deal. Your name?"

"Vorth."

"Well, Vorth, if you serve us as you say, the bronze's scales will be yours."

The draconian picked up the leather bag and tucked it in his belt. Bowing once, he said, "The militia split into three groups. One is following the river, heading for Duntollik. A troop of centaurs went north, probably to rouse their clans. A third party went north and east toward the King's Road."

The Akkad-Ur steepled his fingers and stared thoughtfully through the eye holes of his mask. So, they were trying to raise the Plains against his army. The thought pleased him. The more people they pulled into the war, the better would be the battle and the greater would be their defeat. Let them run themselves ragged trying to draw help from every corner of the Plains. Their doom was inevitable.

"So be it. There is one other small matter I will offer

you. A bounty. I wish to have an escaped prisoner returned to us. A woman Knight of Solamnia. She will probably be with the militia heading for Duntollik. She is a skilled warrior, so her capture will not be easy. I will pay one-hundred steel coins for her alive."

"What about dead?"

"The person who brings me this woman dead will meet the same fate."

"Ah." The bozak flicked his pointed ears. "I will remember that."

His business with the draconian finished, the Akkad-Ur gestured to his guards and dismissed the draconian. He watched as the bozak stamped out.

Something stirred in the deep shadows at the back of the tent, then a grubby and weary-looking man stepped out of the sleeping area and tread softly across the carpets.

"Mercenaries again?" he said behind the Akkad-Ur. "How long will these last?"

The Akkad-Ur did not turn around. "As long as they are useful. If they prove troublesome, we can put them in the front of battle and crush them in the middle." He heard the splash of wine and held out a hand. A wine cup was pressed into his palm. "You really should stay downwind of me," he remarked.

His visitor ignored the comment. "To the militia," the man said, coming around to face the general. He raised his cup in a toast. "They are a courageous and tenacious foe."

"They have been more of a challenge than we anticipated," agreed the Akkad-Ur. "Yet the Rose Knight fled. That surprised me."

"She did not run away. She is making a strategic withdrawal. As long as you have the dragon, she will not go far."

"She cares a great deal for that dragon," the Tarmak mused. "Does that bother you?"

"No. It is a dragon."

But the denial paused just a heartbeat too late and came a little too emphatically. The Akkad-Ur knew this man well and realized the truth behind the words. "When the time comes, you may kill the dragon," he offered.

"She would never forgive me," the man said. "That's hardly a way to win a woman."

"Why win her? Just take her."

But the man realized he'd said too much about a subject he preferred to keep personal. He drank deeply of his wine and deliberately spilled some down his filthy tunic. "I have to explain the smell of wine. You're torturing me, remember?"

"Why continue this ruse?" The Akkad-Ur said, pouring more wine. "The Knights are ours and the woman is gone. Come and take your rightful place beside me."

The man stared at the red liquid in his cup. "I have considered that. But I don't believe the Rose Knight and the militia are quite through. I prefer to keep undercover until she is back in our hands and we have defeated the forces of Duntollik."

The Tarmak shrugged. "As you wish."

The man drained his cup, set it down, and stood in front of the Akkad-Ur. "Does the dragon know yet?"

"No. But he is growing restive. He has asked to see her several times."

"It would, I believe, be a good idea to get her back."

"I have already sent the bandits after her. Do you want more?"

"Let's try the Solamnic Knights."

"Tell me."

The man did, and when he was finished, an appreciative and knowing smile lifted the Akkad-Ur's mouth. "I will do as you suggest."

"Good. Now you'd better hit me. Just once, please. Make it look believable."

The Akkad-Ur clenched his fist and punched the man on the cheek bone, not hard enough to break bone but enough to leave a colorful bruise and a black eye.

The two bowed to each other, and when the guards were called back into the tent, the man extended his arms. He was bound and shoved forcefully out the entrance. Dirty, dripping with blood and wine, and seemingly hurting in every limb, he returned to his companions in the slave camp.

Early the next morning, the Akkad-Ur called back his trackers and left the badlands behind. The army was not far from the King's Road, the old road that bisected the eastern Plains from west to east and ended eventually in the kingdom of Silvanesti. One of his scouts had told him earlier that the Qualinesti elves were on the road moving east toward the Forest. While he would not mind sending them to join the dead, he did not really worry about them. From more recent reports he knew the elves were exhausted, low on supplies, and disheartened. Slaughtering them would be no honor and hold no glory. They were going to Silvanesti and would soon, he knew, have their hands full of Dark Knights, refugee Silvanesti elves, and nowhere to go. He could deal with them later if need be. In the meanwhile, he sent scouts out to check on the elves' progress and sent his army marching west toward the east fork of the Toranth River. They would follow the river north and west, cross the King's Road, and enter Duntollik from the east.

He was still working on his maps at noon when his guards brought the Solamnic Knight commander before him.

The Akkad-Ur looked from his camp chair at the sweating Knight and gestured to a second chair set beside the small table under an awning. The Tarmaks had stopped for a noon break to rest the horses and allow the army to eat a quick meal.

Sir Remmik's stare could have set the table on fire. He did not move. He did not look cowed or fearful, only suspicious.

"Please, Sir Knight," said the Akkad-Ur. "Sit down. I merely wish to talk to you."

The guards saluted and walked some distance away, leaving their Akkad-Ur alone with the Solamnic. A young Tarmak boy approached with a tray and quickly laid the table for a meal. He set out two cloths, two mugs, and a pitcher of something steaming. He laid food on the cloths, bowed to the Akkad-Ur, and hurried away. No one else came to join them.

"Sir Remmik, sit down. The food is not poisoned or drugged. I will not harm you. I only intend to talk to you."

The Knight lifted one eyebrow. "I have not bowed to your tortures. I will not bow to your blandishments. By our Oath and Measure I cannot cooperate with you."

"Really? Others have. I just assumed these oaths of yours were mere . . . guidelines."

Sir Remmik recoiled as if insulted. "Who has cooperated with you? Tell me their names!"

The Akkad-Ur gave a cold chuckle. Carefully, reverently, he removed the golden mask of his office, laid it on a stand, and turned barefaced to look at the Knight.

Sir Remmik's eyes narrowed. Without the gold mask, the Tarmak looked much like the others. His features were sharply aquiline, framed by long gray hair and thick gray eyebrows. His eyes stared back with a piercing intensity and intelligence that Sir Remmik found rather disconcerting in a barbarian. Yet without the mask, the Akkad-Ur seemed more . . . human . . . more approachable. Radiating caution, he walked around the table and sat down across from the Akkad-Ur. He kept his hands on his knees and touched nothing.

The Akkad-Ur poured the hot liquid into the cups, inhaling the powerful spicy scent of kefre. "I have taken a liking to this beverage. I don't know why. You could polish armor with it. But it has a certain body. My cook heats some for me in the morning and keeps it hot through the day." He pushed a cup toward Sir Remmik, who ignored it.

Leaning back in his seat, the Tarmak swallowed a long drink. "There are meat rolls, olives, cheese. It is a simple meal for the trail, but better than you've had for a while. Eat."

The Knight sat stonily in his seat, his face set in grim lines. His eyes strayed to the bronze dragon crouching a hundred feet away, out of earshot. He could not see the barb that kept the dragon imprisoned with the Tarmaks, but he saw the effects every time the dragon tried to move his front quarters. It obviously pained him.

"I have a task I would like you to perform for me," the Akkad-Ur said.

"No." Sir Remmik's tone was harder than steel.

The Akkad-Ur took a bite of his roll, chewed and swallowed before he replied. "You do not know what I want you to do."

"It doesn't matter."

"It might matter to the people of Duntollik. You have

seen our army in battle, and you know some of what we are capable of doing. I would like you to go to the leaders of Duntollik and ask for their surrender."

Sir Remmik leaped to his feet. Disbelief and anger warred for his self-control. Resisting the impulse to leap on the Tarmak and strangle him, the Knight turned his back on the Akkad-Ur and crossed his arms, the figure of adamant. "I will not betray an innocent people."

The Tarmak sighed. "I am not asking you to betray them. I am asking you to tell them the truth, that we are coming and that we will destroy their homes and villages if they do not surrender to us. You know we can do it. You know we *will* do it. If you can persuade them to surrender, you will be saving many lives."

"You would have to let me go," Sir Remmik said without turning around. "What makes you think I would obey your orders?"

The Akkad-Ur gave a dry laugh. "Someone else asked me how he could trust my word. Well, Sir Knight, I have learned enough about you to be confident that if you gave me your word that you would deliver my ultimatum to Duntollik. I could trust you to do so." He drank some more of his kefre and went on. "I have messages for you to carry. I will give you horses and three of your Knights to accompany you, and I expect you to take them to the leaders of the people of Duntollik. What you do after that is up to you."

"What about the rest of my men?" Sir Remmik demanded.

"They will stay with us. If you care to return with a reply, I will consider releasing all of you. There are hardly enough Knights left to pose a serious threat to my army."

Remmik tried to hide a grimace at the reminder of his missing Knights. Slowly he turned to face the

Akkad-Ur. His face was red under the sweat and the stubble of a gray beard. For a long, painful run of minutes he stared into the distance while his mind worked over the possible traps and pitfalls of such an offer. The Tarmak silently ate his meal and waited.

Finally Sir Remmik's eyes focused on Crucible again. The dragon had not moved and still sat staring north in the direction of Sanction. The Knight's brow lowered. Tight lines settled around his nose and mouth. "Sir, if I may ask, do you know where the militia is?"

"Most of them are headed for Duntollik," the Akkad-Ur answered. His eyes bored into the Solamnic, but Sir Remmik did not flinch or even seem to notice.

"I see." The Knight stood for another minute, his thin frame as unbending as an oak tree. At last he sighed a long breath of resignation. "I will go," he said. "My only wish is to bring order to this troubled realm. On my word as a Solamnic Knight, I will deliver your message. I will not guarantee that they listen to it."

"Agreed."

The Akkad-Ur sent the proper orders to his subordinates and with pleased graciousness offered a seat and food to the Knight once again.

Once again Sir Remmik refused it. "If I may, I will wait with my men for your horses and your messages." At the Akkad-Ur's dismissive wave, he started to leave, but his steps were slow as if he fought an internal debate that dragged at his intentions. He stopped in a decisive movement that set the Tarmak guards' hands to their weapons.

Ah, thought the Akkad-Ur, the bait has finally been taken.

"If I may ask," Sir Remmik said slowly, "were your people involved in the ambush of our Knights the night of the storm before your invasion?"

"We sent a small party of warriors who volunteered to enter the city early, yes. And yes, they were the ones who killed the honor guard."

There was a pause, then the Knight went on. "Did you have inside information? An informant?"

"Of course. We could not have taken the city so easily without someone on the inside. She's been feeding us information for over a year. Even now she is on her way to gather more valuable information on Duntollik."

Sir Remmik's lean face paled and he looked truly pained. "And the Wadi?"

The Akkad-Ur laughed a rough, patronizing sound of derision. "Why do you think only the Solamnic Knights were captured and everyone else was slain?"

The Knight Commander obviously reached his own conclusion, for he stepped back, storm clouds building behind his gray eyes. He forced a slight bow and turned on his heel. The guards hurried to catch up with him.

The Akkad-Ur watched him go, satisfied with the interview. His informant thought the Knight would certainly lead their trackers to this woman and possibly bring her back as a hostage to save the other Knights. But after looking into Sir Remmik's eyes and seeing the red rage within, he felt sure the Knight would not hesitate to impose his own Solamnic justice. He had better warn the warriors sent to trail the Knights to be on the alert.

Dreams and Arrows

18

*L*insha. A voice whispered her name over the rustle of the flowing river. She did not hear the voice as much as feel it caress her mind.

Startled, she sat up straighter, for the voice sounded familiar. Her eyes scanned the riverbank to her left and right, but she saw no one in the heavy gloom. This was a night of a dark moon, a night of dense shadows and velvet darkness. The only light came from overhead where the stars glittered in brilliant clusters, freed from the moon that often stole their fragile light. Around her insects hummed in the grass and on the river, a mist was rising from the water, pale and ethereal, reflecting the distant starlight.

Linsha. Wake up, my lovely.

Linsha's heart skipped a beat and tripped forward in a rapid pulse. Her breath caught in her throat.

A pale figure stood in the middle of the river perhaps ten feet away. It had no solid form. It looked to her like an outline of a person drawn with silver ink. The mist swirled about its feet and rolled upward, defining its limbs and filling out its shape with a spectral glow

181

as pale as starlight. The last to appear was his face, as handsome as she remembered. She fancied she caught the faintest hint of blue in his eyes.

Linsha pitched a rock at him. "For the gods' sake, am I dreaming you again?"

He watched the rock sail through the area of his chest and shook his head. *Is that any way to treat an old friend?*

"What do you want now, Ian?" she demanded. "You're supposed to be dead. Why do you keep coming back? What enigmatic warning are you going to give me this time?"

He laughed, that same roguish rumble of good humor she remembered from Sanction. It seemed another lifetime ago she had loved him—or thought she had.

He held out his arms to her. *Come kiss me, Green Eyes.*

"Drop dead, Ian."

Thanks to you, my lovely, I already have.

"Right. So what do you want now? Still want to warn me about some nameless rogue?

You are in a bad mood. Even in your sleep. Anything to do with that dragon of yours?

Linsha leaned forward, another rock in her hand. "He's not my dragon," she snapped.

So you say. He grinned again. *I don't have to tell you to be wary. You already know. Listen to your heart. No, I just came to tell you to wake up. Wake up, Green Eyes. There is trouble coming.*

"Wake up!" A real voice, a human voice spoke in her ear. "Linsha, wake up."

Linsha nearly leaped vertically off the rock she was sitting on. She turned huge eyes to the speaker, snatched his padded jacket, and yanked him closer. "Don't you *ever* sneak up on me like that again!"

Sir Hugh calmly put a hand on her wrist and pushed her away. He moved quietly and sat down beside her on the rock.

"Sorry. You were mumbling something. I thought you were dreaming."

She turned back to look at the river, but the spectral form was no longer there, only the mist that flowed in currents above the water. Had she been dreaming? She didn't think she'd been asleep. She knew how to sleep sitting up or even standing up when necessary—every active Knight learned that trick, but she'd never fallen asleep on guard duty before. Of course she was still bone-weary from days of work and worry and travel. Perhaps Ian had been only a dream. Yet . . . she had felt his presence so intensely, just as she had in Sanction those years ago.

"Did you see something on the river when you came?" she asked softly.

He looked at the mist and the shadows and said, "Like what?"

"Nothing. I suppose I was dreaming." She was not about to explain Ian Durne to Sir Hugh. The young Knight still believed in her. She was not going to shatter that illusion by telling him about her love affair with an assassin from the Knights of Neraka.

But if she had been asleep then, she was very awake now. Awake and vividly aware of the night. She sat up straighter, her senses reaching out around her. Something did not feel right. What had Ian said? Trouble is coming.

Brush rustled somewhere to her left. Gravel crunched softly under a heavy foot. Linsha reacted instinctively. She lunged against Sir Hugh, shoving him off the rock onto the ground. She landed heavily beside him just as a crossbow bolt cracked into the rock where they had been sitting.

Both Knights shouted a warning to the sleeping camp.

The effect was immediate. Another sentry blew a horn. The sleepers in the camp, trained by months of danger, slept fully clothed with their weapons close at hand. The shouts brought them instantly awake and on their feet just as a mob of dark figures charged the camp. Voices rang out in war cries and challenges. Swords clashed in the dark.

More crossbow bolts slammed into the rocks around Linsha and Hugh, then three dark forms barged out of the brush and dashed toward them, swords and bucklers raised for an attack.

"Damn! They're carrying scimitars!" said Sir Hugh, who only had a light long sword and a padded jacket.

Linsha, who had managed to scrounge a heavy rapier and a brass-hilted poniard before she left Sinking Wells, wasn't any happier. "Damn," she muttered. "They're draconians."

They leaped to their feet and stood back to back. There was no time to retreat up to the camp or make an offensive move. The draconians were on them in a blink of an eye, screeching and smashing in for a quick kill.

In the dark Linsha could not easily identify what type of draconian they were. They were not skilled fighters. That much was clear, for they got in each other's way and used their curved scimitars to hack and beat down their opponents. They'd probably stolen the blades and their armor, too. Thankfully two of them were short for draconians, which meant they were probably baaz, the warped, evil perversions of brass dragon eggs. The other was taller and heavier. A bozak perhaps.

"If you kill one, pull your weapon out fast!" she cried to Sir Hugh.

He managed a grunt in reply and fended off another wild swing at his head from the bozak.

The draconians jeered at them and pressed harder. Their scimitars slammed into Linsha's blades until both her arms ached and quivered from the force of the blows. Her left arm, wounded in the melee with the Tarmaks, flared with pain every time she used the poniard to stop a swing.

Fortunately her rapier was a well-built weapon, strong enough to survive the blow of a scimitar, balanced for speed and slashing cuts, and not too heavy for good point work. Linsha often preferred a good rapier and had trained with one for years. Using all of her skill she forced one opponent to back away and, ducking under another wild blow, she slipped by his arm and rammed the point of her blade into the draconian's chain mail vest. The sharp point burst through the chain links, slid between his ribs, and pierced the heart.

She yanked the blade out of the body as it toppled over, but she had no time to watch what happened to it. The remaining two draconians pressed their attack harder, and in the dark it was difficult to see, to watch the enemy's face and muscles and look for the subtle clues that often gave away his next move.

Behind her she heard Sir Hugh gasping as he swung his long sword at the bigger draconian. He sounded tired, and she knew she was wearing down fast. At least they were fighting only two draconians now. She parried a wild thrust and jabbed with her poniard at the creature's midsection. It snarled and deflected the blow with its buckler.

All at once it paused, its long nose sniffing the air. "You!" The baaz hissed. "You are the one! The woman with the bounty. Vorth! This is the one the Brutes seek!"

The second and larger draconian hissed in glee. Giving his large wings a powerful flap, he leaped up and came crashing down to smash Sir Hugh into the rocky riverbank. Linsha could not look. She had her hands too full to help. The first draconian, seeing steel coins in his mind, switched from trying to kill her to trying to disable her. Her came at her using his buckler like a ram to push past her blades and shove her backwards. She tried to get a point under his guard, but his larger size and weight bore her back. She banged into Sir Hugh behind her, twisted to get out of his way, and tripped over something hard in the dark. Her foot caught on the thing and she fell over it, landing on her right arm and side. Pain ripped up her ankle and through her back. Her elbow hit a rock so hard her entire arm went numb, and her sword fell out of her nerveless fingers. By sheer force of will she kept a grip on the poniard and made her body relax over the uneven lump she realized was the first dead baaz. It was a terrible gamble, but she hoped greed would overcome bloodlust in her attacker.

The draconian hooted with derision. Lurching over her, he grabbed her hair and yanked her head up to see if she was still alive.

As fast as a Tarmak, Linsha pulled back her good arm and rammed the poniard through the joints of the old armor into the draconian's gut. Hot blood spilled over her hand. The creature screeched and tried to pull away, but the point of the long dagger slid up through a lung and hit an artery. In moments, the baaz's heart failed.

Although Linsha tried to pull the weapon out of the dying creature, she wasn't fast enough. It toppled over her, ripping the handle out of her hand, died, and, like every one of its kind, its body promptly turned to stone. Linsha's weapon became trapped in a petrified statue.

Pinned between the two dead draconians, Linsha struggled to free herself, then fell back panting for air and feeling nauseous from the pain. The stone body that held her down was too heavy for her to move alone. She either needed help or an hour's worth of patience to wait until the draconians' bodies crumbled to dust. Frantic for Hugh, she squirmed around to see him. What if he was dead already? But when she finally worked her upper body into a place where she could catch sight of him, she paused, taken with surprise.

Hugh had fought off the bozak's air attack and had disarmed him. He had lost his own sword as well, and as Linsha watched, the two opponents went after each other with tooth and bare fist. Bozaks were known to be dirty fighters, but she was astonished to see Sir Hugh fought dirty as well—with head, teeth, elbows, fists, knees, and feet. He used moves the trainers never taught Solamnic Knights. Kicking and punching, he slowly drove the draconian away from Linsha and away from the fallen swords.

The bozak looked wildly over his shoulder for help, but there was none. The riverbank was black around them and apparently empty.

In that second of inattention, Sir Hugh slipped a foot under the scimitar, kicked it upward, and caught the grip with his hand. He brought it around in a vicious arc that took the draconian's head off at the shoulders. The head bounced once and rolled to the water's edge.

"Get down, Hugh!" Linsha shouted.

The Knight dove for cover behind the rock just as the skin on the bozak began to crumble. Unlike the baaz which turned to stone and eventually disintegrated, dead bozaks swiftly deteriorated into skeletons which a minute later exploded in a hail of shrapnel and bone fragments. Linsha threw an arm over her face just as the dead draconian blew apart. Shards of bone whizzed over her head.

There was a polite smattering of applause from the top of the bank.

Linsha and Hugh looked up to see four figures standing on the bank watching them. Someone had built up the campfire, and it illuminated the watchers from behind in a yellow glow. All four held swords and one carried a loaded crossbow. Linsha sagged back with a groan. In all the rush of battle, she had forgotten about the camp.

"Well done, Sir Hugh!" Falaius called. "I see you have taken care of things down there. Is Linsha injured?"

"I don't know," she answered for him. "If someone would help me get this blasted draconian off—"

Mariana sprang lightly down the bank, and with Linsha's help from underneath and the aid of Sir Hugh's strong arms, they lifted the heavy stone baaz off Linsha and heaved it aside.

With a grin Sir Hugh pulled Linsha to her feet. As she came upright, she tried to put her weight on both feet and was immediately reminded of her injured ankle. The damaged joint refused to hold her. She gasped and fell forward against Hugh's chest. His arms automatically went around her, and they clasped each other close. She wondered briefly if she should pull away, then he looked into her eyes and in the same breath they started laughing in relief and in the pleasure of being alive.

Mariana studied them both for a minute in her cool, detached way and rubbed the sweat from her face. "Linsha, go soak your ankle in the cold water for a while until I can attend you. Sir Hugh, stay with her and try to wash some of the blood off so I can see to your injuries."

"What of the others?" Linsha asked.

"They're alive. Your warning alerted us in time. Most of our attackers were human and not skilled. Falaius thinks they were just bandits. You had the greater number of draconians."

"Just lucky I guess," Sir Hugh said, still holding Linsha and still grinning like a lunatic.

Mariana raised an elegant eyebrow. She had seen this reaction before. People sometimes felt drunk after a mortal battle. "Fine. I have a few other people to attend to, then I'll be back." She strode up the hill into the firelight.

Sir Hugh's head dropped to Linsha's shoulder. "Is she gone yet?" he groaned. At her reply his whole body seemed to sag into her arms.

By fits and starts and careful hops, Linsha and Hugh worked their way over to a grassy patch by the water's edge and collapsed side by side.

"By Helm's sword, Hugh, where did you learn to fight like that?" Linsha said while she pulled off her boot.

He splashed water over his hands and face and pulled off his padded jacket to make a pillow for them both. "The streets of Palanthas," he replied, stretching out on the grass beside her. "I used to run with a gang before the Knights saved me." His voice dropped as his energy seemed to be draining away. "Thank you for saving me."

Linsha sank her ankle in the cold flowing water. She lay back and closed her eyes. "I still owe you, Hugh."

Her ankle was cold, her entire body hurt, and the grass was chilly beneath her. But the exuberance of relief was gone and in its place flowed unadulterated exhaustion.

"Linsha?"

"Hmmm?"

"Who is Ian?"

"He's dead, Hugh."

"Oh."

The last word was barely a sigh.

—————————

Mariana came back half an hour later and found them both asleep in the grass. She propped her torch up between several stones and moved among them to check their condition. Except for the old bruise on her face, Linsha looked well enough. She slept peacefully and barely moved when the half-elf lifted her ankle from the water and shifted her back enough to rest her foot on the land. The ankle looked bruised and a little swollen, but it was not broken, and the cold water had helped. Mariana wrapped it tightly and left her friend to sleep.

For a moment she paused by Hugh's head and let her gaze dwell on his features. He looked so relaxed in the innocent pose of sleep, so peaceful and boyish. If she had not seen him fight the draconian bare-handed, she would not have believed it of this young man. She brushed a hand over his forehead where his light brown hair had stuck to a bloody swelling. He was a well-built man, strong, and handsome enough with the heart of a true Knight. Would he and Linsha ever—?

No, the half-elf corrected herself almost as soon as the thought surfaced. Linsha's heart belonged to someone else. Of that Mariana was certain. The Rose Knight might not realize it yet, but her love's eye looked somewhere beyond the men at hand. As for Hugh, Mariana suspected he bore an attraction for her. Looking at him now, asleep, battered, bruised, bleeding in several places, dirty, and sweaty with just a hint of that lunatic smile still on his lips, she decided that was not a displeasing notion. Perhaps in the months ahead when this war was over they could spend time together that didn't involve fleeing, fighting, and burying the dead. They could find someplace quiet where they could just be together. Until then, Mariana thought with a sigh, they would have to be patient.

Carefully, so as not to disturb him, she examined his limbs and his torso for wounds that needed mending. She found cuts and scraps, a black eye, a bite that would need careful observation, bumps and bruises, and two slashes that needed stitching, one on his forearm and a second on his ribs. He had been very lucky. Using warm water she had brought down from the campfire and a small healer's kit, she washed the slashes and gently stitched them closed by torchlight. He did not move through either stitching, and she assumed he slept through the whole procedure. But when she finished the last knot on his side, his hand caught hers and pressed her fingers to his lips. She looked down in the dark planes of his face and saw his eyes watching her.

Mariana smiled.

"Thank you," he whispered. "You're a woman of many talents."

She brushed her lips over his forehead. "Sleep now, Hugh. Morning is coming."

He blinked at her, then his eyes slid closed and he dropped back into sleep, still holding her hand.

Mariana waited a little while before she slid her hand free. She snuffed out the torch in the water, and in the darkness she found the long sword and the rapier

191

on the graveled bank and the poniard resting in a heap
of dust. She placed them carefully by her friends' sides.
Satisfied, she sat down on the large rock nearby to keep
watch.

The Grandfather Tree

19

Linsha awoke to sharp points digging into her skin and a small weight bouncing on her chest. She opened bleary eyes and looked directly into round, golden brown eyes surrounded by a ring of creamy feathers. A sharp beak clacked a greeting.

"Oh, good. You're awake," chirped the owl, bouncing up and down again for good measure.

"Varia," Linsha croaked. "Where have you been?"

"Yes, I see you had a busy night."

Linsha pushed herself up to a sitting position and looked around. The mists of night had vanished. The sun was shining brightly on the water. She was still lying on the bank, but there was no one else in sight.

"Where is everyone?"

"Getting ready to go," Varia replied, hopping up onto Linsha's shoulder. "Messengers arrived at dawn. Centaurs." The owl bobbed again in excitement. "The tribes and clans of Duntollik are already meeting. They heard we were coming and wanted someone to come now to talk to the chiefs. If they agree, we're supposed to go the Grandfather Tree for the gathering of the warriors."

Linsha's forehead wrinkled in thought. This was a great deal of information to force into a brain that was still trying to work out what time of day it was.

"The Grandfather Tree? What is that?"

Varia's eyes glowed gold with delight. "I will not spoil the surprise. It is one of the true wonders of these Plains."

Linsha felt too lousy to argue. "Fine. So where have you been?"

"Following the Tarmaks. They are about three days' march behind."

"Is Crucible . . . ?"

"He is still alive and still a prisoner. They keep him in the center of the army and keep guards around him. I cannot get close." She fluffed her feathers, a habit she had when something bothered her. "Someone else is following you now."

Linsha rubbed her eyes and took a deep breath. Memories of the night before were coming back with painful clarity, and she remembered something one of the draconians had said, something about a bounty.

"Bounty hunters? Did the Tarmaks put a bounty on me?"

"It's possible. I saw maybe twenty or thirty humans and draconians riding in the Tarmak army, and other small bands are roving along the trails in this area. But no, this is someone else. Sir Remmik."

"What?" Linsha sat bolt upright and stared at the owl in astonishment.

"Sir Remmik and three Knights. I saw them last night. They are following your trail. I think they're going to Duntollik, too."

Linsha was too dumbfounded to speak. What was the Knight Commander doing free of the Tarmak army? Had Sir Remmik and some of his Knights escaped?

"I told Falaius about them," Varia went on. "I said you might want to send someone back for them, but he refused. We don't have time. We have to get the Grandfather Tree in two days' time. They'll just have to catch up."

"You talked to Falaius already?" Linsha demanded. "How long have you been back? What time is it? How long was I sleeping?" She struggled to her feet, dislodging the owl from her shoulder.

Varia fluttered to the large rock and perched, waiting while Linsha found her sword and the poniard and shoved them into the scabbards at her belt. "It's still morning," she said. "You've only slept a few hours, according to Mariana."

Linsha, balanced on one foot, glared around at the grassy bank. "Where is Sir Hugh?"

"Oh, he left a little while ago. He volunteered to go speak to the tribal leaders at the Grandfather Tree."

"He left!" Linsha snapped. "Oh, for pity's sake, wasn't anyone going to tell me anything?" She struggled forward on one foot, sore and aching and annoyed with the whole world.

"I just told you," Varia said.

"Stop it, right there," Mariana called from the top of the riverbank. "You shouldn't climb this without help. Your ankle has a bad sprain." She jogged down the slope and put an arm around Linsha's shoulder.

Linsha transferred her glare to her friend. "Why didn't someone wake me up sooner?"

"You were on guard duty half the night, remember? There was nothing you needed to do. Now we have broken camp and are ready to go."

"Sir Hugh managed to get up and be useful," Linsha said, grumbling, but listening to herself, she had to admit she sounded rather petulant.

195

"Sir Hugh was just coming on guard duty when we were attacked. He'd already had some sleep. And he does not have an injured ankle. He can get there faster. Now stop sounding like a fretful child and be grateful you are still alive. Not everyone I know survives a fight with three draconians."

Mariana hefted some of Linsha's weight onto her shoulders and helped her up the steep bank to the grassy grove where they had pitched their camp the night before.

Linsha saw the horses were already saddled and the gear packed. Off to one side in the trees, she saw a pile of bodies—the bandits from the night attack. Everyone in her party was upright and alive. Thank the absent gods for that.

Varia winged past her and came to land on the pommel of the saddle on Linsha's horse. While Falaius and the others mounted, Mariana gave Linsha a leg up then sprang onto her own mount.

Moments later they were gone, and the dust slowly settled over the dead.

Linsha had always found a way to feel at home wherever she went. Her family home was in Solace, to be sure, but she had traveled so much during her lifetime that she had learned to adapt. After all, one place was much like another in the background. Anywhere she stayed for more than a day or two she soon felt comfortable, even in Schallsea where her parents had forced her to go, or Palanthas, or Haven, or Sanction, or Missing City. Everywhere there were the same rocks and dirt and people and plants and animals. Only the trappings and the names were different.

Everywhere she could find something familiar.

Everywhere except the interior of the Plains of Dust. This drear, rugged land even she found difficult to embrace.

While her party had followed the Toranth River the past few days, she had been comfortable enough. Although she much preferred a city, here along the river there was abundant water and forage and prey for the hunters' bows. She found peace in the voice of the swiftly rushing water and pleasure in the wind as it swept through the willows and cottonwoods lining the banks. There were colors to please the eye—green in the rushes and grasses, a touch of autumn gold in the leaves of the cottonwoods, soft reds and tans in the rocks, and the vivid blue of the vast sky.

But that afternoon when the horses crossed the river's ford and trotted over the line of hills at the valley's borders, all of the bright color and rushing life of the river drained away to burned reds and umbers, drifting sand, and the endless solitude of the desert. Linsha had seen the southern end of the wastelands from the sky when Iyesta took her on a flight to Thunder's realm, but this was the first time she had seen the desert from the ground, and she did not like it. It looked empty and hostile to her eyes.

She stopped her horse on a small bare hill and looked out over the barren emptiness. There was nothing to see but sand dunes, windswept rock, and a few scruffy hills.

Falaius came to a stop beside her, his tanned face split with a smile of pleasure. "Isn't it beautiful?" he said. "I have loved this land since my eyes first opened upon it."

Linsha looked at him as if he had just declared his devotion to draconians. She remembered though, before

197

she said anything stupid, that the big Plainsman came from this desolation. What was dismal to one could be home to another.

"Why?" she said. "What do you see that is so beautiful?"

He swept an arm around to encompass the vast sweep of the land. "I cannot name any one thing. The desert is a vast entity unto itself. It simply is, and what you make of it is entirely up to you. You can look at it as a great, terrible emptiness or you can enter it with open eyes and see beauty and subtlety wherever you look."

Linsha tried not to be skeptical as she viewed the desertlands. To her, it still looked like a wasteland, the backside of nowhere. But for Falaius's sake, she tried to find something to appreciate.

"What is that trail over there? Does it go to the ford?" she asked, pointing out a faint track to their north that stretched like a dusty ribbon to the western horizon. Any track that led out of that desolation was worth appreciating.

Falaius's expression grew grave. "That is the trail of the Qualinesti. The centaurs who found us this morning told us they talked to several stragglers at the river. The main body of refugees passed by here about nine or ten days ago."

Linsha glanced up at the hot sun then down at the pale track. She could not imagine what that trek must have been like for the elves. To have lost their lands, their homes, so many of their friends and family; to have to cross that treacherous desert to find other elves who did not want them. What courage that had taken.

"They must have had a great faith in their leaders," she said softly.

"So I understand. You can ask more about them if

you like," the old Plainsman said. "The man who led them across the desert is meeting us at the Grandfather Tree."

"What is this Grandfather Tree?" she demanded. "Where is it?"

"You'll see tomorrow."

He gave Varia a wink and urged his horse downhill.

For the rest of the day, the small party of riders rode in the sweltering heat and dust, deeper and deeper into the great desert. All too quickly the influence of the river and the grasslands fell away behind them and rough, arid lands surrounded them. The sun burned hot in the sky and the dry desert wind blew plumes of red dust and sand from the horses' hooves.

Much of the time Linsha sat hunched in her saddle and dozed. The heat made her groggy, and since there wasn't much to look at, she closed her eyes and let her mind wander on lonely paths. When it became difficult to ride with her swollen ankle in the stirrup, she took both stirrups off and rode balanced in the saddle, her injured foot dangling.

Late in the evening when the sun sank like copper disk into a haze of dusky purple, Falaius led his party into a tiny oasis with a water hole hardly bigger than a mud puddle.

"We are only a few miles from the Run," he told them. "That's the road that rings Duntollik and marks its borders. From there we are only a day's ride from the Tree. But it will be a long ride. Sleep tonight and be ready before sunrise."

Surrounded by sculpted outcroppings of reddish stone, they made a cold camp and bedded down under the stars. Like many deserts, this one did not keep its heat long after the sun went down. By midnight the cold hovered near freezing, and Linsha, keeping watch in

199

the dark camp, had no trouble staying awake. Without a cloak or a warm piece of clothing, she shivered under a thin blanket until Mariana relieved her.

They rose before dawn the next day and were on the move before the sun touched the land. In the east the cold light of dawn slowly turned pale gold and apricot as they rode, and the stars disappeared into the bright light of another day. The riders crossed the Run and hurried on, anxious to keep well ahead of the Tarmak army.

All too quickly the cold of night became a memory. Linsha cast off her blanket, sighed, and steeled herself to face another blazing day of heat and boredom. It was going to take far longer than a day or two for her to feel at home in this place.

Shortly after daybreak the horses climbed a low range of hills and stopped on the crest so their riders could look down on the sweep of the desert.

"Over there," Falaius said and pointed to a place far in the distance.

Linsha tried to see what he was showing her. She blinked and stared hard into the hazy horizon, and all she could find was a dark spot that wavered slightly in the sea of rising heat. He grinned a crooked grin at her and rode on. Curious now, she concentrated on that dark spot for the rest of morning. Whatever it was, it seemed to be large and it sat alone on a high, broad hill. Before long, she caught a clearer glimpse of it and realized with a start of surprise that it was a tree—a huge tree, the only green thing in a realm of browns and reds. She searched her memory for anything she had ever heard or read about a large tree growing in the Plains of Dust, and eventually she remembered reading bits of passages on some old scrolls in the Citadel of Light on Schallsea. The Grandfather Tree was also called the World Tree, which was why she hadn't recognized the name immediately. It grew on an ancient mystic site and was sacred to the god Zivilyn, the god of wisdom, the Tree of Life.

The god of wisdom, Linsha thought. That seemed appropriate. May the absent god of wisdom find a way to help his people find wisdom these next few days.

Late in the afternoon, the travelers spotted a cloud of dust approaching and drew their weapons. This was supposed to be a safe realm, but after the attack on their camp two nights before, they were taking no chances. Varia flew to observe the approaching party and came back wheeling and hooting with pleasure.

It was Leonidas. Accompanied by a half-dozen other centaurs, the buckskin galloped up to join them, his bearded face beaming. Greetings were passed around, and the other centaurs gathered around Falaius talking all at once about the gathering of the clans and tribes.

Mariana fell back to ride with Linsha and talk to Leonidas.

"Many have already come," he told them excitedly. "Wanderer has brought his band. The Ereshu are here, and even many of the Windwalkers have come, and there are more on the way!"

Linsha turned to smile at his exuberance. "Wait! Slow down. Who is Wanderer? Who are the Ereshu? What are you doing here? I thought you went to talk to some of the northern clans?"

"We did! But most of them were already here, so we came here, too. They had a gathering just a few days ago, called by some the northern chiefs. Wanderer was trying to convince them that the Tarmaks meant war. Then Sir Hugh showed up last night and talked to the chiefs. They have agreed that they must fight the Tarmak together. They will not give up the Plains without a fight."

"Do they understand the nature of the Brutes they will face?" Mariana asked.

"Of course. They have talked to me, to the other centaurs with me, to Sir Hugh, and they have an amazing network of spies themselves. Oh," he took a quick breath and plunged on, "Horemheb is there. He's been helping Wanderer gather information about the Tarmak."

"Wanderer." Linsha had to say again. "Who is this Wanderer?"

Leonidas looked at her curiously. "I thought you'd know. I just assumed you know of him."

"Why should I?"

"Because he is the son of Goldmoon and Riverwind. Weren't they companions of your grandparents?"

A flood of surprise swept through Linsha's mind. Wanderer! He would be about her father's age, and now that she thought about it, she vaguely remembered hearing her father mention a young tribesman named Wanderer. But there was something tragic connected to his name. She wondered what it was. "No," she answered softly. "I don't know him."

The young centaur shrugged and went on talking about the tribes and the army that was gathering to face the threat of the Tarmak. The third group of militia that had split off to warn the tribes north of the King's Road had gathered as many warriors as they could and were moving west to join the tribal confederation at the Grandfather Tree. Other tribes were coming, too, including the more settled Wan-kali and the southern nomadic tribes of the Kordath who had suffered much under the lordship of the dragon,

Thunder. The population of the Plains of Dust was such a hodgepodge of nomadic barbarian tribes, centaur clans, and scattered human villages that gathering them all for an immediate offensive was impossible. All the leaders hoped for at this point was to gather enough warriors to defend the borders and drive the Tarmaks out should the blue-skinned Brutes decide to invade. From all indications, the invasion was just a matter of time.

After a while, Leonidas reached the end of his news, and Linsha and Mariana told him about the attack on their camp and the possibility that the Tarmaks had put a bounty on Linsha. He waved off the danger of any more bandits.

"Not this close to the Tree. This area is too well patrolled. If anyone wants to get close to Linsha, they will have to go through half the Plains tribes to reach her." He chuckled. "When I saw Sir Hugh last night, I wondered what had happened to him. Fought a draconian barefisted, did he? He looks like he went through a sausage grinder. And you," he said to Linsha, "don't look much better. There is a mystic healer in Wanderer's band who is very good. I will ask if he will see you."

"You don't have to," she hastened to say. "I don't need a healer."

He tilted his head to look at the owl on her shoulder. "Maybe you do and maybe you don't. But you would like him anyway. He is a good man. He has a kestrel."

Although the kestrel piqued her interest, Linsha did not give the tribesman much more thought. There were too many other things to think about and see. As they had talked and the miles had passed, the Grandfather Tree loomed larger and larger in the distance. At first she thought it was just a large cottonwood or a willow or something indigenous to the Plains, but the closer the troop drew to the Tree, the more familiar its shape became. They were still miles away when all at once recognition came to her mind with sharp, poignant clarity. It was a vallenwood tree, as shapely and lush as any vallenwood that grew in Solace. She almost cried. Here at last was something dearly familiar, something on the Plains she could embrace and call home.

Falaius glanced back, saw the look on her face, and dropped back to ride beside her. "Beautiful, isn't it?" he asked.

She heard the reverence in his voice and responded in kind. It was beautiful. In fact it was enormous. It was the largest, most magnificent vallenwood she had ever seen.

"They say one hundred grown men can spread their arms and link their hands and just barely encircle it," Leonidas told her.

"Just do not cut wood from it," Falaius warned, "or tear down its nuts or leaves. It is a symbol to our people of life and the ancient ways, and we take these things very seriously."

It was nearly dusk before Falaius and his riders reached the Grandfather Tree and rode under its branches. Awed, they gazed up into the canopy of huge limbs and spreading leaves gleaming in the last light of the day. Dusk had already crept in under the tree's skirt, and small gold lamps glowed like fireflies where various groups camped under the branches.

Linsha stared in delight. She sat for so long, mesmerized by the beauty and comfort of the vallenwood that she did not notice Sir Hugh approach her.

"There you go, sleeping again. Why is it every time I come to look for you, you're gazing off into the distance like a stunned kender?"

Before she could make a witty retort, he took her

horse's reins and led her to a site just under the fringes of the great tree where the refugees from Missing City were regrouping and setting up a camp. He helped her down from the horse, helped her unsaddle it, and led her to a seat on an old tree trunk that had been hauled in for that purpose. He left her there while he took her mount to the picket lines and gave it some food.

She noticed a pot of liquid heating on a small cooking fire and inhaled with deep appreciation. Someone had found some kefre.

"That's for later, for the sentries," Mariana told her, catching her look of yearning at the pot. "Wanderer has invited us to a meal in his camp. Food before business. It's an old tribal custom."

Linsha felt her stomach rumble. It had been too long since she'd had a warm meal that filled her belly. "I appreciate old tribal customs," she replied heartily.

"Good," Sir Hugh said behind her. "And you can get there on your own. I am not carrying you all over this camp." He walked around beside Mariana and tossed Linsha a walking stick he had cut and shaped to her height. "No, it is not vallenwood. If you look carefully at the grain you will see it is olive. There is a grove of wild olive not far from here."

Linsha tried it and found she could hobble around well enough to ease the pain in her ankle. Her expression of gratitude was thanks enough for Sir Hugh. She winked at the Knight and, using her stick, limped away to take a closer look at the Grandfather Tree's huge trunk. She glanced over her shoulder just once and saw the half-elf and the Knight sitting close together on the old log and quietly talking. It was as it should be.

The Feast of Dragon Blood

20

Crucible paced at the end of his chain and snorted a deep, rumbling rush of anger. The chain infuriated him. It was only bolted around one leg and it certainly was not strong enough to hold him, but it was the principle of the matter. The Tarmaks had put it on him to make a point, that he was chained to them and that he was not going to leave until they decided to let him go. He whipped his tail around in an agitated fit of rage, nearly squashing three inattentive guards, and stamped back to the tree that held the other end of the chain.

The movement set off the pain in his shoulders again. He twitched and squirmed to rub his back against the tree branches, but his efforts only made the pain more irritating. The barbed dart was starting to drive him mad. Every time he moved his forequarters, every time he lifted his wings or shrugged his shoulders or took a step, the barb rubbed a little deeper into muscles that were already swollen and inflamed. The wound was a constant source of nagging pain and frustration.

His thirst was beginning to annoy him as well. He

was a bronze dragon, a creature of land and water whose affinity for lakes, rivers, and seas always kept him near places of abundant water. These stupid Tarmaks did not seem to understand that. They had been marching beside the swift Toranth River for several days, and all they had allowed him to drink was a few buckets of water. Buckets! His throat and skin were so parched that he could have drunk a stock pond dry.

He twisted around to look at the river only a few hundred feet away. It was nearly dark, but he could smell the water and hear its rustle. He glared at the tree and made up his mind.

One quick precise beam of his breath weapon seared the tree in half lengthwise and melted through the chain. As the two halves of the large tree sheered sideways and crashed to the ground, he tugged his foot loose and galloped toward the river, ignoring the shouts of the Tarmaks behind him. Water splashed in sheets around his feet. He charged out into the fast-flowing current to the deepest channel of the river, stretched out his legs, and lowered his bulk into the cool water. He drank and splashed and drank again until he could feel his body relax and his thirst ease. Eddying around him, the water cooled his wound and washed the dust from his torn wings.

Finally the dragon submerged himself as deep as he could go in the river's bed and let his head rest on the water's surface. His eyes closed.

"Are you quite through?" a harsh voice shouted from the riverbank. He opened one eye and saw the Akkad-Ur standing on the bank, his guards around him holding torches and longbows.

"No," he grumbled.

"I could have my guards kill you," the Akkad-Ur warned.

"Don't bother," said Crucible in acid tones of resentment. "I will go nowhere. I just need water." His lean head floated near the bank like a large and bilious crocodile. "If you want to keep me alive so you can kill me later, you have to let me have more water than a bucket's worth."

The Akkad-Ur jerked his head at his guards to lower their weapons. He watched Crucible thoughtfully for a few minutes then said, "You should tell us if you are in need."

Crucible's hooded eyes glared balefully at him out of the darkness. "Very well. I need you to get this thing out of my back and let me go."

"Food and water will be sufficient."

"Then it had better be riverfuls of water. Not buckets."

"We are close to the river's ford. We will soon be entering the realm of Duntollik," the Akkad-Ur informed him. "What will you do when we enter the desert?"

Crucible snorted a huff of hot air and steam in a small geyser. "I know where we are," he growled. But he did not answer the question.

The Akkad-Ur shrugged. "Good. Then you know we will soon expect you to fight. When battle comes, I will place you in the front to decimate their forces. Whether there is water or not."

Crucible glowered at the Tarmak from his watery bed, his ears flattened to his head. "You can put me anywhere you want, but I will not kill innocent people."

"All dragons kill. They are the children of Kadulawa'ah. It is in their nature."

"Who is Kadulawaha?"

"The goddess of the Descent," replied the Akkad-Ur, ignoring the dragon's mispronunciation. "The rebellion of the sky gods was instigated by her and her children."

208

Crucible hissed another geyser of steam. "We are the children of Paladine. Keep your blue-skinned mythology to yourself."

The Tarmak crossed his arms and regarded the big bronze like an interesting specimen he was about to pin to a board. "I do not understand you. I offer you a partnership. I will give you lordship over Missing City. I will give you treasure, authority. I will give you freedom, if you join us willingly."

"I have seen how you deal with your allies," responded Crucible with a snarl. "The treasure you offer is stolen, the lordship rests on the bodies of my friends. The only freedom you will give me is death."

The Akkad-Ur went on without a pause as if he had not heard him. "And yet you throw it all away for a woman. A human woman who will age and die in only the blink of a draconic eye. You are a fool."

"Then I am a fool, for I will not fight for you."

"Then your woman dies."

"She is not my woman."

The Akkad-Ur crossed his arms. "I see. Then perhaps it will not bother you if I told you she is already dead."

Crucible's head reared out of the water, creating a wave that washed up the bank as far as the Akkad-Ur's sandled feet. His eyes glowed a fierce yellow; his wet horns glittered in the torchlight. His rational mind told him he was being baited, but his more passionate draconic nature burned with rage. "What do you mean?"

"Nothing, really," the Akkad-Ur said coolly. "I was merely making a point. You care very much for this woman."

But Crucible would not be placated. "What have you done to her? I want to see her now! Show me she is still alive!"

"I think not. I will leave that to your imagination. Is the Rose Knight still alive, waiting to come rescue you at her first opportunity? Or did she die in the slave pens after my officers made use of her?"

Crucible's roar shook the camp, sent the horses plunging in panic, and the Tarmaks running for their weapons. He sprang upright in falls of cascading water and sprang at the Akkad-Ur, who was still standing calmly on the bank. He reached a shallow shoal not far from the water's edge when the pain hit him. It exploded between his shoulder blades, seared up his neck and down his back, and burned into his brain like a firebrand. His strength turned to ash, and his legs fell out from under him. He crashed into the mud and gravel writhing in agony. Red ribbons of pain twisted through his mind. The dragonfear pulsed from the dragon's body in almost palpable waves, but this time the Akkad-Ur was ready. When the terror squeezed his belly and his men fell to their knees around him, he twisted his fist and brought his spell to an end.

The pain stopped and Crucible lay still, gasping in the shallow water.

"I fear you have forgotten, Dragon," said the Akkad-Ur, "who holds the end of your chain. The dart of the Abyssal Lance in your back has now moved another inch or two closer to your heart. It is nearly buried beneath your scales. Is this what you want? To die in consuming agony on a muddy riverbank?"

Crucible groaned. "I just want to see her."

"No. I think another form of persuasion would be more effective to curb your belligerence and change your mind about your participation." He snapped his fingers and two tall Keena priests in sleeveless robes came out of his tent carrying a large iron box suspended between two poles. They set the box down by the Akkad-Ur's feet, bowed, and handed him a pair of heavy leather gloves. Their faces expressionless, they stood back to watch.

The bronze raised a suspicious eye. He waited warily while the Akkad-Ur donned the gloves and unlocked the box. Using some care, he lifted the hinged lid and reached inside. He pulled out an oblong orb large enough to fill both hands, as sleek as polished metal, and the color of pale gold. A brass dragon egg. He set it on top of the box and angled it to his satisfaction.

Crucible recognized the egg and felt a bolt of dread go through him that was almost worse than the barbed dart. "No," he whispered.

"We keep these quite warm to incubate them," the Akkad-Ur informed him. "We have fourteen left. We had more, but we have used them for various things. I find the inherent power of magic in the embryos to be most useful."

The Akkad-Ur pulled out a large dagger. In front of Crucible's horrified gaze, he stabbed the blade into the top of the egg, pulled it out, and stabbed again. He paid no attention to the albumen and blood that trickled out from the break. Carefully measuring and stabbing, he cut a circular hole in the egg and pried off the top. An attendant brought a large cauldron.

Grief stricken, Crucible could only stare as the Akkad-Ur tipped the egg over and poured out the contents into the cauldron. He choked back a cry as a bloodied, half-formed embryo slid out and fell with a splat into the ruined contents of its egg.

"There are thirteen more," the Akkad-Ur said. "We will kill each one before your eyes if you do not obey my every command."

Crucible glared at him, hate in his glowing eyes.

"Do we understand each other?"

The dragon forced a nod. What he had just seen left him speechless.

The Tarmak turned his back on the dragon and raised his dripping dagger over his head. "The feast of dragon blood will be prepared tonight! Who will partake of the offering?"

A roar answered him as every warrior around him raised his weapon and shouted.

The two Keena collected the heavy cauldron and carried it to a large fire. While Crucible watched, grim and shaking, they chopped the embryo to bits, mixed its body back into the egg, and added powders and liquids until they had made a foul looking soup. Other priests gathered and began chanting and beating drums while the ghastly soup cooked. The call of the drums sounded through the huge camp and brought the Tarmaks crowding around the clearing. When the potion was cooked to everyone's satisfaction, the head priest pulled out the small, underdeveloped dragonet's skull, filled the brain pan with liquid, and gave it to the Akkad-Ur.

Bathed in torchlight, the Akkad-Ur faced the east and raised the skull in salute. "To the godson, Amarrel, Keeper of Dragons, Champion of the White Flame, beloved of the goddess, we who are about to fight in your name, salute you!" So saying, he brought the skull to his lips and drank the contents in one long swallow. The Tarmaks howled their approval in time to the beating of the drums.

Crucible turned away. He heard the warriors rush forward to get their smaller shares of the potion, but he could not watch it. He didn't know why they cooked and ate the baby dragon or what purpose it served for them. All he knew was the baby had been killed because of him, because he had been greedy for water and lost his temper. If Iyesta had been alive, she would never have forgiven him.

His thoughts went back to iron box. It was heavy and rather large. Where would the Tarmaks store thirteen of those things? And how did they keep them warm? He tried to dredge out of his memory everything he had seen in the massive column of Tarmaks, wagons, beasts of burden, horses, chariots, and the slave train, but he could not remember seeing anything large enough to haul thirteen of those big iron boxes. Maybe they were scattered throughout the column on various baggage wagons. He didn't know. Maybe the Akkad-Ur was bluffing and only a had a few while the remaining eggs stayed safely in Missing City. It did seem rather ridiculous to bring fourteen dragon eggs on an invasion. But how could he know for sure? Did he want to risk any more of the eggs?

Linsha and the dragon eggs. Two invisible lengths of chain far stronger than anything the Tarmaks could forge from steel.

Growling deep in his throat, Crucible curled up in the shallows of the river and brooded on revenge.

The Tree's Gift

21

"E xcuse me, Lady Linsha, my name is Danian. I have been asked to see you."

The Rose Knight looked up from her plate into two pairs of captivating eyes, one pair human and clouded beyond use, the other pair avian, beady black, and sparkling with intelligence. She felt Varia lean forward on her shoulder to stare at the other bird. The bird was a kestrel, a sleek and lovely predator.

The sight of the kestrel tweaked her memory, and she remembered. Leonidas had said something about a healer with a kestrel. He hadn't mentioned the man was blind. Intrigued, Linsha set aside her plate and climbed carefully to her feet. To her surprise she looked down on the healer. He was somewhat short for a Plainsman with a build that was slender and ropey like a pine tree toughened and stunted by the desert wind. His dark hair was cut short and his skin was deeply tanned.

The evening meal was almost over and the tribal bards and clan storytellers were preparing for the evening's entertainment. The feast had not been fancy, but the two tribes who had hosted it had worked hard to prepare a satisfying and hearty meal for the day's new-comers. It was tribal custom to start any gathering with a feast and songs that lasted far into the night before a large meeting was called. Linsha appreciated the food, and she knew the storytellers and singers would regale the crowd with war songs and tales of great bravery to excite their minds for coming battle. In truth, she didn't want to hear them. Perhaps she was getting too old for battles, but she had long ago given up looking for glory among the hacked and maimed bodies on the field.

"Healer," she said to Danian, "I don't know what you can do to help my ankle. The injury is several days old. But if you would like to leave this crowded place and come to our camp, I would be pleased to talk to you."

He cocked his head as if listening to something then nodded. "I will tell Wanderer I am leaving and we will go."

She watched him with interest as he wove his way unerring through the busy, crowded space under the tree set aside for feasting. If she hadn't seen the milky fog that obscured his eyes, she would never have guessed he was blind.

"The kestrel helps him see," a stranger said beside her.

Startled, she looked at the people around her and realized a taller, much younger man was waiting close by. By his unkempt red hair and paler skin, she knew without asking this boy was an outlander, a stranger like herself to the Plains.

"Who are you?" she asked, her astonishment making her question more abrupt than she meant.

He offered her a bashful grin. "My name is Tancred. I am not from around here. I am Danian's apprentice."

She gave him a smile back. "You sound as if you've had to repeat that a few times."

"A few. I ended up here by accident a few weeks ago, and I am still trying to explain myself."

Her brows lowered in confusion. "A few weeks ago? And you are an apprentice with a tribal healer? Already?"

"He is a healer and a shaman. And yes, I am his apprentice. It was all rather unexpected."

Linsha looked back to watch Danian. "He knows animism, as well. Or does his bird talk?"

"His bird does not talk," Varia replied in her ear with only the slightest hint of condescension in her tone.

They watched the healer talk to a tall, powerful looking man near the back of the crowd. The Plainsman nodded once and glanced Linsha's way. She caught his eye and made a bow as best she could with a walking staff and an owl on her shoulder. She had not had a chance to talk to Wanderer that evening, but she hoped to sometime before the confrontation with the Tarmak.

Danian came back, as unerringly as before, and with Tancred by his side, he followed Linsha out of the feasting grounds to the militia's camp. She could only hobble very slowly, even with the help the staff, but the two men made no complaint or comment. When they reached the camp, Linsha saw the site was empty at the moment, for everyone else was enjoying the food and the music on the distant side of the tree. The small fire had burned down to orange embers but was still hot enough to keep the pot of kefre warm for anyone who wanted some.

Danian obviously "saw" the camp, too. He steered Linsha to the fallen log seat and had her sit. "Tancred, stir up the fire so we can see."

Varia fluttered from Linsha's shoulder and perched beside her on the log, her round eyes fixed on the healer and his bird.

Linsha said nothing. She watched the healer carefully while he knelt in front of her, removed her boot, and examined her ankle with his fingers. He seemed to know what he was doing, in spite of his sightlessness. His long fingers stroked and prodded her joint, twisted it back and forth, and gently massaged her foot.

"It's not broken," he announced. "But I think you know that." He twisted his neck to look up at her. "It is badly sprained, but I might be able to repair some of the damage with your help."

"Mine?"

"Of course. You have a mystic talent, too. Not quite as good as Tancred's for healing. Different." He cocked his head as if pondering an unexpected discovery. "Still, I think it will be enough to help you get back on your feet."

"But I haven't been able to use mine for a while. Something is wrong."

"It is the dead."

Linsha stared hard at him "What did you say?"

"The spirits of the dead. They haven't left this world. I think they are feeding off our magic."

"How do you know? Have you seen them?"

"Yes. Some nights ago we were attacked by a raiding party. I had a vision and saw the souls of the dead rise from the bodies. But they didn't leave as they are supposed to do, and when I tried to use my powers to heal the wounded, the dead gathered around me and my magic failed." He paused and cocked his head again. "What is it? You are very quiet. Have you seen the dead?"

"Only one, and he came to warn me. But. I thought I was dreaming." She clasped her hands together. "Until we were attacked by brigands."

Her throat tightened and her head began to pound

217

with a sudden and wrenching sense of sadness for the friends she had lost. Could Danian be right? Falaius had said something similar once, several months ago, about the spirits of the dead remaining behind. Is that all there was to look forward to after death? Wandering this world and devouring magic? What did the spirits do with the power? Why couldn't they leave? Did her father know this?

"Is that how you got this injury?" asked Danian. "The brigands?"

Linsha started slightly and realized she had let her thoughts stray again. "Yes. I tripped over a dead draconian."

"Then let's see what we can do." He leaned forward on his knees and clasped Linsha's ankle in one hand. "Tancred, give me your hand. I want you to close your eyes and concentrate on what I am doing."

The redheaded apprentice tried to stifle a look of apprehension on his face. "Are you sure I can help with this?" he asked.

"Yes, lad. Or I would've asked the sentry over there. Now, Lady," he said to Linsha. "Just focus on your own power, and I will guide it to your ankle. With luck we'll be able to repair this before our magic fails."

Linsha glanced at Varia, who sat so quietly beside her. The owl bobbed her head once. Closing her eyes, Linsha let her body relax muscle by muscle from head to foot. She banished thoughts of death and spirits and turned her mind away from the outer world. Sounds from the feasting and the other camps around her went away beyond a wall of calm silence until all she could hear was the snap and crackle of the fire and the wind rustling the leaves of the Grandfather Tree overhead. Eventually even those fell to a profound silence that allowed her to listen to her own heartbeat. She reached deeper within her and concentrated on the magic power Goldmoon had taught her resided in her own heart. It lay there waiting, a warm, sparkling energy that infused her blood and needed only a gentle prod to go coursing through her body in a healing, energizing wave. She focused the energy down to her ankle and foot, and to her delight, found it was met by another magic far stronger and more assured than hers. It guided her power into the torn ligaments and broken blood vessels, sealing the leaks and repairing the damaged muscles. The pain of her ankle waned swiftly as the joint gently healed.

Then Linsha felt a faint tickle around her face and on her neck like the wings of insects or the light brush of fingers. Her concentration slipped. She recalled this tickling had happened every time she lost control of the magic. Immediately, the power she had drawn from her heart slipped out of her grasp and drained away, leaving nothing but a dull ache to thud in her ankle. Furiously, she wrenched herself out of the failed spell and jumped to her feet.

"Stop it!" she yelled at the darkness. "Why are you doing this?"

There was no answer. She hadn't really expected one. But on the furthest edges of her vision, she saw faint wispy shapes draw back from her, their ghostly hands held out in supplication.

"You want magic?" she shouted at the figures. "Go bother the Tarmaks!" They have plenty of magic!"

The images vanished completely and Linsha found herself standing by the fire and feeling a little foolish.

Varia hooted at her.

She turned to see both birds and men staring at her. Tancred's freckled face was grinning and even Danian's weathered face had an uplifted expression. A sentry nearby and several people within earshot of her shouts also looked over to see what the yelling was about. Linsha felt her face grow hot.

"You're standing without the walking stick," Tancred pointed out.

Still annoyed, Linsha sat down again on the log.

"You saw them this time, didn't you?" Danian asked as he gently manipulated her joint.

"I'm not sure," she sighed. "I thought I saw . . . something. It was very faint."

He wrapped her foot again and slipped her boot back on for her. "Good! We did better than I hoped. Your ankle is not completely healed. You will have to be careful for a few days, but most of the damage was repaired. You have a strong spirit and a powerful will. That is probably why you saw the souls of the dead this time."

Linsha drew a deep breath and let it out slowly. She was suddenly very tired. She could not fathom the mysteries of the dead at this time and didn't have the mental strength to try. But maybe this shaman could help her with something else. She found some cups and poured hot kefre for the three of them, then told Danian and Tancred about Crucible and the Abyssal Lance. She had only meant to explain the barest facts, but the healer started asking quiet questions and before she could stop herself, she told him the whole story of her friendship with the bronze from their first meeting in Sanction to the disastrous night in the courtyard when the Tarmaks fired the dart into his back. Tancred stared at her through the whole telling, his mouth slightly ajar. Danian listened intently and sipped his drink.

"Can you think of anything that could help him?" she asked when she was through. "Falaius said the shamans of your tribes might have an answer."

Danian rubbed a gentle finger down the breast of his

kestrel and sadly shook his head. "I don't know about the others, but I have no experience or knowledge of this kind of evil. This spell is very unusual. You say the dart was fired into his back while he was shapeshifting?" At her nod, he rubbed his chin thoughtfully and added, "Then you will probably have to remove it the same way. But how you can do it without injuring him further, I don't know."

"There is always the Grandfather Tree," Tancred said. A slight blush crept up his fair face.

"The Tree?" Linsha said dubiously.

Danian gave a light chuckle. "Tancred is right. This Tree was a gift from the god. It is old. *Very* old. Its roots go deep. Its branches reach toward the stars. If you are quiet and if you listen, the Tree may sometimes grant you a vision. It is a great gift the Tree gives only to those who are worthy. I would not promise you that it would give you an answer, but it has helped others."

Linsha's green eyes shifted to Tancred and saw his blush deepen. "It gave me a future," he said softly.

"Come, Tancred. It grows late. This Lady Knight and I both are weary. Lady Linsha, I hope to see you again before we depart. If you need me again, send this inestimable owl."

Linsha gave her heartfelt thanks to both men and watched as they walked out of the firelight into the darkness toward their own camp.

"A tree," she said skeptically. "That was something I hadn't thought of."

"Don't discount it," Varia replied. "I have been in the canopy of this Tree, and it is far greater than a mere plant."

Linsha shrugged her shoulders and went to find her blanket. Her ankle, she was pleased to note, was much improved. It was still discolored and a little sore, but she could put weight on it and walk without too much discomfort.

Bathed in the glow of the small fire, she wrapped her blanket around her shoulders and lay down beside the scant shelter of the log. In the distance, she could hear the strains of an old harp. The tree overhead rustled softly in the night wind. Exhausted by travel, injury, and the use of her magic, Linsha fell asleep before the harp music finished and slept soundly the rest of the night.

Linsha awoke at sunrise the next morning and found Sir Hugh, Mariana, Falaius, and all of the human militia stretched out in their bedrolls and still asleep. Only the centaurs of the militia had chosen to stay elsewhere to visit with kinfolk and friends from the northern clans. Obviously, everyone had enjoyed the wine and the food from the night before.

She rose, stretched, and went to build up the fire for a morning meal and was pleased to see her ankle had improved still more during the night. She would wrap it for support for the next couple of days and use Sir Hugh's walking staff, and maybe she would be fit for battle when they finally faced the Tarmak army.

The rest of the day went by swiftly without the pleasures of feasting and dancing. The atmosphere under the great tree turned serious and more grim, as the leaders of the barbarian tribes, the chieftains of the centaur clans, and the leaders of the militia met and discussed the Tarmak army. Scouts and messengers arrived and departed in an almost constant stream, bringing news from reinforcements that were on the way and word of the progress of the invaders into Duntollik. Spies reported seeing a metallic dragon in the midst of the

Tarmak army and claimed he had burned several small farmsteads along the river and was killing livestock.

Linsha attended the meeting with Falaius, Mariana, and Sir Hugh, and with their help and input told the tale of the fall of Missing City and the deaths of the two dragonlords. Rumors of Thunder's disappearance and Iyesta's death had circulated through the Plains, but this was the first time the full tale had been told in front of the gathered tribes. She also explained Crucible's presence with the Tarmaks and asked for any help that might relieve him of the dart, but as Danian predicted, none of the shamans or healers present knew what to do. It was a terrible disappointment.

By midafternoon, Wanderer, Falaius, and a centaur named Carrebdos of the Windwalker clan emerged as the leaders of the Plains confederation. They met alone for a time to discuss a defense of the eastern Plains then called for the other chiefs to voice their ideas and suggestions. Slowly a plan came together.

Linsha was still sitting on the fringes of the gathered leaders listening to the talk when four riders in tattered Solamnic uniforms rode under the Tree and asked to speak to the tribal leaders. She knew who they were in a heartbeat and eased out of their direct line of sight. She worked her way forward to better hear what they said, keeping others between her and the riders so they would not spot her. Warily, she watched while they dismounted and were greeted by Wanderer and the others. Falaius, she noted, did not look pleased to see Sir Remmik.

The men and centaurs talked quietly for a few minutes while everyone watched. Sir Remmik, his lean face impassive, handed a scroll to Falaius and waited silently while the scroll was read and passed around. A rumble of displeasure began to grow among the leaders.

223

"Do you believe these words?" Linsha heard the Legion commander say to the Knight.

Sir Remmik's patrician gaze swept over the crowded onlookers as if taking their measure. For just a second Linsha saw his eyes hesitate when he looked in her direction, then his gaze swept on over the faces of militia, tribesmen, and centaurs. A small shiver slid through her. Had he seen her?

"I do not recommend them one way or another," Remmik replied. "You, too, have seen how these Tarmaks fight. I was given orders to deliver them and little choice but to obey."

"And will you return with an answer?"

He nodded. "I have no choice. The Tarmaks still hold the rest of my Knights. I will not abandon them to torment and death."

Wanderer snatched the scroll back from a chieftain and tore it fiercely in half. "The answer is no."

Sir Remmik took the gesture without surprise. He glanced at the leaders again and said, "Is that the answer of all of you?"

Centaurs and humans alike raised their fists and shouted their war cries until the air under the tree shook and people from outlying camps came running.

"We will fight," said Falaius.

Sir Remmik bowed once and mounted his horse. But he did not leave immediately. He reined the animal around to face his former allies. In a move that surprised them all, he brought his fist to his chest in a salute and half bowed from his saddle.

"I respect your decision," he said. "You have made the honorable choice." Ignoring the possibility of a reply, he left the gathering at the Grandfather Tree and, followed by his Knights, cantered his horse east out into the desert.

Linsha sadly watched them go.

"They didn't even stay for tea," Sir Hugh said quietly beside her.

Night came cold and windy, accompanied by clouds rolling in from the southwest. As soon as the meetings and the talks were over, the leaders and their people returned to their own camps to spread the news and prepare for war. Lanterns were lit under the Tree, but because of the wind, campfires were kept to a minimum. Most suppers that evening were eaten cold. No one suggested a feast. Guards were posted around the Tree and by the picket lines, and almost everyone retired to their beds early that night.

Linsha was no exception. Varia was off hunting somewhere, and Linsha was still tired from the past days and weary of company. With an apology to Mariana, she moved her blanket out to the edge of their camp where she could see the sky through the fringe of the great tree's canopy. A combination of leaves and sky seemed pleasant to her while she rolled up in her blanket and stretched out on the grass to sleep.

The problem was she couldn't fall asleep. Despite the weariness that weighed down her body, her mind would not stop thinking. She lay on her back, her eyes wide open, and stared up at the Tree above her.

Perhaps it was the noise that disturbed her. It wasn't a manmade noise. The camps under the canopy were quiet. If she turned her head, she could see the dark, motionless lumps of sleeping men and staked tents, a few glowing lamps, and the occasional movement of a sentry. No, it was the wind that provided its own racket. Without anything to really slow it down, the wind stampeded across the desert, roaring and howling and kicking up dust before it. It swept over the hill where the Tree grew, blowing through the grass and brush and pushing through the Tree's canopy. The roots of the ancient tree went too deep for a mere blustery wind to disturb it. After all, it had survived the great storm of the early summer. But the Tree still moved and creaked and slowly swayed in the night wind. Its leaves rustled and shook; its branches rubbed and banged together; the trunk groaned like an old man in the impudent rush of the wind. It sounded to Linsha like an entire forest of vallenwoods rather than just one tree.

She looked up into the treetop at the dancing, swaying branches and tried to think about Danian's words. What had he meant when he told her the tree sometimes granted visions? What sort of visions? Were they prophetic visions or visions given in response to some sort of prayer? The barbaric tribes of the Plains were very spiritual people, heavily dependent on their connection to the natural world around them. They believed everything had a lifeforce that was attached to everything else. It was little wonder they looked on this Tree with nothing short of adoration. But could it truly give answers? Would prayer help?

Linsha was not very good at prayer. She had grown up in a world that had lost its gods just before she was born, and while her parents raised her with the belief that someday the gods would return, she had not found much use in praying to deities who weren't around to listen. If the rumors of this One God were true, maybe she would learn to pray, but until then she would have to make do with simple speech. She had told the story of Crucible to the gathering in the presence of the Tree. If it truly listened, then it already knew what she needed. There wasn't much point in belaboring it.

Her hand slid up to her neck and found the gold chain with the dragon scales under her tunic. Her fingers closed around them, and she drew some comfort from their reminder of her friends. The wind roared and rushed around her. Her eyes slowly slid closed.

She wasn't aware of sleeping, but after a while she became conscious of the fact that a light was shining red through her eyelids. Thinking it was dawn, she sat up in her blanket and stretched her neck and arms. She was still sore and stiff, and she didn't feel rested at all. Reluctantly, she opened her eyes . . . and choked on a cry. Her eyes blinked with sudden tears. She crawled to her knees and knelt on the blanket, her heart pounding.

The light she'd thought was the sun actually emanated from a huge metallic dragon crouched on her belly only feet away from the edge of the Tree's canopy and Linsha's blanket. Her large expressive eyes gleamed down on Linsha with pleasure. Her sleek head and polished horns glowed with a pale translucent gold light of their own.

"Iyesta!" Linsha whispered in delight.

The dragon inclined her head to Linsha until her gleaming nose almost brushed Linsha's head. Giving a slight nod, she lifted her neck and plunged her nose into the leaves of the Tree's canopy. Gently the apparition snipped two leaves from the vallenwood and let them fall to Linsha's side.

The bond formed between a dragon and a human is worth the effort to forge it, the dragon's voice said inside her mind.

"How?" Linsha begged. "How do I help him?"

The Tree of Life will guide your hand.

"Will you stay and help me?" Linsha cried.

There was no answer. The wind roared and the light vanished, leaving Linsha rubbing her eyes and crying

227

in the darkness. She groped frantically for the leaves, found them, and held them tightly in her hands. With tears running down her cheeks, she leaped to her feet and limped out from under the tree into the open where the chill wind tore at her clothes and whipped her hair around her face. She turned around and around to search for any sign of the big brass dragon and saw what she expected. Nothing. The night hung densely dark under the clouds. There was no hint of a golden light, no sign that Iyesta had truly been there. The sentries still paced on their rounds, the horses dozed in their picket lines, the men and women of the gathering continued to sleep undisturbed. The vision of Iyesta had been hers alone.

Her face still wet with tears, Linsha took the leaves and crawled back under her blanket. She wasn't certain what Iyesta meant for her to do with these leaves, but they had been granted to her for a reason, and until she understood more, she was not going to let the leaves off her person. She curled around them and lay still, listening to the voices of the wind and the Tree.

The next thing she knew it was dawn and Varia was waking her.

A re you going to make a habit of this?" Linsha said to the owl sitting on her chest.

Varia trilled a bit and clicked her beak. She peered into Linsha's face, so close the woman could see the tiny feathers on her eyelids. "You didn't sleep well?"

Linsha pulled her blanket tighter around her shoulders and closed her eyes again. "No. I had the oddest dreams."

"I have news that is not a dream. Sir Remmik and his Knights did not go far. They are camped in a small ravine only an hour's ride away."

Linsha's eyes creaked open. "What? They left yesterday afternoon. They should be miles away by now. If they were returning to the Tarmaks." She sat up to think. "Did they look all right? Was something wrong?"

"They looked much the same to me . . . but—" The owl broke off. She looked down at Linsha's lap. "What are those? Are those leaves? You're not supposed to pull things off the Tree!"

A big grin lightened the worry lines on Linsha's face. She picked up the leaves and held them up to the cold light of dawn. "Zivilyn be thanked. It was not a dream! These were a gift from the Tree!"

"The Tree?"

Linsha lifted the leaves in the palm of her hand. They were still as green and fresh. "Iyesta said I could use them to help Crucible."

"Iyesta . . . " the owl said in disbelief.

"Well, a vision of her. It must have been. She picked the leaves from the Tree and gave them to me."

The owl's eyes widened to dark circles. "What are you supposed to do with them?"

"I don't know."

Varia looked relieved. "As long as you did not pick them." Then her demeanor changed again, and she fluffed her feathers and shifted her weight from one foot to another. "Linsha, there is a Knight waiting out there at the farthest guard post. He wants to talk to you."

"So why doesn't he come into the camp?"

"Because he only wants to talk to you. I overheard him talking to the sentry who would not leave his post to bring a message until his relief came. So the Knight is just sitting out there waiting for someone to get you. I thought I'd better warn you."

"Who is it?"

"Sir Korbell."

Linsha cast a quick glance to the east where the clouds had rolled away during the night. The sun's rim already warmed the distant horizon and cast its level light under the skirt of the Grandfather Tree. People were stirring in the camps and smoke was beginning to rise from cooking fires.

"When do the guards usually change?"

"Around now."

Linsha nodded, her mind already made up. "Then let's go see what he wants."

"Linsha, don't go alone," Varia said. "I don't like this. Sir Korbell is one of Sir Remmik's bootlickers. Take Sir Hugh with you."

"He has guard duty," Linsha replied while she rolled the leaves carefully in a scrap of fabric and tucked them under her shirt. "I don't need an escort. I'm only going to talk to one Knight."

"What Knight?" Mariana's voice said behind her. The half-elf came, stretching her long limbs, and joined her friend in the growing sunlight.

Linsha quickly told her about the Solamnic Knight waiting to see her out by the guard posts.

The captain agreed with Varia. "Don't go alone. I'll go with you. And just to be on the safe side, Varia, why don't you keep a watch for us but stay out of sight?"

Pleased for the company, Linsha picked up her walking stick and went to get her weapons and the bridles for the horses. The two women decided not to bother with saddles and retrieved their horses from the lines. By the time they were mounted bareback and ready to leave, the relieved guard from the outpost found them and reported the Knight's message. Varia fluttered up into the Tree where she could watch them ride out to meet the Knight.

About two miles away from the Grandfather Tree they found the guard outpost where the Solamnic Knight was waiting. He stood by his horse, his arms crossed and his face sour while the new centaur sentry watched him like a vulture hoping for a meal.

"Sir Korbell," Linsha said, her voice deliberately even and inoffensive.

The Knight saluted her as a Knight of superior rank, although he did not look pleased to do so. "Lady, Knight Commander Sir Jamis uth Remmik requests your presence for a meeting at our campsite."

Linsha looked down at him and frowned. She was in no mood for games. "Pull the other one, Korbell. It has bells on."

"This is a legitimate request. He would like to talk to you before we return to the Tarmaks."

"Why?" Mariana snapped.

Sir Korbell did not look pleased to see the captain either. "I requested that the Rose Knight come alone."

"Well, I guess that bit got lost in the passing," Mariana said coldly. "If she goes, I am going with her. So tell us why Sir Remmik wants to talk, or we'll turn around now and leave you with this fine centaur who would rather spit you on his spear than look at you." A ferocious glare twisted Sir Korbell's face before he fought it off and tried to look reassuring. "As you choose. The Knight Commander has information about the Tarmaks he wants to pass on—and a message from the Legionnaire, Lanther."

Linsha did not move a muscle. "Why didn't he give it to me at the Grandfather Tree?"

"The gathering was too crowded, too busy. Sir Remmik wants only to talk to you, and quickly. We must get back to the others."

"Uh-uh. I seem to remember the last time I saw Sir Remmik face to face he accused me of aiding the enemy and breaking my oath to the Knighthood. I can't imagine why he would want to see me alone except to try to arrest me again."

"Sir Remmik told me to tell you he gives his word he will not arrest you."

Linsha and Mariana exchanged a long, thoughtful look. "It's a risk," Mariana said under her breath.

"I know," Linsha replied in a like manner. "It smells to Palanthas like a trap."

"You know him better than I do. Would he betray you?"

"Before the war? No. Sir Remmik was a man of his word. His honor meant much to him. Now? I don't know. He has suffered much."

"So have you. So have we all!"

Sir Korbell cleared his throat with a forceful rasp. "There is little time," he reminded them.

The half-elf turned her back to him and said to Linsha, "What will you do?"

"He says Sir Remmik has a message from Lanther." She sighed, knowing her mind was made up. "Perhaps he has information worth listening to."

"We must go with care."

"Agreed." Linsha turned to Sir Korbell. "How far is your camp?"

"About four miles east of here," Korbell replied with bad grace.

"All right," she said, hoping this would be worth the ride. "We'll come."

Without further speech, Sir Korbell kicked his horse into a trot and rode into the sunrise, obviously expecting the women to follow him. He rode fast in a straight line back the way he had come, with no effort to lose his tracks or mislead anyone who might be following them.

Linsha and Mariana followed side by side. The strong winds of the night before had dropped to a mere breeze in the light of the new day, and the sky shone a brilliant cloudless blue. It would have been a pleasant ride, if it not for the person who awaited them.

As Sir Korbell had said, the ride to the Knights' camp was only a few miles away. In less than an hour they rode into a shallow ravine worn away by wind and rain and found Sir Remmik standing by a small fire waiting for them. He smiled a steely smile when he saw them, and his gray eyes were cold as deep winter ice. The two women slowed their horses to a walk and approached cautiously. Walls of weathered rock rose about ten feet on either side of a floor just wide enough for the two riders to pass through. About fifteen feet away from Sir Remmik, they stopped their horses and studied their surroundings. The camp sat in a widened curve of the wash, still dimmed in morning shadow by the eroded walls. They could see Sir Remmik standing by a small fire and Sir Korbell dismounting by several horses tied nearby. There was no sign of the other two Knights.

Linsha felt the hairs on the back of her neck rise. She and Mariana glanced at each other, both conveying the same sense of alarm.

Sir Remmik held out his hands to show he held no weapons. "Please dismount, Majere."

Linsha's hand slid closer to her sword. She suddenly wished she hadn't left her saddle behind. If they had to make a run for it, she was going to want a sturdier, less slippery seat. "I don't think I will, Sir Remmik. Just tell me what you want."

"Very well. Is it true that you have been passing information to the Tarmaks for a year and a half? Is it true you helped in their invasion and with the battle for the city? Is it also true that you gave away vital secrets about the Scorpion Wadi and its defenses that led to the slaughter of the militia?"

Linsha's mouth fell open in shock. Her face burned a fiery red. She was so taken aback by his sudden and vehement accusations she could not make a sound.

Mariana had no such trouble. "How dare you!" she shouted. "Where did you hear that dung heap of lies? How could you possibly believe it of one your own Knights?"

A loud, insistent alarm started going off in Linsha's head. Sir Remmik would not have lured her out here just to shout vile accusations at her. He had to be planning something. "Mariana," she whispered out of the side of her mouth. "We've got to get out of here."

The half-elf was in complete agreement. She backed her horse out of Linsha's way and was about to wheel it around when Sir Remmik raised his hands to stop her.

"No! Wait! You misunderstand. I had to ask."

The two women were so surprised they pulled their restive horses to a stop and stared at the older man. His words had been clipped as if he loathed saying them, but his tone had been almost conciliatory.

"Where are the others?" Linsha demanded.

"On guard duty, of course," Sir Remmik said. "This is a Solamnic Camp."

Linsha made no effort to move her hand away from her sword or lessen the look of distrust on her fair face. She only lifted her chin and asked, "What do you want, Sir Remmik? I know where those accusations come from, and how badly you'd like to believe them. But I will not sit here and be insulted."

The Knight commander lowered his hands. An expression crossed his face as if he had just tasted bitter gall. "I know. I have had much time to think during the ride through the desert. I am no fool. The Akkad-Ur is treacherous and ambitious. He betrayed Thunder, the mercenaries, and the gods know who else to take our city. You have given me reason to doubt your loyalties in the past, but the more I thought about it, the more the Akkad-Ur's interest in you raised my suspicions. His tale rings true: there is a spy in our midst. And I believe that spy helped murder Sir Morrec. But I am guessing his words hide a poison that has been working against us for months." He stepped away from the fire and pointed a finger at Linsha. "Tell me now, Majere," he said forcefully, "give me *one* reason to believe you now. Just one."

Linsha felt the silence ring in her ears, for she hardly knew what to say. Only two words came to her mind and they were enough for her.

"The dragons," she said in a loud, clear voice.

She was about to add more when something thin snaked down from above, looped around her chest, and pulled tight, pinning her arms to her sides. She saw a similar rope catch Mariana before she was yanked off her mount and dropped heavily on the rocky ground. Their horses squealed in fright and bolted out of the ravine.

Remmik shouted something to Sir Korbell and drew his sword, then Linsha heard an odd whining noise and a thunk. Something heavy fell to the ground. She twisted her neck and saw Sir Korbel flat on the dirt with a long Tarmak arrow in his chest.

Winded and angry, Linsha struggled to escape from the ropes and climb to her feet, but two blue-skinned Brutes dropped down from the top of the ravine and closed in on her before she could stand upright. Linsha got in one well-placed kick before a Tarmak fist landed on her jaw and knocked her almost senseless. She knew Mariana was struggling just as hard, but neither she nor Mariana could fight efficiently when they were lying on their backs with their arms roped to their sides.

Her head ringing from the blow, Linsha felt herself flipped over to her belly and her hands tied behind her back. Her feet were tied next. The men then dragged her to Sir Remmik, who was still standing by the fire. He had been disarmed and was flanked by two more warriors. They brought Mariana over bound the same way.

Linsha glared up at the Knight Commander through

the sweat and dust and blood around her eyes. "You bastard!" Her green eyes were dark like the clouds before a violent storm. "You gave your word."

He stared down at her impassively. "I have nothing to do with this."

More Knights were shouting, and the two who had been keeping watch were shoved into the camp, stumbling and cursing. They were followed by four more Tarmak. The Tarmaks disarmed them, trussed them, and left them bound beside Linsha and Mariana.

The leader of the Tarmak force strolled over to Sir Remmik and shook a finger under his nose. "That one," he said, pointing to Linsha, "is ours. She is not to be harmed." He grinned. In his own guttural language he issued orders to his warriors, and they began to round up the horses and tie the prisoners on the animals' backs.

Linsha closed her eyes and fought to bring her heart and her breathing back under control.

"So the Tarmaks have come to your rescue once again," Sir Remmik said, his voice full of acid.

"Shut your gob, you stupid fool," Mariana retorted. "You led them to us and handed Linsha to them on a platter. You just can't see it, can you? The Tarmaks don't want to rescue their spy. They want her to help keep Crucible under control."

Sir Remmik did not reply.

Neither did Linsha. She was angry beyond words. Angry at Sir Remmik, angry that her body was hurting in every muscle again, angry that she had walked into another trap. Worst of all, it appeared she was going to be taken back to the Tarmaks and the Akkad-Ur where they could use her to coerce Crucible to obey.

At least this time she was returning to Crucible with some hope. The leaves of the Grandfather Tree

237

lay hidden in her undertunic, and the words of
Danian and the image of Iyesta lay hidden in her
mind. All she had to do was put them together and
deduce what she was supposed to do. Maybe Lanther
could help her. She had a feeling she would be seeing
him all too soon.

he Tarmak army was still on the move when the trackers returned with their prisoners late in the afternoon of the next day. The forces of the Akkad-Ur had crossed the river two days before, but rather than follow the example of the elves and strike straight across the interior desert, the Tarmaks turned southwest to follow the Run around the southern border of Duntollik. Although this route would also take them through harsh desert lands, it provided a road for guidance and it paralleled the Red Rose River, the western branch of the Toranth, for over a hundred miles. It led to the small towns of Stone Rose and Willik and eventually to Duntol, the largest city in the area. The Akkad-Ur, a veteran of many campaigns, knew he did not need to pursue the band of militia and their tribal reinforcements into the wilds of the desert. Eventually, the defenders of Duntollik would have to come to him.

Under orders from the Akkad-Ur, the trackers took the prisoners directly to the slave gangs and turned them over to the Tarmak overseer. The overseer cut them loose from the horses, chained their feet, and forced them to march in front of him until the Akkad-Ur called a halt for the night at sundown. As the army settled into its camp for some rest, the overseer separated the rest of the Knights of Solamnia and added them to Linsha's group, which he kept under heavy guard in a place a little apart from the other slaves. The Knights milled around for a short while then sat apart from Linsha and Mariana and waited.

Linsha, too, waited with some trepidation. Although no one had said anything, she was certain they were being kept aside for the Akkad-Ur to interrogate. After all, she and Mariana had been with the tribal confederation for two days, and Sir Remmik and his escort had ridden through the camps. They all were probably due for some questioning, and Linsha doubted it would be pleasant.

She wondered, too, about a reunion with Lanther. She had missed his presence and his crooked smile, but they had not parted in the best of circumstances. Would he be angry? She could see him standing at the edge of the slave camp, his arms crossed, his weight shifted to his good leg, his rugged face glowering at the Tarmak guards as they watched the prisoners.

Thoughts of Crucible crossed her mind as well. She and the others had been brought in slung across the backs of their horses. It was hard to see anything when your nose and face are being bumped and rubbed by the rib cage of a horse. She hadn't seen Crucible, but she knew he was still there by the distant sound of a dragon roar shortly after the army made camp.

The night grew later, and still there was no sign of the Akkad-Ur or anyone else of authority. No one brought them water or food or gave any indication that they were supposed to do anything more than wait. A new moon slowly settled to the west, and a cold breeze sprang up. Sometime near midnight, Linsha thought she heard an owl cry far away. And that was all. The warriors of the Tarmak slept, while the prisoners shivered in the wind and waited for day.

The army was awake and preparing to move in the early light of morning when the Akkad-Ur and his guards rode down the lines to the rear of the camp where the wagons were being loaded and oxen hitched to their yokes. Among the dust and the crack of whips, they rode swiftly, their blue-painted skins an odd contrast to the yellows, browns, and dusty reds around them. They stopped their horses by the small group of prisoners and dismounted.

The overseer was already busy with the tasks of the day, but he dropped his work on his second underling and hurried over to the greet the Akkad-Ur.

Mariana, Linsha, the Knights, and Sir Remmik climbed warily to their feet, as their guards moved aside and formed a loose square around them. The Akkad-Ur's escort filled in the line behind the prisoners and he strode to their front.

The busy slaves and drivers close by seemed to sense something was about to happen and they stopped work to watch. Lanther crept closer, his face grim.

"Sir Remmik, did you fulfill your task?" the Akkad-Ur demanded of the Knight.

"I did," he replied coolly. "The answer was no. They are determined to fight."

"Good. It is much better that way."

"Akkad-Ur," said the Solamnic commander in a firm voice. "You told me if I returned with the reply, you would free my men."

The Akkad-Ur inclined his mask. "That is true. However, you disobeyed me, and you had to be brought back by my men. I did not ask you to apprehend this woman."

Sir Remmik threw a scathing look at the guards around him. "I did not. I arranged a meeting with her to discuss Solamnic matters. Your warriors interrrupted that meeting and apprehended all of us."

"Solamnic matters!" The Akkad-Ur sneered. "What have you left to discuss with a traitor?"

Sir Remmik drew himself up to his full height and gave the Tarmak his chilliest patrician glare. "The possibility that she is not a traitor," he said. "And that you are a liar."

"It is unimportant. The Solamnics are no longer of use." The Akkad-Ur raised his hand. Swords flashed in the sunlight as the Tarmak guards drew their long blades. Before anyone could move, they slew six of the unarmed Knights. The rest scrambled in a sudden panic to escape from the tall warriors. Sir Remmik yelled at his men to stand their ground, and he leaped like a madman on a warrior attacking a wounded Knight.

Shouts and cries of horror came from the watching slaves, who crowded closer.

The Knight Commander was so distracted trying to defend his men that he did not see the Akkad-Ur attack the women. The Tarmak descended on Mariana and Linsha like an executioner, pulling a vicious-looking spiked battle-ax from a strap behind his back. "As for you," he bellowed at Linsha, "you tried to escape, but you will never have that opportunity again!"

Even while he spoke he turned slightly, lunged, and stabbed the spiked end into the half-elf's stomach. He wrenched the point upward through her stomach and into her lungs. Blood splashed over his hands.

Sir Remmik heard Linsha scream, an appalled cry of fury and grief that wrenched his attention around to her. He turned and saw Mariana vomit a bout of crimson blood. Her hands groped at the metal spike in her abdomen, but she was already dying. Her skin went deathly pale beneath the splattered blood. She sagged to her knees, her face a mask of disbelief and agonizing pain. When the Akkad-Ur pulled his ax out of her body, she pitched forward at Linsha's feet, and her blood pooled on the graveled ground.

Reacting without thought, Linsha kicked the ax from the Akkad-Ur's hand and sent it spinning to the ground. She landed another kick on his stomach that doubled him over and launched herself after the fallen weapon.

But Sir Remmik was faster. The Knight Commander snatched the ax from the dirt and threw himself at the Akkad-Ur just as the guards reached him. The two combatants fell to the ground locked together in the Knight's death grip. The golden mask slipped off and clanged to the ground.

There was a shout and abruptly everything stopped. The Tarmak guards froze, their swords pointed at Sir Remmik's throat. The Knight paused, the ax blade pressed to the Akkad-Ur's neck. A silence closed in, and the tension crackled through the violent tableau.

Sir Remmik stared bleakly at his men. Besides Linsha, only three other Knights were standing and two of them were badly wounded. The rest lay motionless on the blood-soaked ground. His eyes switched to Mariana and recognized that she was dead as well. Regret clouded his gaze, then he looked up and found Linsha's green eyes staring at him unflinching, the anger and sadness still burning in the depths of her clear green gaze. The very uncomfortable feeling that had begun to creep over his thoughts on the trail to the Grandfather Tree was now forged into a solid conviction.

"You are not in the service of the Tarmak," he said

to her alone, ignoring the swords at his throat and the general in his grip.

The Akkad-Ur answered for her. "I wish she was. She is the most stubborn and loyal female I have ever had the pleasure to meet."

Sir Remmik's eyes closed. He was breathing heavily under the weight of the larger Tarmak across his chest. "So, you were lying to me," he said to the Akkad-Ur.

"It was effective. You brought her out where my men could recapture her. You have been a most useful tool. But now—" he dared a gesture at the warriors around him. "We are in a standoff. You wish to kill me, and they wish to kill you. What do we do?"

"Let my men go," Sir Remmik said forcefully. *"Honor your word.* You have dishonored me and slaughtered my unarmed men without reason. You have betrayed us. Release the Knights—*all* of them. Or we die together. Now."

"There is no need for both of us to die. You surprise me. I can count on one hand the number of men who have brought me to my back. Would you fight me to free your Knights and yourself?"

"What? A duel?" Sir Remmik hissed, his hand still firm on the axe at the Akkad-Ur's neck. "I could just kill you now."

"And you and your Knights would die a moment later."

"You will kill them anyway."

"By the sacred gold mask of Kadulawa'ah that I wear, I swear I will free your men if you choose to fight."

"If I fight, you must free Linsha as well."

"Very well." The Akkad-Ur smiled a feral grimace. *"Ket-rhild!"* he said to his men. "A challenge!"

The guards stood back, talking excitedly. The Tarmaks were a warrior society who placed much emphasis on honor and the glory of single combat. And they always enjoyed watching their leader slaughter an inept human.

Sir Remmik pulled his weight off the ax and stood up. He did not look at Linsha again.

One of the guards lifted a curved ram's horn and blew three blasts that were quickly answered from somewhere near the front of the line. The entire Tarmak army stopped what it was doing and paused while the high ranking officers hurried to the call of the Akkad-Ur. Meanwhile, the other guards hurried away from the dead Solamnic Knights and reformed a larger square in a clear, open area. Sir Remmik was quickly and firmly escorted to the square and placed in a corner. He was given a stool to sit on, honeyed wine to drink, and a light offering of food to revive his strength. Weapons were brought to him for his inspection. The Akkad-Ur occupied the opposite corner and received the same preparations.

***

While all this bustling activity was going on around her, Linsha crouched beside Mariana's body and bowed her head. There were no tears in her eyes, because she was too numb, too full of disbelief. Her head ached with unshed tears, her belly churned with rage. She could not accept that Mariana was dead. All she could think about was how she would tell Sir Hugh.

Hands gripped her arms and pulled her gently to her feet. She saw a glimpse of Lanther's vivid blue eyes and buried her face in his shoulder. "I should never . . . have let her . . . come with me," she said. "She wanted to make sure I would be safe." Her throat ached with a grief she could not articulate.

The Legionnaire wrapped his arms around her and held her so tightly she could hear his heartbeat. "She was your friend, Linsha," he said in a choked voice. "You would have done the same for her."

She rested there for a brief space of time, appreciating his comfort and strength. Then a groan of pain penetrated the hum of noise that surrounded them. It drew Linsha's attention back to the wounded Knights and her duty. She pulled herself back under control and wiped her face on her sleeves. Relieved to have something else to think about for the moment, she took Lanther's hand and hurried to help them.

One Knight was unharmed and greeted Linsha with gratitude. Together, he and Linsha moved the two wounded men into the shade of a clump of tall thornbushes and began to examine their wounds. The overseer sent a few slaves to carry away Mariana and the dead Knights and bury them in the desert sand before the vultures arrived.

Linsha and the Knight did what they could for the wounded, but she did not give them much hope. Their wounds were severe. They had no healers, no herbs, no bandages, and unless the Tarmak took pity on them and let them ride in wagons, they had little chance of surviving the next march.

"Let me keep a watch on them," the Knight said to her. "Go and witness Sir Remmik's duel. Someone should be there for him."

Linsha was sure Sir Remmik would rather have anyone else than her witness his duel. "I don't think—" she began, until she remembered that one of the wounded Knights was this man's best friend. Her eyes strayed to the bloody spot where Mariana had died, and she nodded without a word.

Taking Lanther's hand in hers, she went with him

to the square of Tarmak guards waiting patiently for the duel to begin. She looked at Sir Remmik, and her eyes bulged. If she hadn't been feeling so miserable, she would have sunk to the ground in hysterical laughter. The Tarmaks—much to Sir Remmik's obvious disgust—had stripped off the remains of his tattered uniform and painted his skin blue with the paint they all used so liberally. They had expected him to fight naked, but he had managed to rescue his pants and stood glowering while the warriors finished painting him. The moment they finished, he tried to scrape it off with the blade of his sword.

Linsha hurried around the square to his corner. "Sir Remmik!" she hissed. "Leave it on! It helps heal wounds!"

He scowled at her, but he left the paint alone after that and turned his attention to the sword the Tarmaks had given him.

Across the square from the Knight, the Akkad-Ur had finished his preparations. He gave a curt command and strutted to the center of the space. He wore nothing but the blue paint and the feathers twisted into his long hair. His golden mask rested in the hands of one of his guards in the corner. He carried nothing but a sword.

Seeing the Akkad-Ur without his mask, Linsha guessed both man and Tarmak were close to the same age. However, the Akkad-Ur stood a good foot-and-a-half taller than Sir Remmik and had a healthy, muscular build. The Knight had lost weight the past few months and was certainly not in top physical condition. Nor had Linsha known him to participate in any of the training or conditioning sessions the arms master used to hold at the Citadel. She feared this duel would not last very long.

The Akkad-Ur must have thought so too, for he

did not bother to look at Sir Remmik when the Knight Commander walked forward to meet him. Without any preliminary speeches, rattling of drums, or bowing to one's opponent, the two foes lifted their swords and the battle began.

Sir Remmik struck first with a speed and a ferocity that took everyone by surprise, including the Akkad-Ur. He lunged forward, his blade swinging in a wicked arc that forced the Akkad-Ur to take several steps back and swing his sword in a defensive parry. The blades clashed and swung again. The Knight pressed his slim advantage and kept after the Tarmak with a solid barrage of thrusts and swings that allowed his opponent little opportunity for offensive moves. Even so the Akkad-ur did not allow him past his guard. Back and forth across the square, they fought in a bitter struggle that looked surprisingly well matched.

For a while Linsha feared Sir Remmik would wear down from his grueling attack. He was sweating profusely and breathing hard, but the Knight showed remarkable stamina and more skill than she had known he possessed. He ducked and wove and lunged like a much younger man and did not seem to be tiring. Above the crash of the swords and the cheers of the watching Brutes, Linsha felt Lanther move close behind her. He stayed at her back and watched the fight avidly. He seemed to be strangely agitated, for he was breathing heavily and his hands jerked and swayed as if he was swinging a sword in his mind. His eyes were focused with brilliant intensity on the fighters in the square. When she put a hand on his arm, he started and stared at her as if she shouldn't be there. A particularly loud cheer brought both of them around to look in the square.

Despite Sir Remmik's powerful attack, the Akkad-Ur had drawn first blood. His blade flashed past

Remmik's and the Knight staggered back with blood running down from a slash across his thigh. He regained his balance just in time to avoid a lunge by the Akkad-Ur, who came after him grinning like a wolf. Sir Remmik waded back into the fight, followed by the cheers and insults of the watching Tarmaks.

Soon Linsha noticed both combatants were sweating in the heat of the morning, and both looked like they were tiring. Their swings were slower and less controlled. Their tactics became more brutal. When their swords locked, they used fists and elbows to punch and hit. Sir Remmik lashed out his foot and kicked the big Tarmak in the back of the knee, bringing the warrior down. When he tried to follow through with a powerful swing meant to cut his foe in half, the Akkad-Ur locked both feet around the Knight's and tripped him into the dust. They rolled away from each other, spitting dust and blood.

The Akkad-ur sprang back to his feet, all arrogance forgotten, and brutally assaulted Sir Remmik with his sword, forcing the smaller man backward with sheer brute size and strength. Sir Remmik barely avoided slamming into the one of the guards and managed to duck under the Akkad-Ur's arm long enough to cut him on the ribs. Now both foes were bleeding, and the excitement of the watching Tarmaks had reached a fever pitch.

The fight went on in a dust-stirring, swirling chaos of attacks and counterattacks until the Tarmak's advantage began to show. Sir Remmik was on the defensive now and bleeding from several wounds. The fury and agility he had shown earlier was gone, and in its place was a second strength born of desperation. Pressing, he lunged again, but his aim was off and the Akkad-Ur slammed his blade aside. The Akkad-Ur moved in close and punched the hilt of his sword into Sir Remmik's face. Blood spurted from the Knight's nose and lip, his head snapped back, and he staggered. Stunned as he was, still he kept a grip on his sword. He jammed the point into the ground and used it to prop his weight while he twisted sideways and kicked the Akkad-Ur just below the breastbone. The Tarmak, already off balance and weary, did not have quite enough strength to force his body away from the blow. It landed solidly on his torso and drove the air from his lungs. He fell to the ground, gasping for air.

Sir Remmik summoned his last vestiges of his will, raised his sword, and rammed the point into the Tarmak's chest, seating it between the ribs with his final strength.

A look of pained surprise contorted the Akkad-Ur's face. He shuddered once and jerked in the throes approaching death. His breathing stilled; his muscles collapsed. His arms and legs sank down to the sand as his body relaxed into lifelessness.

Exhausted and trembling in every limb, the Knight Commander sank to his knees and leaned his weight on the upright sword. The Tarmaks stopped in mid-shout. A long and terrible silence enclosed the square.

The Akkad-Ur was dead.

The Betrayer

24

Only a moment passed after Sir Remmik's sword stabbed the Akkad-Ur before Linsha reacted. Darting from Lanther's side, she shoved between two surprised guards and snatched up the Akkad-Ur's large sword to defend her fellow Knight. The sword was so long for her that she had to use both hands to hold it, but she did not hesitate to stand over Sir Remmik and raise the sword between her and the Tarmaks. Sir Remmik and the warriors stared at her.

Horns blared a frantic call nearby, shattering the stunned silence. Tarmak voices exploded in fury and alarm, for the watching Tarmak warriors had hardly expected this man to defeat their general. Weapons in hand, they shouted in loud, brutal voices and charged Linsha and Sir Remmik.

A strange voice shot like the crack of a whip over the uproar and stopped the warriors in their tracks. They glared and stamped and grumbled their frustration, but they held their places and did not advance closer to the two humans.

Linsha gripped the sword harder. She could not

251

see over the taller Brutes, so she did not know who had spoken the command, yet she had the oddest feeling she had heard that voice before—in the dark and the rain, echoing thunder and lanced with pain. Her skin prickled and the hairs raised on the back of her neck. Keeping her eyes on the bloodlusting warriors, she gave Sir Remmik a hand up and stood at his back while he pulled his sword free. Together they waited for the next move.

The voice snapped another order in the Tarmak language, and the guards reluctantly made way for a man to walk through. Not a Tarmak. A man. A very familiar man.

Linsha's sword point fell to the ground. She froze, pinned by disbelief. Like an animal caught in a trap, she watched Lanther walk into the cleared space. The limp was gone. The slouch vanished. With the agility of an actor changing costumes, he threw off the countenance of the quiet, crippled Legionnaire and became something very different, something very dangerous. She lifted her eyes to his and saw a strange cold glint in their blue depths, a light she had never seen before. It made her think of glaciers, of ice so cold and dense it hid most of its frozen bulk beneath the surface of the water. Linsha began to shake.

"You," she groaned.

Sir Remmik drew himself up to his full height. "Now I see the truth," he said in the tones of a man who knows he is about to die.

Lanther did not reply at first. He knelt by the head of the dead Akkad-Ur and cut off one the general's braided lengths of hair. The warriors watched him avidly, ready to spring on the humans at the man's least command. But he only bowed his head sadly for a moment in respect for the dead Akkad-Ur, then rose to his feet, his hand still clutching the braid of hair.

"It has taken you long enough, Remmik," he said. "And still you only know half the truth."

"Who are you?" Linsha asked in a daze.

First Mariana was murdered and now Lanther, her trusted friend, revealed himself to be an enemy. Her mind could hardly deal with such blows.

His lips lifted in a cold smile. "I am Lanther Darthassian, son of Bendic Darthassian, who served as Lord Ariakan's ambassador and liaison to the emperor of the Tarmak empire."

"You're not a Legionnaire then," she said, her thoughts whirling in confusion.

He laughed. Standing straight with his shoulders thrown back and his head held high, he stood taller than many men, but not quite as tall as most of the Tarmaks. When he pulled his lank hair back out of his face and tied it behind his head with a strip of leather, his entire expression turned more harsh and arrogant.

"Of course I am a Legionnaire. I was once a Knight of Neraka, as well. Long enough to learn the arts of the dark mystics, long enough to realize the Knights of my father's day no longer existed. They are weak and ruled by a greedy, self-centered clerk. So I joined the Legion. They are not so rigid, so suspicious."

Linsha felt a flicker of anger ignite in her head that burned away some of the confusion. Her eyes narrowed as she thought about what he had said, and had not said, and the truth became bitterly apparent.

"You are the spy who helped the Tarmaks."

Lanther lifted one eyebrow.

"You are the spy we have been looking for all along."

Sir Remmik stared at her, but she ignored him, focusing on the friend who had suddenly become a cold-blooded stranger, a stranger who betrayed Iyesta and her city and who leaked information that led to the massacre of hundreds of people. Again, Lanther agreed.

Linsha felt the betrayal like a knife in her gut. How could she not have seen it? He had been lying to her for a year and half and she never caught on. Never even suspected! What a fool she had been. She had given him her friendship, her trust, and her help. The only thing she had not given was her love. At least she had not fallen for him like Ian. Gods, would she ever learn? Images of their time spent together ran through her head, memories of things they had done, talked about, and witnessed as friends. She saw again in her mind the way she had seen him many times, the way he walked, his gestures, and the tones and timbres of his voice. Suddenly another memory settled into place like a puzzle piece into a long-empty hole. When he had spoken in the language of the Tarmaks, his voice had changed, becoming harsher and more guttural. Her hurt fueled her anger to a flame.

"It was you, wasn't it?" she said in a rush of fury. "I thought the voice sounded familiar, but I just excused it as my imagination. *You* were the one who led the ambush on us in the storm. *You* took the dagger from me and stabbed Sir Morrec."

Lanther glanced at Sir Remmik with a sardonic twist to his lips. "Yes. Sir Morrec was a more dangerous leader. I needed to dispose of him. I was also hoping to keep the Solamnic Knights occupied and get you out of the Citadel before Thunder destroyed it. Sir Remmik played nicely into my plans."

The Knight Commander went deathly pale, aware at last of the depth of the lies he had accepted.

Linsha lifted the sword again and shoved the point

at Lanther's neck. "Why?" she screamed. "Why did you do this? Why pretend to be a Legionnaire, a defender of the city, a friend to all of us? What kind of a bastard are you?"

"I am an adopted son of the Tarmak nation, and I owe them my allegiance. My honor. And I am a loyal servant of her dark majesty, the Queen of Dragons, the Lady of the Night, the goddess Takhisis." His fingers gripped the sword point and forced it aside. "Beyond that, I will have to tell you later. We have much to do today."

He snapped something to the guards beside him and Linsha found half a dozen swords suddenly poking the skin at her throat. Stinging frustration and anger battled with her common sense. She could see the pulse of his blood throb in the vein of his neck. It would be possible to ram her sword home into his traitorous throat . . . if she was ready to die with him.

Cursing under her breath, she lowered the Akkad-Ur's sword and dropped it on the ground. Sir Remmik let go of his as well.

Lanther nodded to the warriors standing around the small group and spoke to them in their own tongue.

The Brutes growled like a pack of wolves and turned on the three Solamnic Knights with all the anger and vengence they had kept in check. The two wounded Knights hardly knew what hit them, but the uninjured Knight stared in horrified terror at the warriors descending on him and tried to throw his body over his friend. All three men died together, pierced and hacked by a dozen swords.

Linsha turned away, her eyes clouded with tears. "Paladine preserve us," she whispered.

Lanther took her arm and steered her in the direction of a group of watching Tarmaks on horseback.

From their size and the deeper color of their body paint, she guessed these were some of the officers. "Let us go," he ordered. "We need to inform the army and a bronze dragon of a change in command."

"You?" Linsha spat.

"Of course. It was my plan to conquer the Plains of Dust. I fully intend to carry it out. The Akkad-Ur was my friend and my general, but I was his second-in-command."

Although he was shoving her ahead of him toward the officers, she twisted her head around and saw Sir Remmik being escorted behind her. In the churned sand of what once was a dueling square, she saw four warriors pick up the body of the Akkad-Ur and carry him reverently to a wagon. Good riddance, she thought with grim hatred. She was still stunned by Lanther's revelation, but at least the truth was out. She knew who the spy was who had betrayed Iyesta and Missing City, she knew who killed Sir Morrec, and somewhere in a very small corner of her brain a tiny selfish thought noted with satisfaction that Sir Remmik now knew all of this, too.

She stood silently, conscious of many eyes upon her, while Lanther spoke to the Tarmak officers. His use of the Tarmak language was fluent, she observed, and the manner of the officers in his presence was respectful and attentive. What had he done, she wondered, to earn such consideration from such a martial race? To say he was intelligent was putting it mildly. He had hood-winked an entire city, the dragon's militia, Thunder, the circle of the Knights of Solamnia, the Legion of Steel, and even one small intelligent owl who had allowed herself to trust him. He was also cunning, ambitious, and probably a highly skilled warrior. He had survived the Dark Knights, after all, and while his limp was fake, the scar on his face was not. Instead of being a trusted ally, he had become a dangerous enemy. Linsha knew she had to gather her wits and find some way to escape from his grasp.

* * *

Crucible was waiting with barely concealed impatience by the edge of the Tarmak camp when a capricious wind whisked by and brought him a scent he had not caught in many days. His horned head snapped alert, and his nostrils flared to search the breeze for another hint of that smell. There it was again, coming from somewhere near the east end of the camp where the Akkad-Ur had disappeared some time ago. It was growing stronger. He leaped to his feet, his torn wings partially unfurled, and watched intently down the long lines of waiting Tarmaks and half-loaded wagons.

From his height, he saw her coming long before the Tarmaks around him realized the party was approaching. A low, rumbling growl started in his chest and vibrated up his long neck. Something was wrong. He could not smell or see the Akkad-Ur, but he could smell blood, and he saw Linsha following someone he had never liked. All at once he clamped his ears to his head, furled his wings tightly against his sides, and laid his belly on the ground, his front legs crossed. He did not know what had happened, but he had survived enough odd circumstances to sense when he needed to tread with care.

He watched through slitted eyes as the Tarmak officers, with Lanther, Linsha, and Sir Remmik in their midst, came into the place where the Akkad-Ur's tent still stood. He tried not to show any surprise when the Tarmak guards by the tent saluted Lanther. What was going on? Crucible studied Linsha avidly to see if she was well and unharmed, or if she could give him any clues, but all she did was return his gaze with infinite sorrow. Her hands were tied, and her tunic was spattered with fresh blood.

Crucible heard someone speak and jerked his attention away from the woman. To his astonishment and dismay, Lanther strode over to Linsha and dragged her in front of him.

"The Akkad-Ur is dead, killed in a duel with the Solamnic Knight, Sir Remmik," Lanther said in a voice loud enough for everyone to hear. "I am now commander of the army. I am the Akkad-Dar, and I hold the secret of the power over this dragon."

Crucible's eyes narrowed even further. This man was not a Tarmak, yet not one of the Brute officers or warriors offered an argument, and no one in his right mind would approach a dragon with a statement like that if he did not have some way to back it up. Unless, of course, he had a death wish.

The bronze dragon tapped a taloned foot on the ground thoughtfully. "Do I have this correct?" he asked in a frigid voice. "You are a traitor and you are now in charge of this army? And they are willing to go along with it?"

Lanther gave Linsha's arm a shake. "Tell him so he understands."

In hard, grim terms she told the dragon what had just transpired, including the deaths of Mariana, the Akkad-Ur, and the remaining Solamnic Knights.

Crucible felt his temper rise as surely as the magma in Mount Thunderhorn. He struggled to fight it back. This was not the time. Not when Linsha stood there in the traitor's grasp. Not when that foul barb still penetrated his back. He needed patience and time.

"I suppose you, too, know the spell that controls the barb," he said to Lanther, sneering down his long nose.

For an answer, the man lifted his fist and spoke a word. Pain stabbed down Crucible's back and almost broke his self-control. He howled and swung his head around to snap at his back, and as quickly as it came, the pain vanished. His golden eyes smoldered in fury, but he restrained himself from retaliating. He knew it would not help.

"You see?" Lanther said with an arrogant smile. "I created that spell, and I control it far better than my predecessor. Be warned, Crucible. I could kill you with a word, and that word would still be viable even if I die."

The dragon snaked his head down and glared at the man nose to nose. "How is it that you, and your . . . *predecessor*—" he spat the word— "wield magic when no one else in this land is able to do so?"

Lanther chuckled. "Just know that I can."

He suddenly swung around and pointed his hand, palm out, toward Sir Remmik. As he muttered a string of unfamiliar words, he curled his fingers into a fist.

The Knight screamed and grabbed his head both hands. With a convulsive jerk, he fell to the ground, his eyes rolling wildly, and writhed in the dirt as if his very bones were on fire.

Crucible was impressed. He guessed this was the same curse the Akkad-Ur had used on Linsha, but he had had to touch her. Lanther could inflict that kind of agony from a distance.

Linsha leaped forward and grabbed Lanther's arm, deflecting his spell from the tortured Knight. The connection broke. Sir Remmik shuddered once and lay on his back panting, his face twisted in lingering pain.

Crucible tensed, wondering if he would have to

protect Linsha and risk Lanther's wrath, but Lanther looked down into her green eyes and grinned. He locked his strong fingers on her chin, pulled her close, and kissed her full on the mouth. An unexpected, wild feeling of rage welled up in the dragon that had little to do with self-preservation. He hissed, a sharp, searing blast of air that sounded like a gnome's steam engine about to explode, and reared up on his hind legs. His wings unfurled and his lips pulled back from his teeth in a snarl.

He was stopped by Linsha. She wrenched away from Lanther and threw herself in front of Crucible's towering form. Grabbing a flapping wing, she yanked it with all her weight. "No!" she yelled at him. "No! Not now! Be patient."

"Yes." The new Tarmak general sneered. "Be patient. Your time to fight will come soon enough."

Crucible bowed his neck and leaned down to nudge Linsha away from his wing. "I will listen," he hissed softly to her. "I will listen to you. But if he touches you again . . ."

Harsh laughter rang in the clearing. "What a touching scene!" Lanther was about add more when the sound of hoofbeats distracted him.

A slim Keena in the dark robes of a priest trotted into camp and saluted the new Akkad-Dar. "Majesty," he said. "Urudwek's body has been brought to us and is safely sealed for mummification."

Lanther turned away from Linsha and the dragon. "Very well. Then let us leave." He stepped away and raised his voice for all the onlookers to hear. "Commanders, I want this army on the move before the sun passes midday! You two!" He pointed to two guards. "Put Sir Remmik in the slave cage. No food or water. I will find a good use for him."

"And the woman?" one asked.

"Tie her to a horse. She rides with me."

The Tarmaks bowed and hurried to their tasks. Shortly thereafter, the large army pushed on, leaving the fords behind and following the Run toward the distant town of Stone Rose.

Crucible estimated that at the rate they were moving, they would be in the small town in six or seven days—if the militia and tribesmen did not stop them somewhere along the way. Disgruntled, he stamped along behind Lanther's retinue and thought about everything Linsha had told him and a few things she knew nothing about. By the First Eggs, he wished he could sear Lanther where he stood. This was the second—no, there was that Lonar in the Crystal Valley. So this was the third man Linsha had liked and trusted who had lied to her, betrayed her, or even tried to kill her. It was enough to give any woman reason to never trust another man as long as she lived.

He ground his sharp teeth together and fought down his despair. By the absent gods, how would he ever find the courage to tell her?

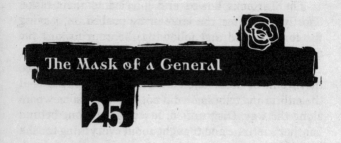

The Mask of a General

25

The next few days became a blur to Linsha—hot days on horseback and cold, uncomfortable nights spent tied in Lanther's tent. The new general did not try to kiss her or touch her again, but he would not let her near Crucible, and he never let her out of his presence. Linsha wished sometimes he would, even for just a few minutes. She was starting to loathe this man she had once considered her friend. She stared at him sometimes as they rode, still in shock that he had turned on her so suddenly. She half expected him to slouch in his saddle, turn around with his crooked grin, and tell her it had all been a joke. A poor joke, but a joke nonetheless. And then he would limp to her side and apologize. But it never happened. The Lanther she knew was a lie, a fabrication that was gone forever, and she began to grieve for that person as surely as she grieved for Mariana.

She saw Sir Remmik a few times during those bleak days. The older Knight had been locked in a small barred cage used to discipline disobedient slaves. The cage was loaded on the back of the wagon that hauled most of the furnishings, ropes, and walls of the general's tent, and in those rare moments when the Akkad-Dar was distracted and the wagon was unwatched, she tried to slip Sir Remmik a water bag or a fragment of food. The Tarmaks gave him water and bread in the evening, but it was not nearly enough to last through a long day. Sir Remmik swallowed his pride and took what she could give him with mumbled thanks. He would say nothing more to her for fear of being beaten. In spite of his earlier animosity to her, she feared for his well-being. At least the traces of the blue paint remaining on his skin protected him from sunburn and helped heal the wound on his leg and the many cuts and bruises from the fight.

When she wasn't worrying about Sir Remmik or Crucible or Varia during the long days of endless riding, Linsha often wondered what Falaius and the militia were doing. Had they gathered enough people to confront the Tarmaks? Would they attack before the army reached Stone Rose? Or would the town be sacrificed? Where were the inhabitants of this land? Thus far she had seen no sign of tribesmen, centaurs, or anyone. The desolate land they traveled was seemingly empty of people. There were no travelers, no caravans, no shepherds herding their flocks, no nomads to watch them pass by. Even when they stopped near the river to replenish their water supplies and water the stock, they did not see boats or local fishermen. This was not a heavily populated land, Linsha knew that, but this close to the river, there should have been someone.

The Tarmak scouts did not seem to be finding anyone either. Whenever they returned to report to the Akkad-Dar, she sidled close to listen and heard enough to make her suspect the local inhabitants were fleeing the coming of the Tarmaks. They were wise, she thought.

But this empty peace would not last much longer. Of that she was sure. The people of Duntollik had not maintained their free realm between three dragonlords by sitting in their homes and running at the first sign of trouble. Somewhere out there on the Plains the tribes and clans were mustering to confront the Tarmak invaders, and she doubted they would wait much longer.

Three days' march to the southeast of Stone Rose, another tributary of the Toranth River joined the Red Rose in a confluence of shifting sand bars, twisting currents, and treacherous shoals that changed the character of the river to a staid, meandering waterway with enough water to float a boat. The southernmost tributary, the Khol, was named for a village in its proximity and stretched lazily through the southern reaches of the vast desert. West of the confluence, where the Red Rose ran alone, the river was not a pretty sight in anyone's imagination, for it was shallow, thick with silt, and meandered through rusty colored mud flats and sand bars. The Red Rose, Linsha learned, had been named by local centaurs for its reddish color and for the odd stone rosettes that could sometimes be found in the weathered gullies and canyons of its watershed. Its banks supported only tough cottonwoods and thick willows and beds of rushes that harbored every biting insect known to the Plains. But it was water, and water was more valuable in the desert than gems.

Even though the Run paralleled the river, the majority of the Tarmak army did not see the confluence of the Khol and the Red Rose simply because it was too far from the Run for the wagons, chariots, and slow-moving oxen to detour. However, a day later they reached a section of the road that passed a great northern loop of the Red Rose and saw for themselves the muddy, red-hued river and its striated banks of red sandstone. After several days of skimpy water rations, everyone was pleased to see it. No one minded a little mud.

Especially Crucible. Without waiting for Lanther to agree, he galloped down the bank and plunged into the water, wallowing snout-first into the mud and sending waves of muddy water washing up the bank. Linsha laughed for the first time in days, and Lanther, who knew more about dragons than the Akkad-Ur before him, grunted and said, "He could have done that a little farther down stream."

That evening, they saw the first rider on a hill to the west, silhouetted against the setting sun. Lanther send a band of the mercenary brigands after the rider, but he disappeared before they could get near him.

At dawn there were two watchers on the distant hill.

Lanther sent out Tarmak trackers and put his army on alert. They broke camp quickly, and every Tarmak carried his weapons on the march. They did not see a concentrated band of the enemy that day, but they saw watchers on every distant hill and occasionally a troop of centaurs would canter by on a parallel track and observe the Tarmaks as closely as they dared.

Linsha observed the sentinels and felt her nervousness increase by the hour. The Tarmaks' opponents were out there, waiting for the most advantageous time or the best place to attack. Were they going to launch an ambush? Or use the old familiar form of advancing lines? Would they attack at dawn? She could only wait and try to keep her worried frustration from boiling over.

At dawn the following day, signal horns blared all around the camp, alerting the warriors and bringing the commanders running. They stopped and stared at a sun-capped hill on the western Run not far from the sprawling camp and saw at least seven mounted riders and three centaurs standing in the middle of the road as if they were attempting to block the Tarmaks' path. One carried a truce flag.

Lanther buckled on his sword and strapped the gold mask of the Akkad on his face. Taking Linsha with him, he mounted his horse, called his guards, and rode up the hill to meet the waiting riders.

Linsha kept her face expressionless as the group of Tarmaks came to a halt ten feet away from the truce party. She scanned the faces in front of her and saw Falaius, Sir Hugh, and several of the militia she recognized. The others were tribesmen and centaurs from Duntollik clans. She gave Sir Hugh a scant nod and tore her eyes away from his questioning expression. She hoped they would not get a chance to talk. She did not want to have to explain Mariana's death to him under these circumstances.

The rider carrying the flag nudged his horse forward to meet the Akkad-Dar. He held his hands out so the Tarmaks could see he was unarmed. The only thing he carried was the torn scroll Sir Remmik had given to the leaders at the Grandfather Tree.

He handed it back to Lanther and said, "I am bidden to return these to you and offer you the same terms. If you surrender to our commanders, we will not slaughter your men. You will turn over your weapons to us and return to Missing City."

Lanther laughed behind his mask and took the torn scroll. "Very well. Your message has been delivered. I give you the same answer you gave me. No. Go back to your commanders and tell them to meet us on the field of battle."

The tribesman turned to go, but there was a sudden commotion in the group of riders behind him. Sir Hugh, his face thunderous, urged his horse through the clustered party and yanked it snorting and prancing to a stop directly in front of Lanther's horse. The Tarmak guards drew their swords.

"Who are you?" Sir Hugh demanded. "I've seen the Akkad-Ur! And unless he shrank a foot, changed his voice, and cut off his braids, you are not he! Who are you?"

The guard beside Lanther answered with a thick accent, "This is the Akkad-Dar, the golden general of the western armies, Lord of Missing City, Sword of the Emperor. Bow when you speak before him!"

"In a pig's eye," Sir Hugh snarled. "What happened to the other one?"

Linsha felt the tension around her tighten even further. If Hugh didn't back away, she was afraid these guards were going to start the battle on the hilltop using him as their first target.

"He's dead, Sir Hugh," she said quickly. "Sir Remmik killed him in a duel. But we have found the traitor."

Before she could continue, Lanther pulled the mask from his face and gave Sir Hugh a sardonic salute.

Exclamations of dismay and anger burst out from the militia who recognized him.

Linsha's eyes sought Falaius's face among the tribesmen. He had been the one who worked the closest with Lanther the Legionnaire; he had been Lanther's commander and supporter. Had he ever guessed, she wondered, that this crippled Legionnaire from City of Morning Dew was in reality a spy, an assassin, and a dark mystic? From the look of angry surprise and dawning comprehension on the old tribesman's face, she had to guess not. Lanther's subterfuge had been perfect.

Falaius's voice cut over the noise like a saw. "Sir Hugh, let us go. We have our answer." He wheeled his horse back over the hill without waiting for the others. The rest of the party followed.

The young Knight looked at Linsha uncertainly, then he and the flag carrier spurred their horses after the group.

As soon as they were out of arrow range, Lanther and his guards rode to the crown of the hill to look down the road. Ahead of them the Run dipped down the slope of the hill and could be seen like a pale ribbon winding through a broad, low-lying valley. On the far side, across a flat stretch of dried mud flats, small sand dunes, and rocky scrubland stood a large force of men, centaurs, and others waiting in quiet ranks on the rise of the opposite hills. To the left curled the river, its sluggish water glistening in the morning light. Beds of reeds and clumps of scraggly willow lined the shores, where Linsha could see ducks and small birds feeding in the shallows. She saw another, larger bird glide across the river and disappear into one of the willows, but she could not tell from this distance if it was Varia. She turned away from the river and sighed.

"Linsha," Lanther's voice cut through her thoughts. "You were in the gathering. How many warriors did the tribes muster?"

Linsha stiffened. She had been dreading this and had hoped he would not press the issue of divulging information. "I have no idea. Thanks to Sir Remmik and your trackers, I left the gathering before all the forces had arrived."

He twisted around in his saddle and fixed his eyes on her face. Linsha glared back.

"Was there a tribesman there by the name of Wanderer?"

"I don't know."

"Did the Windwalker clan come?"

"I don't know."

"What is their favorite color?"

"Tarmak blue. They can't wait to see how it mixes with blood red."

His eyebrow curved up and his lip twisted down in a sarcastic sneer, and he yanked her horse closer to his. "Good. You were listening. Then listen to this. It does not really matter how many face us today. We are the Tarmak. We will prevail. There is nothing on this plain that can stop us. Not elf, not centaur, not human. Not even dragon. If you wish to see that bronze of yours survive this day you will obey me. As much as I would enjoy to have you fight by my side, you will stay in the camp under guard, and if you so much as twitch a muscle, I will let him die. Is that clear?"

Linsha matched his expression with a sneer of her own and nodded. It was clear enough.

Lanther abruptly switched to Tarmakian and began passing orders to his officers. They turned the horses around and cantered down the road to the waiting army, taking Linsha with them. By the time they reached the camp, their plans were set and the leaders of the hundreds were waiting by the road to receive their commands. Horns blared throughout the camp. There was noise everywhere as thousands of Tarmaks roared their joy at the prospect of the coming battle. The boredom and tedium of the long march was about to come to an end in bloodshed and conflict.

Lanther hauled Linsha off her horse and left her fuming in front of his tent while he went inside to ready himself. For a little while she curbed her agitation and watched the warriors hurry about their duties. Some gathered weapons, arrows, spears, and hand axes. Others refreshed their body paint or tied fresh feathers in their hair. The charioteers were told to unhitch their horses and ride, for the ground was too uneven and cluttered for chariots. On the heavy, powerful Damjatt horses they would form a cavalry that would attack the centaurs. Very quickly the Tarmaks began to form lines for the march into battle.

Linsha glanced around. No one was watching her except Sir Remmik in his cage. He gave her quick nod and jerked his head toward the river.

But the river was not where Linsha wanted to go. A short distance away, behind the tents and wagons of the Akkad-Dar's retinue, crouched Crucible. His head was raised and swaying slightly as if he was breathing the clean wind from the desert. A powerful desire swept over Linsha to go to him, to talk to him, to tell him why she had left and what had happened since. After the Akkad-Ur's death, she had not been allowed near him, and she had missed him more than she imagined. There was a wagon close by. If she could just . . .

A Tarmak warrior stepped out of Lanther's tent and grabbed her arm. At least at first glance she thought he was a Tarmak. Then she realized he was too short and his hair did not have the numerous braids with the white feathers decorating their lengths. Lanther had removed his clothes and painted his skin blue. The gold mask glinted in the sunlight, and his weapons hung from an ornate battle harness of leather and gold strapped over the Akkad's cuirass decorated with the brass dragon scales. His fingers dug painfully into her arm as he hauled her to the wagon where Sir Remmik's cage sat.

His guards unfastened the cage, pulled the Knight commander out, and pushed Linsha inside on her hands and knees. The cage was too short for any occupant over the size of a small kender to stand up inside.

"Stay here," Lanther ordered. "I want you to see our army return victorious with the blood of our enemy on our hands and their heads on our spears."

Linsha and Sir Remmik exchanged a long look, then to Linsha's surprise, the older Knight raised his right hand and saluted her.

His hand had hardly dropped when Linsha heard the whisk of a sword blade slice the air and a thunk as it met solid flesh. Blood spattered over the side of the wagon. Struck with horror, Linsha clamped her hand to her mouth to stifle her scream as Sir Remmik's head dropped off his neck and fell to the ground. His body swayed once as if greatly surprised and then it, too, collapsed to the earth in a small cloud of dust.

"Why did you do that?" Linsha cried, her face bloodless to her lips. Her head was spinning, and she feared she was going to vomit. She was accustomed to bloodshed in battle, but this second abrupt, vicious murder that came unlooked for was almost more than her over-stretched self-control could bear.

Lanther lifted his sword and watched the blood run down the blade. "It was a quicker, cleaner death than my men would have given him. He earned that for his courage in the duel. And now you will always remember his salute to you as the last thing he ever did."

"But why? Why now?"

"I told you I would find a use for him. I will send him back to my enemy, so they will know what we intend to do." He snapped an order to his followers and sprang onto his horse. "And now, my lady, to see a dragon." He laughed and cantered away, his guards close behind.

Sick at heart, Linsha watched the Tarmaks heave Sir Remmik's body onto the back of another horse and tie him upright in the saddle. It was not an easy task, for the horse was spooked by the bloodstench and refused to stand still. When they finally had his body tied to their satisfaction, they fastened his head to the saddle horn, led the horse up the hill, and let him go with a slap to the rump. The last sight she had of her old nemesis was his headless corpse disappearing over the top of the hill. It became a memory that would haunt her for the rest of her days.

Crucible's roar of protest rumbled through the camp like thunder, drawing Linsha's attention back to the moment. She cast aside any thoughts of shock, hurt, and anger to concentrate on the battle and the dragon she wanted to help. The leaves of the Grandfather Tree were still hidden under her tunic near the dragon scales. Somehow she had to get free of this cage and work out a way to use the leaves to free Crucible of Lanther's spell. It sounded easy enough in words, but in reality she had no solid idea how to proceed.

One step at a time, she told herself. First, she had to get out of the cage.

Over the uproar of shouting voices, trampling feet, and rattling weapons, Linsha heard the heavy tread of the dragon go by. She could not see him from her position in the wagon, but she listened as he passed and realized he was being unnaturally quiet. He no longer growled or roared or argued. Was he seething or had Lanther found a way to control him beyond the barb in his back? She craned her neck as far as it would go and finally found a way to see the hillside. She just caught a glimpse of Crucible escorted by Lanther and his bodyguards. Her worry grew more desperate.

Still on her knees, she lashed out at the door of the cage with her booted heel, but the door didn't budge, and the two guards shouted at her. One slammed his shield on the cage to make her back away. They did not look very pleased to be left behind to guard a woman. Linsha responded with a Tarmak phrase she had heard the guards shout at slaves and was rewarded with a loud barrage of words and a second slam by the shield.

Suddenly the Tarmak's war horns blared across the lines of waiting warriors, and a thunderous shout shook the camp. The guards turned around to watch as the long lines of blue-skinned Brutes broke into a trot and moved up the hill. In loose groups of a hundred, they moved past the camp, up the long slope of the hill, and down the crest out of sight. Several troops of heavy cavalry cantered by and veered north to move up the valley in a flanking maneuver.

Linsha's fingers tightened around the bars of the cage as she watched them go. They were so tall, so strong and graceful that she could not help but fear for the people she knew and liked on the other side. Did they stand a chance? What were they doing at this moment as the Tarmaks appeared on the hilltop and swarmed down into the valley in seemingly endless thousands? She had seen Sir Hugh and Falaius, but was Leonidas there? Where was the healer Danian and his red-haired apprentice? She hoped they were close by, for she knew they would be needed before this day was over. And what would they do about Crucible? She knew Falaius had explained to the chiefs and tribal leaders about the dragon's predicament, but what if they were forced to kill him to prevent him from destroying their men in his throes under the spell?

She glanced at the guards again and moved surreptitiously over to the door. The small door that opened into the wooden cage was firmly tied with a thick rope. The Tarmaks hadn't bothered with a lock, since anyone inside the cage who wished to get out needed a very sharp knife or an axe—neither one of which she had—to get through the thick bindings. She studied the guards, but they were too far away, and they were more likely to jab her with their spears or swords than get close enough to be conveniently strangled. She sat back on her heels, taut with frustration.

In the distance, from the other side of the hill, came the music of horns and drums, then a vast, ringing roar of war cries overlaying a thunder of pounding hooves and trampling feet. There was a great crash as the armies collided, and abruptly the sounds disintegrated into a cacophony of shouts, screams, clashing weapons, and a dragon's roar.

Linsha's guards took an involuntary step toward the noise.

She glared at their backs, wishing she had a handy supply of knives, when she caught a slight movement in the farthest edge of her vision. Somewhere, off to her left, something had moved in the trees down by the river. She turned slightly to get a better look. There were a few trees and only a little ground cover between the Tarmak camp and the riverbank, but she was sure something had moved down there where a clump of young willows had taken root in a depression about halfway between the edge of the camp and the river. She looked harder, and then she saw them—a dozen men or maybe more creeping through the high grass toward the camp. They were well camouflaged with mud and grasses and could barely be seen against the browns, greens, and reds of the landscape.

Linsha whipped around to check the guards, but they were still engrossed with the sounds of battle. Nearby, other Tarmak servants, a few slaves, and more guards moved about the tents and the wagons, unaware of the enemy stalking their camp.

She heard the soft, unmistakable sound of arrows whizzing by and saw both Tarmak guards pitch forward with arrows protruding from their necks. The men in the grass sprang to their feet and sprinted up the slope toward a rough line of brush just as two centaurs galloped out of the trees. A small brown shape flew with them and winged directly to Linsha's cage.

"She's here! She's here!" Varia screeched to the centaurs.

A young buckskin and an older chestnut the color of polished cedar raced past the men and galloped through the outskirts of the camp to the wagon where Linsha was caged. Both carried bows that they nocked, drew, and loosed as they ran.

Shouts erupted in the camp, and Tarmak guards came running only to die in a barrage of well aimed arrows from the men hidden in the brush.

"Where are the others?" shouted the red horseman, whom Linsha recognized as Horemheb. "Where is the other Knight?"

"Dead," said Linsha. "It's just me."

The buckskin Leonidas sliced through the ropes on the door of the cage and yanked it open. Linsha shot through it like an arrow and jumped from the wagon onto Leonidas's back. The two centaurs wheeled and charged back the way they had come, firing their bows as fast as they could. The few guards left in that part of the camp fell back before them.

Linsha held onto Leonidas with her hands and knees as he ran down the slope into the trees. Once into the copse of young cottonwoods the two stallions turned and used their bows to cover the retreat of the men. A few Tarmaks tried to chase them and died on the grassy slope.

As soon as the last man was in the trees, the entire

group ran for the river to a denser stand of willows. There, behind the cover of the trees, they splashed into the water and waded across the Red Rose to the opposite bank where horses waited patiently in the shade. Linsha watched, impressed, while the men waded out of the river and mounted their horses. They were Plains barbarians, locals probably, who knew the twists and turns of the river and where to find crossings among the dangerous mudflats and shoals. They grinned at her through their mud masks and congratulated each other in their own tongue.

"How long have you been here?" she asked Leonidas. She knew they would have been spotted by the Tarmaks if they had tried to cross in daylight.

"Since last night. We left the horses here and crossed over before dawn."

She heard a flutter of wings and held out an arm. A delighted owl dropped from the sky, landed on her wrist, and scooted up to her shoulder.

"Varia told us you were still alive and where you were," Horemheb said. "It made it much easier to strike fast and get out. But what happened to the other Knight and the captain? We thought they were with you?"

Linsha leaned her face against Varia's soft feathers and took a deep breath. "Lanther killed Sir Remmik this morning. He sent the body on horseback to your lines. Mariana was killed by the Akkad-Ur four days ago."

A sudden silence surrounded her, and she closed her eyes so she would not have to see the shock and sadness on his face that so deeply mirrored her own feelings.

"Oh no, not Mariana," Leonidas whispered. "And *Lanther?* He is the traitor you and Falaius tried so hard to find? *He* killed Sir Remmik?"

Linsha could only nod. She had not yet cried for Mariana, or for her loss of Lanther's friendship. Although she could feel the burning, prickling of tears in her eyes, she fought them back. This was not the time. Not yet. Not while Crucible was caught between two armies.

"Leonidas, please. I will tell you everything later, but now I have to get to Crucible. Lanther forced him to into the battle, and I fear what he might do if that barb overcomes his self-control."

The riders and centaurs turned upstream and trotted back in the direction of their own army. They passed the hill on the opposite bank, and the valley opened up where they could see a great cloud of dust that billowed and swirled above the struggling armies. The noise increased to a muted roar of voices and the myriad sounds of violent impact.

"Look!" Leonidas said. "They've fired the grass!" He pointed north toward the far end of the valley.

The tribesmen, Linsha knew, sometimes set grass-fires to thwart enemy flanking or cut off retreat. She looked into the valley where the Tarmaks fought with the Duntollik confederation, but she could not yet see Crucible. There was too much dust hanging in the air. Varia trilled something to her and dived off her shoulder into a glide that took her swiftly over the river. Linsha watched her beat her wings to rise to a better height and skim off to the west.

Meanwhile, the plainsmen led the centaurs on a narrow trail along the low bank of the river that skirted beds of reeds and muddy pools to another ford between the gravel bars and sinking sands where horses could cross the river without too much difficulty. They trotted across, sending fountains of silty water splashing into the air, and clambered up the shallow bank onto the northern side.

Varia came flying back as fast. She didn't bother to land on Linsha's shoulder but hooted urgently, "Come!" And flew back toward the surging, raging mass of men and Tarmaks.

Leonidas needed no urging. He galloped after her, placing an arrow in his bow as he ran. Horemheb followed at his heels, the others right behind him. They crossed the flatlands Linsha had noticed earlier and raced up onto drier land.

A breeze picked up at that moment and swirled the dust around the armies. Sunlight glittered on thousands of swords and weapons and helms. Drums boomed over the fighting, and dozens of colorful flags swirled in the wind.

Linsha strained to see Varia overhead and finally picked her out moving toward a space near the center where the Run crossed the valley. The wind gusted again, and she caught a glitter of sunlight on metallic bronze scales. She tapped Leonidas's shoulder and pointed.

"Get me a sword!" she yelled over the uproar.

By this time they reached the fringes of the fighting where the wounded were retreating and plunged in among the dead and injured. Leonidas fired an arrow at a moving Tarmak, bent low, and yanked a sword out of a dead warrior's chest. He tossed the sword to Linsha and reloaded his bow in one smooth movement. The small troop slowed their gallop to a canter as the fighting around them increased. Several of the plainsmen fell back, diverted by attackers. One was pulled down and killed by two Tarmak. The centaurs plowed on through the struggling mass toward the place where Varia hovered.

Suddenly they heard a fearsome roar over the pandemonium of the field. They saw the bronze dragon rear upright out of the mass of Tarmaks. His wings beat wildly, and he shook his head back and forth as if in great pain. His jaws fell open, and a brilliant beam of light shot from his mouth into the sky. Warriors of both sides screamed and shouted in terror and fell back around him. Dragonfear spread in ever-increasing ripples that sent weaker men running in terror.

Everything around the dragon turned to chaos. Leonidas and Horemheb and their surviving escorts were slowed to a difficult trot as they fought their way through seething mass of battling Tarmaks and tribesmen, fleeing warriors, and the dead and the wounded that littered the ground. Linsha hacked and slashed at any blue skin that got too close and defended the centaur's right while he loaded and fired his bow in rapid succession. Around them the dust and smoke grew thicker until Linsha could barely see more than a few yards through the swirling, stinking air.

All at once the space cleared out before them as the fighting shifted away from the dragon, and they saw Lanther standing in a circle of his guards, his face still masked and his fist raised at Crucible.

The dragon screeched in hideous pain. His tail lashed out and caught two of the Tarmak guards, slamming them off their feet. But Lanther was so intent on his spell that he did not notice.

"Is that him?" Leonidas snapped, struggling to fight off the dragonfear. "The short blue-skin?"

"Yes," Linsha replied. "Kill him if you can."

The awe and terror emanating from the enraged

dragon did not affect her this time. Her mind was already too full of powerful emotions.

The young centaur's bow sang and an arrow slipped neatly into the gap left by the guards before they could regain their positions. It caught Lanther high in the shoulder and spun him off his feet.

Linsha saw him fall, and she prayed to any god that would listen that the spell would be broken and Crucible would be free to escape.

But the arrow that struck the Akkad-Dar was not fatal, and Linsha could see him struggle to rise. He lifted his hand again and snapped a loud, clear command. Linsha did not need to understand it to know what it meant. Her heart sank in despair.

Crucible screamed a long, terrible sound. He dropped to all four feet then collapsed to his side on the ground where he writhed in agony, his heavy body crushing anyone hapless enough to get in his way.

"Crucible!" Linsha shrieked. She threw her leg over Leonidas's back, and slid off, her sword still clutched in her hand. She had lost too many friends and given up too much to lose this dragon now. She didn't think she could bear another death, especially his. Desperate to save him, she ducked past his thrashing tail and ran toward his head.

Leonidas started after her, but a squad of furious Tarmak guards charged him and he was forced to turn and defend himself. Raising a war cry, he and Horemheb joined in the furious battle.

Linsha heard Leonidas's war cry in a distant part of her mind. She knew a battle was surging around her, but all she could see, all she could think about was the dragon thrashing and moaning on the churned up earth. She reached his head and yelled his name, but he gave no response. His eyes were closed, and his lips

281

were curled back in a snarl of pain and bitter anger. His breathing was fast and irregular. She tried again to call him and beat her fist on his nose.

This time one eye cracked open.

"Crucible! It's me! Don't move!"

She scrambled up on the dragon's leg and climbed toward his shoulder. Another spasm of intense pain racked his body. Her feet slipped out from under her, but she scrabbled up high enough to grab the ridge on his neck and hold on until his shaking stopped again. Scrambling and clawing her way along his slippery scales, she pulled herself up the peak of his shoulders and balanced herself on his wing joint. She had no problem finding the entry wound. The crossbow bolt had disfigured and blackened his scales between his shoulder blades and left a raw, bloody hole.

"The barb!" she screamed. "Where is it? I can't see it!"

"It's gone," he panted. "Inside . . . too late."

"No!" She shouted. "Not yet! Fight it! Don't let him win!"

She noticed Varia dip down and circle close to her head, and the sight of the owl helped calm some of her raging thoughts. Holding on to Crucible's wing joint, she forced her mind to slow down, to relax, to seek a calm where she could think. What did she have that she could use to help the dragon? Two leaves from an ancient tree, two dragon scales, her own small talent, and the words of a tribal shaman.

"Did Danian say anything more to you about the leaves?" she yelled to Varia.

The owl hooted a no. "Although," she added, "the Grandfather Tree was a gift from a god of neutrality. Perhaps the leaves can be used to help neutralize a spell of evil."

Linsha plunged her hand into her tunic and pulled out the rolled packet of leaves and the chain with the dragon scales. Leaving the scales dangling, she flipped the fabric around the leaves so they unrolled in her hand.

The two leaves were still fresh looking, colored a lovely blue green, with five deep lobes on each leaf. Linsha stared at them wide-eyed as if she had never seen them before while her mind bloomed with a sudden inspiration. The long, lobed leaves resembled nothing so much as hands. The hands of a god. The Tree of Life.

Zivilyn, god of wisdom, she thought with all the strength she could muster, *help me help this dragon.*

Then the words of the shaman returned to her memory, and she knew what she should do. . . if the dragon could survive it, and if the centaurs could keep the Tarmaks off her long enough.

"Crucible!" she yelled. She slithered down the dragon's shoulder and returned to his head. "Crucible!" She yelled again to get his attention.

He looked worse now. His breathing was still rapid and shallow, and his scales looked dingy. The golden light of his eyes had faded. He still writhed in pain, but his movements were weaker and not as frantic, and he did not respond to her voice.

She kicked him hard on the nose. "Crucible! Listen to me! I think I have a way to get that barb out. But I need your help. Don't give up now! Help me."

One eye slowly opened wider and rolled toward her. "How?"

"The barb entered your back while you were shapeshifting. I want to try to get it out, but you have to change again."

"The Akkad-Ur warned me the barb would kill me if I tried to shapeshift," he moaned.

283

"It *will* kill you if you don't!"

"Tell him to change to something smaller!" Varia cried overhead. "That way the barb will be easier to reach." She paused then hooted a warning. "And tell him to hurry! The grassfires are getting closer."

"Make yourself smaller," Linsha ordered. "Just not too small or the barb will reach your heart before I can get it."

"I don't know if I have the strength," he gasped.

Varia fluttered down to the dragon's face and looked into his eye that was almost as big as she was. *You have to try! Change to your man-shape, Crucible. Do it now, or you will die.*

When she sees me, she will hate me, he replied. *I have betrayed her trust.*

She should be allowed to make up her own mind, the owl insisted, *and she won't be able to do that if you are dead.*

The bronze lifted his head and nudged Linsha with his nose. "I am sorry," he groaned. His eye closed again, and a faint glow of light began to glimmer on his scales.

Linsha raced around to his back. She could still hear the sounds of the battle behind her and the wild yells of the centaurs; she could smell the thickening smoke of the grassfires. But she shut out the stink and the noises and the fear and placed a vallenwood leaf on each hand so her fingers matched the lobes of the leaves. She focused her thoughts inward. Although she feared there were many dead souls on the battlefield, she hoped perhaps she could use her healing ability just long enough to help ease the pain as she pulled out the barb.

The glow of light brightened and began to sparkle. The spell was slow, for Crucible was weak, yet it appeared to be working. The dragon was suffused in the golden light from head to tail, and his wings quickly shrank and vanished. His large body began to grow smaller within the aura of light. Linsha was forced to squint in the brilliant glow as she watched for the small reddish barb.

When Crucible shrank to something close to fifteen feet, Linsha spotted the tail of the barb penetrating the glowing area that she guessed was his shoulders. It glared through the beautiful light like an ugly splinter, its color dark with blood. She did not hesitate. Her leaf-covered hand shot through the coruscating energy of his being.

Linsha gasped. She was suddenly inundated by the power of Crucible's being in a massive rush of memories, thoughts, emotions, and worst of all, his pain. Her consciousness reeled from the overwhelming assault of the dragon's wounded mind, and she felt herself slipping both physically and mentally away from him. She was losing him.

No! No-no-no-no-no-no.

It was the only word she could dredge from the chaos of her mind, but it worked. Short and emphatic, it served as an anchor for her will and gave her a grip from which to reach deep into the wells of her ability. From her blood and her bones, she drew the strength to push her own awareness to the forefront and to focus on her own magic. Using the power drawn from her heart, she touched his mind and reassured him with the warmth of her presence. Crucible fell still. As they joined in mind and body, they became as forged together as two different creatures can be.

The dragon scales around Linsha's neck began to glow, and she felt a new power emanating from the scales. Emboldened, she pushed her arm deeper into the dragon, seeking the dark red impurity of the barb. Her fingers touched it and caught the end before the barb could slip deeper into his back. For just a moment she felt the heat of the thing burn her fingers, then the power of the leaf surged through her hand and into the barb, cooling its foul heat and nullifying its power. She sent her own magic surging out of her heart, down her arm and fingers, and through the leaf into his form. He continued to diminish in size while she gripped the barb in one hand, then with both hands.

The leaves began to crinkle at the edges and turn brown. Linsha gritted her teeth. Her throat and mouth were dry, and she could feel the hungry, tickling touch of souls draining away her power. But the scales fueled her determination, and she did not let go. As Crucible dwindled to the size of a tall man, the leaves lost their vitality and wilted. The heat of the barb returned and scorched her hands. Ignoring the pain, she held tighter and began to pull with all her strength. Crucible's tail vanished. His forelegs shrank to human arms.

An instant later there was loud pop and several things happened all at once. The blinding light vanished in the wink of an eye, leaving Linsha blinking at the spots in her vision. Unable to see clearly, she felt rather than saw the barb pull loose from Crucible's back, and she stumbled backward, the barb still burning her hand. She dropped it like a searing coal and stamped on it. The scorched shreds of the leaves fell from her hands.

A deep groan of pain came from the ground near her feet and drew her attention from the dart. She rubbed her eyes, blinked, and looked down at Crucible's shape sprawled on his belly. He had become a tall man, powerfully built, with dark gold hair, and skin deeply tanned. A torn, bloody wound disfigured his upper back and right shoulder. Blood ran in rivulets down his neck.

Linsha stared at him. Their union created by need

and magic was broken, and in its place a sick, cold feeling crept slowly through her heart and mind. She hadn't thought she had ever seen Crucible in his human shape, but she realized, looking down at the wounded man at her feet, that she had been wrong.

Her hand reached out to his arm, and she carefully rolled him over to see his features. The face she saw was the face of a friend—or someone she had imagined was a friend. The features that turned toward her with a mixture of apprehension, pain, and relief were those of Lord Hogan Bight, Lord Governor of the city of Sanction.

She fell to her knees beside him. "No," she whispered. "This isn't right. It can't be right."

And yet, an unobtrusive part of her mind said *why not?* When had she ever seen them together? But she couldn't believe it completely. She couldn't accept that another man she had liked and respected had lied to her and deceived her.

"Why?" she said in choked-off cry. "Why did you take the shape of Lord Bight? What do you think you're doing?"

Varia came to land on the ground beside the man and hooted softly. "Linsha, he *is* Lord Bight. And always has been."

A tear trickled down Linsha's cheek. She rocked on her knees, her mind reeling. He was a dragon. The dragon was him. "Oh, gods," she cried, and suddenly the flood of tears she had kept at bay for so long broke loose and flooded her eyes. Her vision blurred and swam so badly that she did not see the look of dismay and grief on his face.

He struggled to sit up and reach for her, but she wrenched away from him.

"You lied to me!" she screamed at him with all

287

the fury she had held inside—placed there by Ian and Lanther and by too many trials and deaths. "For ten years I have thought you were human. Did you think it funny to keep me in the dark? To make me such a fool? And you!" She turned on Varia. "You knew, didn't you? All those looks, those remarks to Iyesta, the laughing! You two must have thought I was so amusing, to be so deluded and not have the slightest idea. How dare you!"

Varia wisely said nothing.

Crucible, however, tried to say, "I told her not to tell you. I was—"

Linsha cut him off with a rage as sharp as a sword. "Going to tell me yourself some day? Exactly when? I worried about you and your city. I wanted Crucible to be with you and keep you safe. And little did I know he's been with you all the time! When were you going to tell me? Never?"

Summoning what was left of his strength, he pulled himself to his feet and staggered to the sword Linsha had dropped earlier. He picked it up, although he could barely hold it or even stand upright. Blood was running down his back, and his limbs were shaking.

Linsha glared at him and struggled off her knees. "Oh, no. No, you are not going to fight here. You are not going to die after all we went through to help you. Leonidas!" She bellowed with all her exploding emotions. "Leonidas! I need you!"

It never occurred to her that the young horseman might be busy or dead. Hoofbeats pounded behind her, and the buckskin centaur cantered to her side. He was splattered with blood, filthy with dirt and sweat, bleeding in several places, and looking rather wild-eyed. But he was still alive and kicking.

"What is it?" he said quickly. "The Akkad-whatever-his-name-is has not gone far. I think they're treating his wound. His guards are still around."

Linsha wiped her eyes again and ran a quick glance over the field around her. Close by, Horemheb fought with a Tarmak guard, yet farther away through the smoke and dust she saw only sporadic fighting around piles of dead and wounded. She was surprised and alarmed to see the main battle had moved away from their position. In fact, the Duntollik warriors seemed to be pulling back. To the north she could see the flicker of flame through the billowing clouds of smoke. She strode over to Lord Bight and yanked her sword out of his hand. He was too weak to stop her.

She pointed the tip of the blade at him. "This man is wounded. Take him behind the lines. Get him out of here."

Leonidas looked at Hogan Bight askance. "Who is he?"

"The Lord Governor of Sanction, a tomcat, a dragon . . . who in blazes knows? Just take him out of my sight!"

The young centaur stared at Lord Bight, then at Varia, and finally at Linsha. Receiving no help from any of them, he nodded to Linsha. "I'll get Horemheb to take you. The wind is changing and those grassfires are moving fast."

"No!" Linsha said venomously. "Just take him to Danian. He'll know what to do. I will stay and fight as a Solamnic Knight."

"Linsha," Bight said softly. He lifted a hand and gently touched the bronze scale hanging by the chain around her neck.

"Go!"

Leonidas recognized that tone that brooked no argument and instantly obeyed. He moved in beside the wounded man and hauled him over his withers. With one hand to hold the man on his back, he hefted his sword and whistled once to Horemheb who was busy dispatching a wounded Tarmak. A jerk of his head signaled to the big chestnut to join Linsha, then Leonidas took off at a canter across the valley toward the tribal lines.

Linsha watched them go, weaving between the clumps of fighting men, until she could no longer see them through the smoke and haze. Filled with unspeakable misery, she blinked back more tears and clutched the sword until the hilt dug into the flesh of her burned palm. She knew Horemheb had come to her side, and she knew he could carry her away from the field and over to the Duntollik army. She wanted to go. She wanted to find Falaius and Sir Hugh. Especially Sir Hugh. Besides herself, he was the last Solamnic Knight from their circle. Together they could fight and uphold the honor of the Knighthood. And yet . . . she could not force her body to move. The struggle to summon the magic and free the dragon had taken more out of her than she believed possible. In the turbulent aftermath, she had not felt the effects, but now a heavy cloak of exhaustion and despair settled over her shoulders and drained away her energy, her will, her desires. Her arms and legs felt like lead. Her head was too full of tears and confusion. The day seemed to grow dark around her. Her lungs burned in the smoke of the approaching fires. She had no notion of how long she stood there, rooted to the torn up ground, nor did she notice Horemheb shouting at her. Varia fluttered by her head, screeching a warning, and still she could not move. A tall, dark shape charged at her, and it was all she could do to raise the heavy sword and parry a powerful blow to her body.

Another powerful voice demanded something in the

Tarmak tongue. More shouts echoed through her dazed mind. More shapes moved around her in an odd slowed motion that barely registered on her failing vision. She heard Varia squeal something. Somewhere close beside her, she heard a centaur bellow in pain. She turned her head just as a spear point jabbed her back. The sword fell from her nerveless fingers. She stood, swaying in a dark mist. She caught a glimpse of a golden mask, and a blue painted hand clamped over her face. Varia screeched, but Linsha could not react. An agony sharp and brutal stabbed into her head and sent her senses spinning. She screamed once, and blackness closed over her.

he first thing Linsha became aware of was a deep throbbing pain behind her skull. It was a rhythmic pain as steady as a drumbeat, and it seemed to go on for hours. It took her quite a while to realize that part of the rhythm stuck in her brain *was* a drumbeat, pounding somewhere outside and accompanied by the noises of what sounded like a joyous celebration. Linsha didn't care. Drowned in lethargy, she did not have the will to pull herself out. She lay without moving and sought the darkness and solace of sleep.

Someone walked into wherever she was and without a moment's consideration, rolled her over onto her back.

The movement set off a concert of temple drums in her head. A groan hoisted itself out of her aching body, and she clamped her hands to her throbbing head. For a sickening moment, she thought she was going to vomit.

"Good," said Lanther's voice. "You're awake."

A hand slipped under her head and lifted it just high enough to push a cup of something to her lips.

"Drink this," he ordered and punctuated his demand by forcing the contents into her mouth.

She sputtered and tried to spit it out, but he poured more in until she was forced to swallow a mild, almost sweet-tasting liquid that slid like warm wine down her parched throat.

He laid her head back, and she could hear him moving around the . . . where was she? In a tent? She opened her eyes and was relieved when her head did not shatter from the dim lamplight that lit the tent around her. When she could focus clearly, she looked around and saw that she was indeed in the Akkad-Dar's tent. Darkness flooded in from the open tent entrance, explaining the necessity of the lamps. Outside, the celebration sounded like it was proceeding well.

"Welcome back," the Akkad-Dar said. "You almost didn't survive."

Linsha did not bother to answer. She swept her eyes over the tent again, and this time she saw Varia sitting on a crude perch near the Akkad-Dar's black seat. A chain connected a band fastened around the owl's leg to the perch, and her wings looked like they had been clipped. Varia sat hunched, her feathers fluffed out and her dark eyes vacant. This more than anything else stirred some emotion in Linsha's numb mind. She frowned. The warm drink had had some surprising effects, and she realized her stomach was not churning any more and her head felt somewhat better. She pushed herself to a sitting position on the pallet. But that was as far as she could go. Her entire body felt as if it had been caught in an avalanche and beaten to a pulp with several thousand tons of rocks.

"What have you done to Varia?" Her voice came out in a croak.

"The same thing I have done to you. Cared for you.

293

Kept you subdued. You are lucky I did not kill you both when I discovered you'd found a way to free the dragon. I had looked forward to killing him myself."

Linsha swayed slightly in the effort to stay upright. "How long have you kept us like this?" she asked huskily.

He sat down in his chair and lounged back on the fur pads with all the arrogance of the Tarmak. His skin was scrubbed clean now, and his long hair was pulled back behind his head. A shadow of a beard darkened his jaw and outlined the ragged scar down his cheek. He wore a black tunic and pants, which Linsha found an improvement over the blue paint and linen kilt. There was no outward sign of his arrow wound.

"About four days. Long enough to crush the feeble attempt made by the tribes and clans of this land to stop us and to take the towns of Stone Rose and Willik. In a few days we will attack Duntol. They have no chance, but I am hoping they put up a fight."

"Gods," she moaned. "Leonidas should have killed you."

"Thanks to the One God, he did not. Now, I have a proposition for you." He poured more of the warm, sweet liquid into the cup and brought it to her. Kneeling, he offered it to her with gentleness and the grin she remembered from their time in Missing City. "Drink this. It will make you stronger."

Linsha looked at him. "What is your proposition, Dark Knight?" she snarled.

The reminder of his erstwhile profession pushed the smile off his face. "I was a Dark Knight only long enough to learn dark mysticism and establish my relationship with Takhisis. After she sent me my Vision, I left the Knighthood and returned to the Isle of the Tarmaks. I am the Akkad-Dar."

Linsha snorted her disdain. "You are a traitor, an assassin, and a Brute. They deserve you."

He set the cup down beside her. Swift as a snake, he clamped a hand behind her head and pulled her against him. He kissed her long and hard, then let her fall back on the pallet, panting.

"Urudwek told me I should just take you," he said, jumping to his feet. "But that is for whores. You have earned my admiration this past year. I would rather offer you a choice. Stay with me. Fight by my side. Bear the children of my new dynasty, and you will have my respect and the power of my name. You will be the empress of these Plains. Stay with me, and I will free your owl and allow your dragon friend to live. However, if you refuse me, I will keep the owl and send you back to the slave pens in Missing City. And when I find Crucible as a dragon, cat, or man, I will sacrifice him to the Dark Queen and present his skull to her in tribute."

Linsha looked into his vivid blue eyes and thought that once, perhaps before the death of Iyesta, if Lanther had offered his hand to her as a lover and a companion, she might have taken it. Now it was too late. Lanther was dead to her, and this tall, blue-eyed man that stood before her was a stranger who offered her the wages of dishonor and prostitution. There was no decision to be made.

"There was a man before you," she replied in an almost conversational tone, "who also tried to seduce me. He was a Dark Knight, too. An assassin and a treacherous spy who deceived me and tried to kill me." She sighed. "He died on the side of a volcano. Where would you like to die?"

The Akkad-Dar's eyes glinted with cold humor. "I'll take that as a no." He snapped an order to a guard just outside the tent and watched as a Tarmak warrior fastened shackles around Linsha's ankles and wrists and chained her to the heavy center tent pole. "However, I will give you a little time to change your mind."

He turned on his heel and strode from the tent into the darkness.

Four days later the city of Duntol fell to the Tarmak invaders. Because of its importance as a trade city in the northwest plains, the Tarmaks treated it and its population in a similar manner to Missing City. They massacred all of the members of the government and the city watch, they drove off or killed all the defenders, and they selected many young, able-bodied people to be used for slave labor. They set about repairing much of the damage caused by the battle and swiftly organized a militiary government to run the city.

There was little organized resistance against them. Most of the fighting men and centaurs of the Plains tribes and clans who survived the Battle of the Red Rose had fled into the desert, and those who had not come in time to fight found themselves without an army to join.

Duntollik was no longer a free realm.

Meanwhile, the Akkad-Dar worked on consolidating the Tarmaks' hold of the vast realm he had helped conquer. He left a large contingent of warriors in Duntol to hold the city and made a slow march back across the northern stretch of the Run to pacify the region and accept the surrenders of any chiefs willing to save their people from attack. He led his warriors in several skirmishes against reluctant tribes and in a pitched battle against a large force of the Windwalker clan of centaurs. He left their bodies unburied to insure the word would spread across the Plains that the Tarmaks could not be defeated.

True to his word, the Akkad-Dar searched hard for Crucible, sending out trackers and patrols of brigands to hunt down the dragon. But the bronze had disappeared into the wilds of the vast Plains. No one knew of him. No one had seen him. Everyone believed he was dead. Everyone but Linsha. The Akkad-Dar tried several times to force her to talk about the dragon and where he might have gone, but in spite of his strongest mystic spells, she could not tell him. She simply did not know. The Akkad-Dar knew she liked the dragon, but there was something about the bronze that stirred up powerful emotions in Linsha that shut out many things he tried to use against her. He was both impressed and frustrated.

Finally, he put off his desire for revenge and set his mind on other goals. The eastern half of the Plains of Dust and most of the northern grasslands were his, a huge realm of desert, rivers, plains, and grass. But he only had perhaps ten thousand warriors to defend this land and take what more they could. Kharolis to the west was now free of the green dragon, Beryl, and the Silvanesti Forest might be something to consider. The Knights of Neraka were there now, but they did not need all of those woods. He smiled when he looked at his maps and considered the possibilities. To fulfill these grand plans, he would need more warriors. The emperor at home needed to be informed and more warriors sent. There was much to do before winter set in on the Plains.

The Akkad-Dar left most of his remaining warriors behind to control Duntollik and took only five fast-moving *ekwul* with him back to the Toranth River and the trail to Missing City. He also took the plunder of three towns and a dozen tribes, a large herd of horses, perhaps two hundred slaves captured from the Plains people, and Linsha.

Linsha saw little of the Akkad-Dar during those long days on the trail. The morning after her refusal of his offer, she was locked in the slave cage to ensure she did not escape again. For twenty days she endured the long marches, the hot sun, the cold nights, and the lack of food. She did not see Varia again. At first she was too numb to care what the Tarmaks did to her. Months of fighting, worry, despair, grief, and hardship had taken its toll and finally brought her low. She lay in her cage for days, too sad and weak to move, too worn out to care where they were going.

When the Tarmaks and their caravan finally returned to Missing City, Linsha did not bother to look. What difference did it make? Everyone she knew was either dead or missing. Iyesta, General Dockett, Mariana, Sir Remmik and all but one Solamnic Knight, many of the Legionnaires, most of the militia—they were dead and out of it. The rest, Falaius, Sir Hugh, Crucible, and Leonidas were gone beyond her reach. For all she knew, they were dead, too, killed in the battle by the river. There was nothing left. She didn't even know where the dragon eggs were.

She could barely stand when the cage door was opened and she was ordered to get out. She climbed slowly out of the wagon and stood swaying in her filthy clothes and matted hair. Her guards gave her a disdainful glare and led her into a building she did not recognize. She knew she was back in the city, in the Port District, perhaps, but beyond that she did not know or care. Thus she was flabbergasted when she was escorted into a room with silk hangings and a large bed decorated with colorful pillows. The heavy scent of perfume hung in the air, and candles burned on every flat surface in spite of the daylight that gleamed through one large window. A guard shouted something to someone, then the door was closed and locked behind her.

She studied the room for a moment with growing suspicion and apprehension. Beside the fire was a large metal tub stood filled with water that gently steamed. A meal of soup, bread, fruit, and cheese sat on a small table beside a ewer of wine. Her apathy of the past few weeks cracked just a little, and she searched the room for anything she could use as a weapon.

Light footsteps padded into the room from another door, and the last person Linsha expected to see stepped lightly toward her.

"Callista," she whispered.

The blonde courtesan studied her from head to toe and shook her head in pity. "Lady, I never thought I'd see you here like this, but I've had instructions to clean you up and feed you, and this seemed the best place to do it."

"Instructions from whom?" Linsha snapped.

"The Akkad-Dar." Callista's fair face clouded with dismay. "I certainly never expected to see Lanther's face behind that mask. When he took it off, I nearly fainted from shock."

"Why?" Linsha asked. "Why does he want me bathed now?"

"I don't know. I really don't. He just told me to do it." She pointed to the door. "And he said if you didn't cooperate, the guards would do it instead."

Linsha eyed the door and then the tub. Although

299

she did want to know what the Akkad-Dar had in mind, she had to admit the thought of a hot bath was almost more than she could refuse. She was filthy and she smelled—Callista kept turning her nose away—and she ached in every joint. The thought of soaking away too many days of sweat, dust, blood, and muck was delightful, a feeling she had not had in months. More cracks appeared in her shell of apathy.

Giving a nod to Callista, she tore off her clothes and stepped into the tub. The hot, scented water engulfed her. Using a sponge and soap Callista gave her, she scrubbed and scrubbed her skin until it looked pink again. She washed her hair in a basin of clean water Callista brought, then washed it again just because she could. Between the washings, she ate the soup, the bread, and the fruit and watched Callista burn her clothes. She rather hoped the courtesan had something else for her to wear that did not include skimpy pants and tight-fitting tops, but she felt so languorous in the tub that she did not really care.

It was twilight when Linsha finally stepped out of the cool water and toweled herself dry. She felt better than she had in days, and a little of her energy returned. She stretched her muscles slowly and carefully and tried a few exercises while she warmed near the fire. Callista watched her in amusement.

A thunderous knock at the door startled both women. Callista threw her a clean blue tunic and a long skirt and stood in front of her while she pulled them on. The door slammed open. A Tarmak officer walked in.

"Pack one small bag. You are to be sent as tribute to the Emperor Khanwhelak. The ship leaves tonight with the tide."

"What?" both women said in unison. "Who?"

"No!" Callista wailed. "Wait! No one said I was to go anywhere."

"I just did," the Tarmak informed her. "Now move." He closed the door behind him.

"He can't be serious," the courtesan cried.

Linsha sighed and sank down in a chair. What were the Tarmaks going to do with her? Some of her lethargy returned. Were they going to send her away on the ship too? To where? The Tarmaks' homeland? Why? As tribute? What exactly was "tribute" supposed to do? She could understand why they would pick Callista. The girl was beautiful with long blonde hair and eyes like a summer sky. She would be a rarity in a land of dark-haired women. But what were they going to do with a thin, warrior-trained exiled Knight? Had the Akkad-Dar decided this, or did he have something else in mind for her? She closed her eyes, too weary to think about it.

But several loud crashes and wails brought her back to the present. Callista was not adjusting well to the idea of a sea voyage. Linsha stood up. Just to be sure, she looked out the window to see if there was any escape that way. The window opened to a sheer wall that ran its full length on a busy street full of Tarmak warriors. There was nowhere to go that way.

Silently, she opened Callista's bag and while the courtesan threw in cosmetics, jewels, and bits of clothing, Linsha packed a blanket, the utensils from her meal, a cloak she found in a chest, and a bottle of wine. In a second blanket, she rolled up another cloak, some warm hose, the rest of the cheese and bread she had not eaten, and a small dagger she unearthed in a drawer.

She had just finished tying a carry strap around the rolled up blanket when the guard returned. Behind him entered the Akkad-Dar, looking refreshed and pleased with the proceedings of the evening. He ran his eye over the two women and smiled a cool grimace that did nothing to melt the ice in his eyes.

Both women watched silently as the Akkad-Dar walked to the chair by the table and made himself comfortable. He had the air of a king in his own throne room, Linsha thought, rather than a man visiting a courtesan.

"Callista, you have done well," he said, pouring himself a goblet of wine. "She has cleaned up nicely."

The courtesan tilted up her small nose. "I wouldn't have had so much to do if you had treated her better than a dog," she snapped.

Linsha's eyes widened. She hadn't expected feistiness from this young woman.

The Akkad-Dar chuckled. "The conditions of travel were her choice." He sipped his wine slowly, savoring every drop.

Linsha knew he was deliberately keeping them waiting, but she didn't protest. She was dreading his next move. Her jaw set, she stepped around Callista, picked up her own goblet, and refilled it with wine. Without waiting for permission or an invitation, she sat in another chair by the fire and said, "What do you want?"

She already knew. Why else would he have her cleaned up like this? The fleeting moment of peace brought on by the bath and the wine slipped away, and a heavy despair filled her.

He lifted his goblet to her. "You have had a taste of slave life and time to think. I am offering to marry you one last time. This is the last time. If you refuse now, you will be sent to the slave pens for the rest of your life."

Linsha heard Callista give a small gasp; whether of fright or surprise, she didn't know. She was startled when the young woman took her hand and pulled her out of the chair to the window, away from the Akkad-Dar's hearing.

"Lady Linsha," the courtesan whispered vehemently, "you are going to accept, aren't you? You must."

Linsha kept her expression passive. She turned her back to the Akkad-Dar and asked, "Why? I despise the man. You want me to marry him?"

Callista's beautiful face filled with anger. "I'd rather you shove a knife in him. But if you say no, he'll send you to the pens." She clutched Linsha's arm. "I've seen them. You won't last more than a few days in there."

"I can handle myself in the slave pens," Linsha replied, her voice belying the fear she felt.

"Not if the Tarmaks know the Akkad-Dar has removed his protection from you. If the officers don't take you, the warriors will put you in their war games and fight you until you are killed. *Accept his offer.*"

Linsha did not answer immediately. Thoughts tangled in her mind with regrets and grief and a loneliness so powerful she ached from it. Marry the Akkad-Dar, the man whom she had once known as Lanther. By the gods, how could she do it? Was death preferable?

As if Callista could see the path of her thoughts, the courtesan squeezed her arm again. "If you chose this way, you chose a chance at life. Just do what you can until your destiny reveals itself."

Destiny. Linsha snorted. Yet . . . she did not know where her destiny lay anymore. For years she'd thought her destiny was the Solamnic Knighthood where she would serve with honor until the end of her days. Look where that had brought her! Dishonored, falsely accused, black-listed, abandoned, and now trapped as a captive in a fallen city. There was nothing left but emptiness.

She twisted to look out the open window, and as her body moved she became aware of the slight shift of the dragon scales under her shirt. Although she had deliberately ignored them since the battle on the Red Rose, they had remained hanging on the chain around her neck, warm against her skin.

Her fingers lifted the chain and clutched the scales through the fabric of her tunic. The reminder of the dragons brought such a rush of sadness that she swayed against the window frame.

Callista stared at her worriedly and grasped her elbow to steady her, but she said nothing more, allowing Linsha to reach her own decision.

Lanther was not quite so patient. "The tide is moving, Linsha. I must be away. What is your answer?"

She turned to him, her hand still clutching the scales. "I have a price," she said. "A bridal gift."

His eyebrows lifted. "Your life is not enough?"

"No," she said with an empty voice. "My life is over. Take it if you want it. I don't care. But if you want me, you must pay my price."

"What then? What is it you want?"

Far away in the distant memories of a day that seemed so long ago, she remembered the words of a magnificent brass dragon, her friend, standing by the leaves of the ancient Grandfather Tree. *The bond formed between a dragon and a human is worth the effort to forge it.*

"Oh, Iyesta," she breathed.

Gathering her courage, Linsha Majere faced the Akkad-Dar.

"I want the dragon eggs."

Important Characters and Terms

Solamnic Knights

COMMANDERS

Sir Barron uth Morrec — Former Lord Commander of the Solamnic Circle in Missing City. Killed in an ambush on the night of the Great Storm. See *City of the Lost*, Chapters 7-8.

Sir Jamis uth Remmik — A high-ranking Knight of the Crown, now serving as Knight Commander of the Solamnic outpost in Missing City.

Lady Linsha Majere — Daughter of Palin and Usha Majere, now serving as a Knight of the Rose and Third Commander in the Circle of Knights at the Solamnic outpost in Missing City.

KNIGHTS

Sir Fellion — A Knight of the Sword currently serving in the Solamnic Circle in Missing City. Friend of Sir Hugh Bronan.

Sir Hugh Bronan — A Knight of the Sword currently serving in the Solamnic Circle in Missing City. Close friend of Linsha Majere.

Sir Johand — A Knight of the Sword currently serving in the Solamnic Circle in Missing City.

Sir Korbell — A Knight of the Sword currently serving

in the Solamnic Circle in Missing City. Follower of Sir Jamis uth Remmik.

Sir Pieter — A Knight of the Sword currently serving in the Solamnic Circle in Missing City. Sir Pieter is the youngest knight currently serving in the Circle.

The Legion of Steel

Falaius Taneek — Commander of the Legion of Steel in Missing City.

Lanther Darthassian — Son of Bendic Darthassian and member of the Legion of Steel in Missing City.

Tomarick — A member of the Legion of Steel in Missing City.

Tarmak Characters and Terms

Akkad — Tarmak term for general. Literally translates as "chief" or "topmost." The Akkad answers solely to the Emperor.

Amarrel — The Warrior Cleric, a prophesied holy leader among the Brutes. Lord Ariakan managed to convinced the Tarmak Emperor Kankaweah that he was the Amarrel, thus solidifying his leadership over the Brutes.

Brutes — A colloquial term used by the people of Ansalon to describe the Tarmak.

Damjatt — An indigenous culture on the island of the Brutes that was subjugated by the Tarmaks. They have largely assimilated into Tarmak culture. They are renowned on their island for the breeding and training of extremely large warhorses.

dekegul **(pl. *dekegullik*)** — Officer in charge of one *dekul*. The *dekegullik* answer to the Akkad.

dekul **(pl. *dekullik*)** — A unit of the Tarmak army consisting of 1,000 warriors.

ekwegul **(pl. *ekwegullik*)** — Officer in charge of one *ekwul*. The *ekwegullik* answer to a *dekul*.

ekwul **(pl. *ekwullik*)** — A unit of the Tarmak army consisting of 100 warriors.

Kadulawa'ah — The Tarmak name of Takhisis, Queen of Darkness and Mother of Dragons.

Keena — An indigenous culture on the island of the Brutes that was subjugated by the Tarmaks. They have largely assimilated into Tarmak culture. They are the most philosophically and religiously inclined culture of their homeland, and many Keena find roles as priests, scribes, and scholars.

ket-rhild — Tarmak term for a formal challenge, a battle to the death.

Khanwhelak — The current Emperor of the Tarmak.

Mathurra — A Tarmak soldier.

***orgwegul* (pl. *orgwegullik*)** — Officer in charge of guards and sentries.

Shurnasir — Keena priest among the Tarmak forces in Missing City.

Tarmak — The dominant culture on the island of the Brutes. They subjugated the Damjatt people of the island many years ago and finished their conquest of the Keena people just a few years prior to the Summer of Chaos.

Urudwek — Akkad of the Tarmak forces sent to subdue the Plains of Dust. Official title: Akkad-Ur.

Miscellaneous Characters and Terms

Amania — A young girl living among the refugees of Missing City.

Azurale — Centaur member of the Missing City militia.

Bendic Darthassian — Father of Lanther Darthassian.

Beryllinthranox — Green dragon overlord. Commonly known as "Beryl."

Callista — A beautiful courtesan currently living in Missing City.

Caphiathas — Centaur officer of the Missing City militia and the uncle of Leonidas.

Carrebdos — Centaur. Chief of the Windwalker Clan.

Crucible — Bronze dragon and erstwhile guardian of the city of Sanction.

Cyan Bloodbane — A green dragon most noted for aiding in turning the realm of the Silvanesti into a cursed forest of nightmare. He was later enslaved by Raistlin Majere, but when Raistlin entered the Abyss, Cyan returned to Silvanesti to exact his revenge upon the elves.

Danian — A blind healer dwelling among the Plainsmen.

Dockett — General of the militia of Missing City and unofficial commander of the refugee forces after the fall of the city.

Ereshu — A centaur clan of the Plains of Dust.

Goldmoon — One of the famed Heroes of the Lance. Widow of Riverwind. Now head of the Citadel of Light on Schallsea Island.

Grandfather Tree — A gigantic vallenwood tree growing in the Plains of Dust. It is revered by the local inhabitants. Some even believe it is a manifestation of the god Zivilyn.

Hogan Bight — Lord Governor of the city of Sanction.

Horemheb — Centaur of the Willik clan of Duntollik.

Ian Durne — An officer of Sanction's city guard. See *The Clandestine Circle*, by Mary H. Herbert.

Iyesta — Brass dragon overlord of the eastern Plains of Dust. Commonly known as "Splendor."

kirath — The elite warrior scouts of the Silvanesti.

Kordath — A nomadic tribe of the southern Plains of Dust.

Leonidas — Centaur member of the Missing City militia and close friend of Linsha Majere.

Mariana Calanbriar — Half-elf captain of the Missing City militia.

Mina — A young Dark Knight who has led the armies of Neraka in several successful battles in Ansalon.

Onysablet — Black dragon overlord. Commonly known as "Sable."

Riverwind — One of the famed Heroes of the Lance and husband of Goldmoon. He died fighting the dragon overlord Malystryx. See *Spirit of the Wind*, by Chris Pierson.

Sable — see Onysablet.

Silvanesti — The forest realm of the elves in southeastern Ansalon.

Splendor — see Iyesta.

Stenndunuus — Blue dragon overlord of the central Plains of Dust. Commonly known as "Thunder."

Takhisis — Evil goddess, also known as the Queen of Darkness.

Tanefer — Centaur member of the Missing City militia who goes with Linsha and Lanther to find the dragon eggs in *City of the Lost*.

Tancred — The apprentice of Danian. See *Bertrem's Guide to the War of Souls*, Volume Two.

Thunder — see Stenndunuus.

Varia — A rare sentient owl and friend of Linsha Majere. Varia possesses the ability to speak with a wide vocal range and has a talent for telepathy and reading auras.

Vorth — A bozak draconian.

Wanderer — Son and eldest child of Riverwind and Goldmoon.

Wan-kali — A settled tribe of the Plains of Dust.

Windwalker — A clan on the Plains of Dust.

World Tree — see "Grandfather Tree."

Follow Mina from the War of Souls into the chaos of post-war Krynn.

AMBER AND ASHES
The Dark Disciple, Volume I
Margaret Weis

With Paladine and Takhisis gone, the lesser gods vie for primacy over Krynn. Recruited to a new faith by a god of evil, Mina leads a religion of the dead, and kender and a holy monk are all that stand in the way of the dark stain spreading across Ansalon.

First in a new series from *New York Times* best-selling author Margaret Weis.

August 2004